"Ross's loving attention to detail shows us why it is that the smallest events in our lives are often the most memorable. Her voice is fresh, witty, and incisive."

— Deborah Lichtman, Co-director,
MFA in Writing Program, University of San Francisco

"A smart, sharp collection by a worldly, versatile writer. Ross' ability to look at the world through different sets of eyes is astonishing. She does it with skill, humor, pathos, and with a bracing, refreshing dose of acerbiscism."

— Eleanor Cooney, author of *Death in Slow Motion*

IN THE EYES, IN THE MOUTH

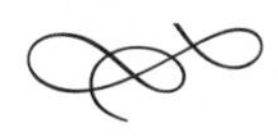

stories by ADRIENNE ROSS

LOST COAST PRESS

In the Eyes, In the Mouth
Stories by Adrienne Ross
 For information, or to order additional copies of this book, please contact:

Lost Coast Press
155 Cypress Street
Fort Bragg, CA 95437
(800) 773-7782
www.cypresshouse.com

Cover and cover art by Bob Ross
Book production by Cypress House

Library of Congress Cataloging-in-Publication Data

Ross, Adrienne, 1933-
In the mouth, in the eyes / Adrienne Ross.
p. cm.
ISBN 978-1-935448-01-3 (pbk. : alk. paper)
1. Interpersonal relations--Fiction. I. Title.
PS3618.O8452I52 2009
813'.6--dc22 2008054941

Printed in the USA
2 4 6 8 9 7 5 3 1

To
the Green Rug Club
and
Amelia

Contents

Landing

ONCE AT A PARTY, Wolfie met a young woman who jumped out of airplanes. "When I start looking forward to the weekend," said the jumper, who had a calm wide face with long blue eyes and pale curly hair, "I know it's time to fall from a very great height." Wolfie, whose own straggly dark hair was pulled back from her thin face, supposed she meant that you've got to have more in life than a subsistence job and time to read the Sunday papers. But compared to jumping out of an airplane, Wolfie figured, a boring job, even a boring life, was preferable.

This line of reasoning fell away, however, shortly after she spoke on the phone with her city friend Renee. Renee was leaving for Greece in a month, and still hadn't found a house sitter who would be sensitive to the needs of her eccentric cats, cats whom Wolfie just happened to be familiar with. "I'll do it," she cried, "I mean, Mitchell and I will do it—oh Renee, I'm dying for a change."

Although Renee was to be gone for an entire year, Wolfie's need was suddenly great. She began to make lists. But Mitchell objected. No way could he find time to visit the city, let alone live there. Maybe he could spare a weekend from time to time, as he had in the past, but that was about it. She'd best forget about him going anywhere during the growing season. If she wanted to live in the air-polluted, crowded, noisy, crime-ridden city, well, she'd best make plans to go and do it on her own.

What had she been thinking? She'd known he couldn't leave, wouldn't leave if he could. They argued. Then they made up and Wolfie changed her mind. Before she could call Renee, however, they had a bigger, more far-ranging fight that she regarded as terminal. Mitchell stomped out of the house, and Wolfie screamed "Fine!" a lot of times in various tones of voice.

She spoke at length on the phone with Renee, and for the next several days packed and sorted, sorted and packed. In the slightly better of their two dilapidated VWs she drove past the Rent-All and the post office, which together signified the town of Filburn, and turned onto the highway. Wolfie drove slowly, even primly. She had a fantasy that Mitchell would follow her in the other car, stopping a couple of times to put in oil—the other car burned lots of it—and head her off at Denny's in Harbor Point, the bigger town with a drugstore, a Safeway, and a gallery for local art. There, over Denny's Cottage Cheese and Fruit Special, which Mitchell loved, he would beg her to come back. This didn't happen. All the way down to the city she thought about the curly-haired woman who jumped out of airplanes.

It was a good thing she drove carefully because the car died a couple of blocks away from Renee's house. Wolfie walked over, her abdomen still rigid from having left Mitchell. She was sweaty and her shirt was rumpled. Her hair was partly pulled back into a rubber band. Her thin, sunburnt face felt gritty when she rubbed it. She was covered with country. She was tired of surprises.

Renee welcomed her with an iced bottle of some delicious fizzy brown stuff Wolfie'd never had before. It tasted like coffee but wasn't. Renee gave over keys, emergency phone numbers, and lots of instructions. She mentioned at least twice that she'd always viewed Mitchell with suspicion, and was ecstatic that Wolfie was leaving him. Also she was pleased and relieved that Wolfie would take care of the cats, Philomena and Oogie.

Renee left on the airport shuttle the next morning, together with her luggage and boxes and raincoat, leaving Wolfie scared and wondering if she'd done the wrong thing.

During the next few days she reacquainted herself with Renee's cats. Under stress of any kind, including Renee's absence and Wolfie's presence, Philomena tended to sleep in awkward and inappropriate areas, flattened out like a little fur coat in front of the refrigerator or on top of the remote control to the TV. Philomena was the flattest cat Wolfie'd ever seen, a wise-faced calico with a vaguely comatose quality. Oogie, on the other hand, had a tendency to disappear for unspecified periods of time, three hours or three days, and to reappear with a soft thwack of the cat door when, according to his own mysterious assessment, things were normal again. He was a skulker, smoky and big-eared. Once Wolfie learned their habits, the cats relaxed. Philomena flopped sedately on a chair, and Oogie, surveying the street from an indoor windowsill, was at all times visible. Wolfie recognized their traits—the trait of getting in your way and the trait of taking off at some inconvenient time—as those of her previous housemate, but unlike Mitchell, the cats were accommodating. They were actually soothing.

With a letter of introduction from her printer friend in Harbor Point, Wolfie soon found a job as an apprentice typesetter and general assistant at a fine book press. She quickly became a fast and efficient worker. Her boss was lenient, her co-workers amiable. The pay wasn't great, but her country habits were frugal. However, she was acquiring new ones. After work and on weekends she took the ferry to San Francisco, or wandered up and down Piedmont Avenue. She slowly explored bookshops, boutiques, cafés, and parks, before returning to Renee's house with a carton of delicious exotic deli food. It was all new, and restful. Everything seemed to work without hassle or breakdowns. Renee's house had a sturdy roof, and glass in all the windows, and she never had to worry about the plastic blowing away or a serious leak undermining the floor. Wolfie had the car fixed and it sat in Renee's driveway, waiting. In Renee's garden, nasturtiums and chard sprang out of the ground. Also, city markets offered a dazzling array of produce. Wolfie had formerly shopped twice a week at Filburn's combo coffee shop and general store, and she and Mitchell had eaten a lot of tacos.

Wolfie's days fell into a pattern, and she was half mesmerized by their regularity. The weather no longer ruled her movements. When the hot, dusty indian summer began, city people acknowledged it merely by a slight change of fashion. Everything was easy. She sometimes fell asleep in front of Renee's TV and woke in the morning wonderfully refreshed, ready for a shower in Renee's tiled bathroom, and a latte and bagel at the café next door to her workplace.

The weekend after the car was fixed, she drove up to visit Mitchell. She wanted to get her sewing machine and some books and her Chinese teapot. Since living at Renee's, she no longer wished for things to work out between Mitchell and herself, but she definitely wanted to make up with him. They'd been together for several years, and she'd loved him in a profound discouraged way. The visit went well, better than she'd expected, and they tacitly agreed on a light, careful, friendly mode of interaction. When she drove back down to the city, the teapot wrapped in newspapers on the seat beside her, she was no longer anxious. The freeway looked friendlier, the gas stations were more distinct, the San Rafael Bridge clicked into brilliant, familiar movie-like focus. She was tired but felt intensely present. She thought, *this is my real life now.* She was an urban resident now.

They talked on the phone, and Mitchell always had

a horror story to relate. Flooding. Drought. A window smashed by a storm. A choked pump, a backed-up toilet, skunks under the porch. City life seemed so calm. At night she heard sirens, and she was comforted by them. It seemed to her that all the apparatus of city government was alert, taking care of citizens and honest working people like herself, extricating them from car wrecks, rushing them to large hi-tech hospitals. She gloated every time she stopped for a red light at a busy intersection. She loved the traffic lights. Stop, go. Stop, go. What a logical and courteous arrangement. The country seemed more than ever hostile, random, perplexing, with too much work expended on minimal results. Too many emergencies. Catastrophic and boring. Wolfie began to realize that she'd left Filburn for many reasons, only one of which was the big fight with Mitchell.

For one thing, she remembered, even after they'd gotten electricity, her life hadn't been that much more comfortable. Their ratty old cars kept breaking down on winding dirt roads at night. Her little flower gardens got rained out as soon as they bloomed, if indeed they bloomed at all. Also, she'd often craved Asian food, bookstores, movies. She'd wanted cable TV, which had all the good shows. She'd wanted a silk dress, and an event to wear it to. She'd yearned for DSL.

From time to time she and Mitchell had cautiously driven down to the city for a couple of days. Weekends in the city were confusing then, and exhausting. The friends with whom they stayed had so much stuff. They had DVRs, microwave ovens, sidewalks. Mitchell and Wolfie had a washer and a dryer in the country, but their clothes never got really clean. Was it the machine? Was it the well? Was it Wolfie?

At Renee's house, there was a tiled shower into which endless hot water poured. Wolfie stood there for many minutes each day, and slowly shed the layers of country skin, a dusty sense of her envelope, a muddy sense. She sat in the big chair, on the couch, on Renee's small, thick Chinese rug. She loved Renee's bed, low and soft, and Renee's bed linens in frivolous prints of flowers and stars. She was lonely, true, but in a pleased, interesting, self-absorbed way. She made it a point to go to the neighborhood café after work, where she drank a refreshing herbal tea and read the local newspaper. Sometimes a handsome older man, with longish white hair, came in and drank a bottle of Anchor Steam beer. He read *The New York Times*. She occasionally felt him glance at her through his tiny stylish glasses while she read, and she glanced at him while he read, but their glances deliberately avoided each other's eyes. This was a bonus, a near-flirtation, something safe to look forward to. Loneliness was richly detailed.

Sometimes Larry, her boss, a master printer and poet, took the whole shop out for pizza and beer after work. These civilized gatherings seemed to Wolfie the easiest and most genial social events she'd ever attended. Loneliness had real possibilities. Days went by during which she didn't think of Mitchell. When she missed her country friends, she phoned them, glad to talk and glad to hang up. It was fall, the end of indian summer. Winter was coming. She could smell it. The nights were cool and she slept well.

As she settled down one evening to watch *Masterpiece Theater,* the phone rang. *Oh, lovely,* she thought, suddenly knowing she craved company. Except for her coworkers and the cats, she hadn't spoken to a living soul in two days. But it was Mitchell.

"I'm coming down to the city to make some sales," he said. He meant his marijuana crop was harvested.

"Oh, good," she said. She hadn't seen Mitchell for nearly three months.

"Can you put me up for a night or two?"

"Sure," she said without thinking.

"Well." Mitchell didn't speak for what seemed like a long time. In her head she wrote a zillion speeches he could have made. *Wolfie I miss you,* he could say, *please come back. I love you, Wolfie. I'm lonely without you. I understand, now that you're gone, how wonderful my life is when you're with me, how grateful I am to know you. You're endlessly interesting, you're hilarious, you're brilliant, you're a supreme lover.* And so forth. But he said none of these things. Just when she was about to scream, he mumbled, "See you Thursday." And hung up.

She prepared for Mitchell's visit. She had a little money now, and she laid in a stash of elegant food. She fantasized that she and Mitchell would walk around the corner to the video store and rent one of his old black-and-white favorites. They'd drink cappuccino. They might even go out to a jazz club. She knew he'd be driving around making deliveries much of the time, but she also knew he was looking for an excuse to hang out with her. From phone calls to country friends, she learned that he didn't have a new girlfriend. So this had to be Mitchell's indirect unsatisfactory way of courting her. Now that she knew he was coming, she was dying to see him. Who knew what would happen? She hadn't thought about another lover, was so satisfied by her new, leisurely, materialistic life that a lover didn't seem relevant, yet as soon as she knew Mitchell was coming into the city she craved intimacy.

He rolled in Thursday night around midnight, about four hours after his estimated arrival. "Got a late start," was his apology. She'd made up a bed for him in Renee's spare room, and he wearily tumbled right into it. So much for a sweet reunion. In the morning she left him a note and a key. At 5:30 p.m., the note was still on the table, but the key was gone. The bed he'd slept in was unmade. His cloth suitcase gaped open on the floor, spilling out two or three wrinkled shirts, a clean pair of jeans, underwear, and socks.

Wolfie turned away from this distressing sight and drifted through the house, assessing Renee's luxury through Mitchell's provincial eyes. She looked with satisfaction at the puffy comforter on her bed. She rearranged Renee's small driftwood sculptures—now augmented by her own collection of fossils—on the mantelpiece, and looked at herself in the mirror. Her black hair was short now, fashionably and smoothly cut in an elegant line just below her ears. Her skin was smoother, clearer. Her shirt hung softly from her shoulders. Nothing sagged, bagged, or crumpled. In the kitchen she opened the refrigerator. She smiled affectionately at the roast duck she'd bought at the neighborhood deli. Two salads, a Greek one with spinach and kalamata olives, and a spicy one with corn and red peppers and cilantro, gleamed side by side out of their plastic containers. She felt incredibly rich. But on the counter, covered with greasy crumbs, were the remains of some toast and eggs. A skillet, sticky with scraps of hardening egg, had been left in the sink: clearly this was Mitchell's idea of cleaning up. A hairy mat, quickly identified as Philomena, hung over the edge of the kitchen table. To Wolfie this was clear evidence of unsettled vibes. As if to confirm her feeling, Oogie was nowhere to be seen.

The bathroom, normally the pristine preserve of one medium-tidy woman, was now awash with wet towels on the floor and wet towels on the racks. He'd used, by her count, four towels. How had he done that? She didn't want to clean up after him, but she'd have to if she wanted to bathe. The old familiar rage bubbled up through her chest and burst out through her mouth. "Fucker!" she spat. Slowly she cleaned up the kitchen, slowly she cleaned up the bathroom. Things were hard again, again accidental, again boring. She had an idea what the rest of the weekend was going to be like, and she hated it. Maybe she should drive up to Mitchell's, and mess up his house, but really, coals to Newcastle, plus the long drive. Or maybe she should stay at a motel, just to indicate her disgust, but she resented being ousted from Renee's house by that same old insensitive asshole it had taken her way too long to leave.

Grumbling with frustration and anxiety, she walked out to the café. Before she left, she set a dish of Oogie's favorite canned cat food on the back step, just in case. In the café she sipped a bracing decaf latte. She sat for a while, imagining what it would be like to confront Mitchell face to face and to try to elicit direct responses from him. The situation reminded her of the grimmest most laugh-track-laden sitcom. Leading man is lovable country bumpkin, steeped in machismo, and though well meaning and good hearted, just can't connect except with one-liners to the gal he's secretly nuts about. Meanwhile, urbane citified leading woman craves intimacy from said guy but also wants to get on with her life, and, most especially, desires not to take any more shit. Classic.

A thin gush of indignation followed that thought, and Mitchell's face narrowed her field of vision. *Mitchell,* she'd say, *please clean up after yourself.*

I know, Wolfie, he answers sheepishly, *I'm a slob.*

Listen, Mitchell, she says, *that's not the point.*

Well, what is the point, babe?

No. This was no good. She was already defending herself. What would the stylish leading woman say?

Mitchell, she'd begin, *I'm glad you're a slob.*

No problem, babe, he grins, waiting for the punch line.

You know why, Mitchell? Because I'll be glad when you're gone. And you know what else? I haven't thought about you hardly at all.

Mitchell looks hurt and dismayed.

Oh, god. Now she was being malicious, and trapped in an all-too-familiar attempt to second-guess the un-second-guessable Mitchell. Much better in Wolfie's view was to jump out of an airplane. That would give her a little perspective. This thought definitely cheered her up and even made her smile at the wall of the café. Between her table and the wall was the white-haired man looking at *The New York Times* through his gold-rimmed reading glasses. He intercepted her smile, and returned it. It came at just the right moment, the moment when she felt herself sinking into sitcom metaphysics.

She stood up and walked past the table of the white-haired man. "Hi," she said, almost sauntering. "Hi to you," he answered, grinning. She looked at her watch as she left the café, striding tall. It was 8 p.m. She was hungry. She thought with pleasure of the duck in the refrigerator, of Renee's comfortable, indulgent house around the corner. At some point Mitchell would come back. Was she ready to have it out? You can't think of these things in terms of pop-culture archetypes, she told herself, you have to get some perspective. But not, no, not from jumping out of airplanes.

Oh, Mitchell I missed you. As she says it, it becomes true. She wonders where that piece of truth came from. They kiss. *Oh, Mitchell. I'm so glad you're here.*

Mitchell is sheepish, pink, pleased. *You're my number one, babe,* he mumbles.

Holding Mitchell's hand, she'll move toward Renee's bedroom, Renee's soft bed, which has now become a bed of steamy sex.

On her way home Wolfie stopped at the video store and rented a copy of *All That Jazz,* a movie Mitchell hated and was mystified by. If he came home late, she could watch the movie. If he came home early, well. In the meantime she was starving for duck and Greek salad. She felt exhilarated, remembering the flattering response of the white-haired man in the café. The almost flirtation had passed into the next phase, the phase of a real flirtation. She contemplated this passage, as evanescent and dramatic as any she'd ever experienced with Mitchell. She knew she'd be encountering Mitchell sometime tonight. So far they hadn't kissed, or even touched. She admitted that along with resenting Mitchell's mess, his impossible slobhood, she looked forward to his sexual availability. It was true she wanted to hold him close. It was also true she'd be glad when he was gone, but in the meantime it was Friday night, after all. Wolfie walked a little faster. Turning the corner she saw Mitchell's rusty VW parked in the driveway, right in back of hers. It seemed like a good omen, but really one never knew what would happen. Had Oogie come back? Had Philomena been stepped on? What's next, Wolfie wondered, not bored at all. A small pulse of alarm was beating in her chest. It was not unpleasurable. Oh god, what's next.

The Transition Consultant

I'M THINKING NOW ABOUT training an assistant, an eventual partner, to take on the death cases. My first choice is the old man. I believe he could become an ideal consultant. First he'd need to thoroughly understand the concept of resistance, and to learn the practical advantage of throwing oneself over the line, so to speak, in order to identify the line itself. This analogy may not be the most apt to describe death work, but I believe the principle is sound. I very carefully brought up this possibility with the old man. He claims he's too old to learn new skills. I told him he would be relying on intuition. He said he's never used intuition. I told him he could learn to tap it. He said he might die any minute. I told him he would die alert and interested in an absorbing job. I added that he could choose his own hours, and he'd benefit others. He asked how he could benefit others when he was dying. "You're a young man," he said to me, with a resigned smirk to indicate polite contemptuous amusement. "It's all very well for you." In fact I am not young, but from the perspective of his advanced age perhaps a man of fifty-some years appears young. But he was engaged in the discussion, and I hadn't ever seen him so animated. His natural pessimism and misanthropy would serve him well in this line of work. I believe clients would be forced into new lines of thought, and respond with innovative ideas—I have seen this before—to his single-minded insistence on rebutting any hint of a new notion or proposition, or even a kind offer.

In the event the old man is adamant in his refusal, I have tentatively decided on a second choice, the old man's daughter. Of the old man's three living children, she's the only one who lives in town. She occasionally accompanies him to his appointments. I've had a chance to talk with her before and after the old man's sessions, and have been struck with her good manners and directness, two qualities not often found together. She pays close attention and is reasonably, although not unnaturally, calm. These qualities inspire confidence. It's my feeling that good listeners, like myself, elicit a good amount of heuristic problem solving by their presence alone. Of course her methods, connections, and results would all be very different from those of the old man.

She recently retired from her modestly successful career running a fine press and print shop. In some circles, I understand, her work is legendary. The old man, always consistent, does not recognize or acknowledge that her work had any value. "Why do they want to print a book with hand-set type?" he asks rhetorically. My answer would be, "Because it's beautiful," but he doesn't wait for an answer. "Nowadays you can print directly from your computer," he goes on. "These art publishers, I tell you, it's a waste of time."

Unlike her father, she's told me frankly that she's looking for something new to do. "I'm sometimes tempted to read in bed all day long," she confessed. Her parodic tone and conspiratorial smile gave me the text: she's completely aware this is a common impulse.

It's not a good idea to stay in bed all day, but getting up is rarely compelling in our culture. My clients, most of them, don't feel good when they wake up. They experience dread in their bodies. It might be a sensation of cold, or of nausea, in the throat, abdomen, or stomach, or it might manifest itself as an almost overwhelming unwillingness to open their eyes. They say they're warm and safe, soft and supple, in bed, under their blankets, but when they get up they immediately feel chilled and stiff. Some can hardly take a few steps into the bathroom because their feet are curled up in a way that repels the floor. Those with daily jobs usually stand under a hot shower for a considerable time before they emerge somewhat more prepared to face their commute. When they come out of the shower they are warm, they can bend their knees and sit up straight, they can swallow, even savor, a cup of hot coffee. The shower has proved itself to be a superior transition tactic for most clients.

For a very few individuals, the best tactic is to simply stay in bed until something, perhaps their bladder or their restless legs or their hunger, impels them up, up and away from the warm tangled mess of bedclothes and spurious safety. Thus the transition is accomplished by waiting it out, that is, by avoiding it until it has passed them by.

The old man, a long-time client, is ninety-five years old. He has lost, and continues to lose, visual and auditory acuity. He has a number of other health complaints. He has no interests, nor has had since he retired twenty years ago from a demanding position as the president and owner of a small manufacturing company. He likes to talk about his company, which he reluctantly sold, as the sole creative force in his life. Indeed, he made a number of innovations in the plastic container industry, and during his stewardship began production of boxes for computer diskettes and also of boxes for storage of other small electronically sensitive objects. He personally invented an ingenious hinge for lids, which enabled them to swing down quietly or to be entirely removed. His pride in these accomplishments was considerable. He's been increasingly despondent, by his own account, passive and dejected, since retirement.

He is the rich patriarch of a large family, numbering nearly thirty people. But with the exception of his daughter, he rarely sees them. He disapproves of his children, grandchildren, and great-grandchildren, all of whom he views as underachievers, coddled and lazy. They bore him, and he bores them. Nearly everything bores him. He never had time to cultivate hobbies, and when he quit working, he says, it was "too late." Naturally, with every passing year, it became more so. Finally, socially handicapped by his disdain for almost everything, and stupefied by tedium, he came to me. My professional title reassured him. It doesn't have the stink of the unconscious. As we worked together, I learned that the transition he had ostensibly come to see me about was the one between life and death. The subject was hardly new to me. In my early days I'd specialized in problems associated with the ending of life. This old man, however, had another motivation, unknown to himself: actually he came to argue with me. He could afford it, and at the time I had an extra slot. Also, I enjoyed the arguments.

Years ago, when I first entered the field of death and dying, I ran a large ongoing grief group. The number of participants went up and down, of course, as some persons left the group to begin a less formal phase of grieving, and as others arrived fresh from a bereavement or an experience that prompted them to initiate a grieving process perhaps long delayed. Still, there were usually fifteen to twenty members in the group, a number that occasionally rose to thirty or dipped to ten. It was clear that people needed to tell their stories, or salient parts of their stories, over and over, and also needed, compulsively needed, to hear the stories of others. The common factor in the stories was the lack of participatory transition. That is, the loved one had just a minute before been seen smiling, speeding away on his motorcycle, racing across the tennis court racket raised, biting into a barbecued chicken leg, shooting a syringe of high-grade cocaine into a vein in her neck, crossing the highway on foot, saying "Good night,

I love you." Transition deprivation then ensued. In the next moment of consciousness the loved one was dead, without even an hour, let alone a week or a month, of adjustment to the new, desolate, absence-of-loved-one state of being.

The condition of shock that followed, inevitably, led me to speculate further on transition deprivation, which, of course, occurs in non-terminal situations as well. A good example, a common example, actually, is abandonment by a loved one. One day she was leaning over my shoulder as I sat reading my mail, her cheek pressed close to mine, her post-shower smell—a fruity waft of lemon soap, coconut shampoo, and sesame body oil—filling my nose and heart with happiness, safety, and warmth. The next day she was packing her purple duffel, which I had given her as a birthday present, crying and blowing her nose. The tissues fell into the wastebasket like snowflakes. Her face was red and blotchy. "I'm so glad I finally told you," she was muttering. "It was hell your not knowing."

Hell? For her, by her own admission, perhaps. Not for me. For me it had been paradise, sweet smelling and eternal. She had had a transition, a lengthy one, too lengthy, as she herself implied, and I had none. Thus deprived, shocked, disoriented, if something like this had happened to you, you would desperately call around. Finally, if you were lucky, you would come for help to a transition consultant. Someone like myself.

Between us, we would imagine a transition in which you participated without awareness. We would reveal or recreate your awareness and move it into present time. Her lateness, her lapses, her morning laziness, are all re-examined and expanded. Your secret knowledge is exfoliated. After several sessions you terminate your work with me, a slightly more alert, even paranoid, but much less disoriented individual.

Transition cannot, of course, be restored to or even

considered by those who are suddenly bereaved. Death creates special problems. Death can be regarded as a separate category under the general title "Transition Work," as in (1) Death Problems, and (2) Non-death Problems. I take no death transition cases, as I no longer consider myself a specialist in any but non-death transitions. I definitely believe the old man capable of becoming a death specialist. The only problem I can foresee, other than his own imminent death, as he himself argues, is that working with him in a more or less collegial capacity may engender competitive behavior on both our parts. I know already he doesn't like to work cooperatively. His deep need to have the only correct opinion or view precludes negotiation, discussion, or rethinking on any topic. If he accepts my proposition, therefore, which I know is not likely, I will have to do some hard thinking about how much I can trust him with clients. If I can trust him completely, I won't have to work with him at all. If I have doubts, I will have to work with him more cooperatively, accept the consequences of his unorthodoxy, and—hopefully—learn from him.

I have no "typical" clients. They all want peace and happiness, of course, but a surprising number of them want distraction or oblivion or surcease from any sort of feeling. Life has become odious to them, too difficult, too fraught with petty decisions that disgust them, too demanding of their collusion, which they interpret as corrupt. I understand this view. They see me as an appropriate person to work with, and I concur. I've spent my entire adult life studying transitions, including sleeping to waking and waking to sleeping, two transitions that are universally acknowledged to be difficult. Other very common transition complaints are work life to vacation life and back again, single life to cohabitation and cohabitation to single living, and so forth. My specialty used to be the voluntary transition between life and death, but now I avoid working with that issue. I didn't always avoid it, however.

In my early work as a grief counselor, working with the recently bereaved, I began to see individuals with terminal illnesses. In this process I naturally came to have a few clients with AIDS. Within a very few years many of my clients were persons with AIDS. It was from them that I learned about the importance of transitions. Their chief problem turned out not to be imminent death. They knew quite well their time was limited. They were well educated about their situations. They wanted help with passages narrow yet profound. One of the first of these clients wanted methods to maneuver the tricky transition between the period of meditating and resting in the afternoon, and the time of going out with friends in the evening, for a light dinner or an excursion to a bookstore. This presented me with a specific experience to construe, about which no generalizations could be made.

There's a certain pace we fall into naturally when we have developed a routine, especially when activities are constrained by a health regimen. This pace, the customized allotting and measuring of time, gradually comes to represent for the client his or her state of well-being. The heart rate is normal, the blood pressure is stable, the breathing is regular. In my work with clients over the years I've come to recognize this optimal physical state as one that occurs predictably when the person has chosen the order of the elements, so to speak, of his or her imposed condition. I read somewhere that this state sometimes occurs among prisoners. The AIDS patient who had a hard time getting ready to go out to dinner experienced her evening diversion, although it was eagerly anticipated, as a difficult interruption in the smooth sequence of medical practices that made up her day. It was with this young woman that I first began developing a series of simple methods and tactics to cope with transitions.

One of the best tactics, as I mentioned previously in connection with the terrible transition between sleeping and waking, is a long hot shower. Before the shower we are unprepared for the activity to follow, i.e., the workday. We're not in a state of mind in which the activity can be experienced. In fact, we're resisting it. During the shower a magical shift occurs, in which the shower is experienced as a preparation for the activity. The activity has become inevitable. We accept the inevitability. Also, we take in the soothing sensory encouragement of the hot streams of water and steam. Moist heat opens the capillaries and the pores of the skin. The brain and limbs become oxygenated, the senses are alert. After the shower we are prepared. We dress ourselves and begin the activity. The transition tactic has worked.

For most persons who are baffled and impeded by transitions between states of awareness, a hot shower is the perfect solution. Its success rate is very high. My first client with AIDS, so many years ago, used a shower as her transition device between resting and socializing.

Other classical transition tactics are changing clothes, or smoking a cigarette. Transition strategies are necessarily more complex and idiosyncratic, e.g., running a series of small errands, or walking the dog, or, my personal favorite, counter-phobic domestic behavior. Counter-phobic domestic behavior involves a distasteful act that has been continually postponed because it's not urgent, yet the doing of it would measurably improve the quality of one's life. As examples I cite cleaning closets, polishing silver plate, washing windows. We are repelled by thoughts of doing such jobs, even as we put them off. But when we are faced with a far more loathsome obligation, such as job hunting or taking a test, we find we can crash through our procrastination and quickly clean the closet while preparing ourselves to schedule the job interview. We are not only vanquishing the terror of a certain kind of transition, and thus restoring or even initiating our control over our time, but also easing and improving our lives. Demonstrating that this can be done is as important as actually doing it, because it gives us confidence in future similar situations.

Due to the cataclysmic change in my own life, the change I neither expected nor wanted, I turned my attention to these other sorts of transition problems, which can be negotiated successfully. I was no longer able to work with death cases or other cases of severe transition deprivation, as I would find myself sobbing uncontrollably while the horrified client, traumatized by his or her own disastrous event, muttered hasty excuses and stumbled out. Since then I have worked exclusively with category 2, Non-death Problems.

The old man is unwilling to be trained in any techniques of problem solving, therapy, or consultation. He refuses to learn to meditate. "It's too late," he says. "How much time have I got?" He refuses to understand the difference between the "I statement," a standard and elementary principle of personal conversation, and an accusation. He interrupts. He scoffs at me and presumably at anyone else he's talking to. So why am I so insistent that he be the death transition expert? I think it's because (a) he's very old, and he's approaching death slowly and naturally, if that term can be applied to aging. He's had the opportunity to think of death, year by year and day by day, as a gradually approaching terminus to his life. And (b) he has some kind of strength or vital spirit that enables him to universalize old wounds and remorse and agonies. This indicates to me that he can be of help to those others who, facing a certain or uncertain soon death, want as it were a balloon to glide over the chasm of transition that keeps them from their final rest.

The crucial part of transition is not the before or the after. Many people see their lives as a struggle to fill the gap, or, rather, gaps, since persons who have trouble with transitions rarely have trouble with only one, unless the one they have trouble with is death, in which case the others fade into unimportance. The crucial part is always the interpretation.

Ultimately these are existential problems, claims the old man, and not accessible to "solutions" except in the most superficial and trivial sense. Maybe he's right, but the sense he speaks of as so thin, so much barely covering the actual intangible dilemma, is the sense in which we (apparently) most naturally perceive and experience our lives. "The skin is not less real than the limb it encases," I argue, well aware of the weakness of my analogy. "You're judging the book by its cover," he says, "and also the map is not the territory." He gives me a look of triumphant fatigue, a look that indicates he's thought out and argued this basic point too many times already.

I try to consult with no more than four clients a day. I allow a full hour to each appointment, and take at least an hour for myself between appointments. I have evolved a little routine for myself to fill this time. First I make notes on the work just done, on a diskette, and file it away alphabetically by the client's first name. I use a special filing box, which was a gift from the old man. Then I tend to my physical needs and take refreshment, perhaps a cup of coffee or an apple. After that I meditate or walk around the block for ten or twenty minutes. Finally, I prepare myself for my next appointment by reviewing the files of the next client. This is time spent pleasantly, an agreeable transition. Afterward I'm refreshed and prepared for the next session. I have performed my obligatory transition. The gap is closed.

My office is in a one-room garden cottage, a structure common to the somewhat old-fashioned city where I live. I'm fortunate to live in a temperate climate where a small cottage can be made cozy with one space heater. The cottage is separated from my house by a small expanse of lawn, and more or less surrounded by tall eucalyptus trees. It's an excellent setting to work in, and I appreciate it. Before I went into business for myself I worked for a number of agencies, whose workplaces were so depressing and grimy and even sordid that I was amazed at the courage and determination that enabled so many sad people, shadowed by this bitter environment even as they left it, to find ingenious and appropriate solutions for their problems. The unobtrusive and cheerful comfort of my office has made it possible, I believe, for clients to work more efficiently, and for me to avoid debilitating stress. That these are important considerations has long been well known. Few therapists or other consultants think it applies to them, however. They believe they can rise above or escape the influence of context. Yet they are often made uneasy by their work and are unable to locate the cause of distress.

My office also functions as an excellent lesson for the clients, in transitions both instinctive and learned. When clients enter the office, they frequently ask to use the bathroom, which is tucked behind the tiny cottage kitchen. Meanwhile, I prepare a pot of tea. When the client emerges, he or she is offered a cup of tea, and reminded, if necessary, to write me a check. My attention is then completely turned to the problems of the client, who, for his or her part, has just undergone the transition between anticipating the session and entering the session. This transition, as I begin by pointing out to them, occurred through their use of the bathroom, their sip of tea, their writing of the check. After these transitional activities, which include both social and kinesthetic adjustments, the client's attention is as completely turned to the work as is mine. This is a valuable model for the difficulties of life outside the consulting room.

I find it convenient to work next door to my living quarters. When my work comes home with me in the form of vexing issues that have arisen during the course of talking with a client, I find that simply walking out to my office, even in the middle of the night, and sitting in my special chair, enables me to generate a few lines of possible resolution of that problem; and then, as I walk back to my house and my bed, to let it go.

The old man tells me he will die soon. He's told me this about every month or so for several years. I don't think he will die soon. This too he traps me into arguing about.

Shakespeare said, "If it be now, 'tis not to come; if it be not to come, it will be now; if it be not now, yet it will come: the readiness is all. . . ."

This quote, hand-calligraphed on fine archival paper and framed under glare-proof glass, hangs in my office on the wall to the left of my desk, the wall without a window. There also hang various certifications that reassure and give confidence to many of those who use my professional skills. The Shakespeare quote always seemed to me a perfect one for those who face imminent death, and also, by extension, those who face any event that they fear. The quote reminds us that an event can be transformed in the mind from a terrifying one to one that can be affected by the particular transition we choose to define it by. This transformation within the mind is not so dissimilar from the change wrought upon the heart by a hot shower.

Nevertheless, people being what they are, and forming attachments as they do, there is a good deal of pain associated with these passages. This is to be expected and even planned for. When a little joy is manifested as well, it may be received with suspicion, because it is ephemeral. Love particularly is coveted and striven for, valued and cherished. It cannot be stolen or traded, negotiated or bargained, because, as we know, it fits only the lover, as the print fits the finger, even though the lover does not create it or cause it, but suffers it, endures it, as it falls like a smothering shroud over one's life, and covers and colors all one's perceptions.

For me, all the intolerable residue of betrayal by my only great love has expanded and diversified. It's, if not transformed, certainly mutated and stretched. It's become the tools and tricks of the transition consultant's trade.

The old man is dead. He died in his sleep, according to his daughter, uttering not even one last cranky word. Some days after the funeral, I spent an afternoon with her. A seizure of grief passed through my body as we talked, and I wept. She remained calm and comforting although she too had tears in her eyes. I made my offer, proposing she begin to learn the fundamentals of death transition. She quickly agreed. When we parted we clasped each other's arms. We were both moved by the connection. It was revealed to me at that moment the existence and nature of my loss. The old man's absence has since repeatedly evoked my earlier, more drastic deprivation, and I believe now I'll never recover.

I never thought I'd miss the old man so much. One time I asked him if he felt okay. I thought he looked a little pale. "No, I don't feel okay," he said, testy, arrogant. "I never feel okay." He paused. "But I don't feel bad."

I don't feel bad either. I can stand under a hot shower feeling the heat in every pore; I can drink a cup of tea between this and that, but I can't cross over to what's gone. I may never really recover. The most pragmatic solution I've arrived at, so far, is to define the transition within new limits, shorter in time and more manageable.

Jack Bailey's Beach Story

I'VE BEEN ASKED TO write a little story about my friend Peach Moy. Peach wrote a movie, the movie won a prize, and now the *Long Arts Magazine* down south wants to do a feature all about her. I was asked to contribute, I was told, because I'm a writer too. Well, I don't like to call myself a writer. I write poems, or short indented pieces, I guess you could call them poems. The word "writer" is a club, you could beat someone to death with it. And then they'd be dead and you'd still have the weapon everywhere you looked.

But okay, I'm willing to write a little something about Peach. She hates movie people, she says, and city noises, too. When she comes up she stays with us or other pals. She sleeps till noon and walks on the beach and goes out to Lorenzo's every night to eat. I don't think it's gossip if I say she looks good up here, and doesn't have the sort of gray peripheral burnt-out look she has in the city. When we visit her down there she's always clutching her calendar, well, they all do down there. They can't help it.

You know, I don't like too much to talk about people's characters. I've always considered it gossip, and I like to think I'm too fastidious to do that. I may not actually be, but I like to think I am. But I could tell a little story about a day we had. A beach day.

Norma drove, I almost never drive anymore. Peach met us at the gate and we walked on the headlands toward the stretch of dunes where some asshole is building a whole tract of slanted glassy houses, each with a view. Probably the guy is a member of the Coastal Commission. Anyway, you walk in that direction along this skinny rocky path. That time of year there's lupine and Indian paintbrush and wild mustard, plus some other little pink guys that Norma knows their name.

A luminous, slightly overcast sky hid the actual sun. The waves were glossy brown where they curved over into foam. The cliffs were overgrown with several kinds of tough, tenacious ice plant and the ubiquitous wheat-like stalks of tall yellow grass.

I had a pint in my pocket that Norma didn't know about, and I was carrying my binoculars. Norma had a backpack on with apple juice in it and bread and cheese and a couple oranges. Peach was all warm in her new down coat that had a city edge our clothes don't ever have no matter what. It's not a thing I especially think highly of, but it is a real thing.

Norma was in a mood, and we'd been bickering. Bickering is a non-sweet way of talking to each other, and I don't prefer it. I had my bottle hid in the biggest pocket of my khaki coat all wrapped up in an old wool scarf that I let the fringes of trail out like the little red herring that it was.

Still: "You've already put away most of a six-pack this morning," she complained in the car, "that's your ration for this evening." It's true, it was just a little after noon. My darling Norma. So we were both glad to see Peach, it tore up that particular script. We started talking fast and interrupting each other in an almost raucous manner as we threaded our way along the path at the edge of the cliff. There was a thin wind against our left sides.

"Look at that sky," Peach shouted out. "It washes right down into the sea without a trace of edge." We looked. It was one of those no-horizon afternoons, you know, where the grayish-yellow sky blends into the yellowish-gray sea and there's no horizon line to be seen. This gives everything a shadowless significance.

"That's the rock where the seals come." Norma pointed it out.

"Seals!"

"Oh, yeah," I said. "They're all down here on a sunny day. Sunning themselves. Some of them lie on their backs."

"Their coats are in an amazing range of colors," Norma added. "You see big ones that are almost white. There's one right now—look—and look there's another one!" We could see their little doggy faces moving smoothly in the line of a wave. We all took turns with the binoculars. Peach was excited, she doesn't get to see wild creatures in the city. Several of them were side-stroking their way around the long rock, deciding probably if this was a good time to rest, or maybe just looking for fish.

When we got to the place where you climb down, the ladies went first, they were both more agile than me. I creaked and stumbled on down like a old worn-out robot. Then we walked on about another half mile. The tide line was sinking and more shells were revealed. We picked them up, of course, and those tiny glassy rocks that if they were much smaller they'd be sand. Norma was collecting driftwood nubs of roundish fruity shapes. They were small pieces, they fit right into the palm of your hand. Smooth like human skin, and they had a warmth. You knew they were living wood, or used to be.

Peach picked up bits of seaweed as we walked. The kind she favored was wispy little tassels and sprigs. They made a stiff crackling sound like dry leaves anywhere. At the place where the cliff runs out into the sea and you can't go on, we turned and found a bunch of new stuff, fresh little disposable treasures. Then we walked on back to where we'd started.

First we built a little fire. Then we ate our bread and cheese and fruit. Of course it was delicious, everything is delicious on the beach. I pretended I had to pee and I walked a little ways down where the women couldn't see me and I had a couple of restorative swallows from my pint. Felt good. Renewed my *elán vitál* and my sweet nature too.

Of course Norma doesn't like me to drink. She goes to those meetings, regularly misses the first half of *Star Trek the Next Generation,* and never a word of what goes on there comes to me. I'm ostensibly the reason she goes. Can you dig it? I've tried to wheedle it out of her, adding an extra kiss here and there, but it's not like a berry pie. Of course she and Peach go out to Lorenzo's where they talk about that stuff and eat a $10 breakfast. I don't think it's gossip if I say that Peach's ex-sweetie drank heavily. I don't think it's gossip if I reveal that me and him are pretty good friends. You can classify this info as background. Just scenery.

Peach was picking up stems of dry grass blown down off the cliff like straws. She put them in a neat stack. Then we dumped out all the stuff we'd collected and began sorting it by color and size and some other more obscure criteria that I don't know how to explain.

Peach started to arrange all her stalks in a checkerboard pattern. I put a dignified-looking piece of driftwood in the appropriate square and said, "This here's the queen." We put each chess piece in its starting position. The paler ones were white pieces, and the darker ones were black pieces. We had plenty of material. Driftwood chunks were the kings and the queens. Shells with seaweed decorations in them or on top of them were bishops and knights and castles. Little rocks were the pawns. We kept substituting and improving on each piece. Every time we got it all perfect, one of us saw a new possibility. "No, wait! Let's use this shell upside down, with this other little shell on top of it, it makes a much better knight!" And then we'd have to make a matching knight. I forgot about the few swallows of vodka in my pocket, and our little fire burnt down past its coals into a sand-scattered darker tinge. Well, I've felt similar concentration before. Sometimes when I'm writing it'll be one word, or one notion, that needs to be changed and then changed back to the way it was and then stared at and then changed again. Finally we saw it would pretty soon get too dark to play, none of us has what you'd call really good eyes.

We left the chessboard with all its pieces on the smoothed-out piece of beach. We climbed up to the top, me behind as before, and snaked our way back to the gate. I spied a couple of ospreys catching thermals along the edge of the water, very, very high. I'd seen ospreys near that stretch before. I looked at them through my binoculars, but there was no way I could have identified them as the same pair, or even as a different pair. In my next life I'll be a hawk, you can count on it.

Peach said, "Well, Jack, was that committee art, that chessboard that we did?"

Norma and I have known Peach pretty well for twenty-five years, which means we've been through some stuff and lost some friends to all manner of implausible accidents and plagues. We've in that time talked a good deal about art, and I'd say that our feelings are well known to each other. I would say there's not a lot of unknown opinions. In my view you got to have an individual vision to write a poem. Try to do it with two poets, and right away you've got another thing, it might be a good thing, but you wouldn't really want to call it a poem. I explained all this to the ladies.

"What about those murals I took you to?" Peach's question jarred my formulation, because I've seen those murals down in the city. Bunch of guys got together, did those on the street. Powerful. Powerful. So while I was thinking maybe I have the wrong take on committee art, she went on, "Well, then, was it conceptual art?"

Another thing I view with suspicion is what I guess they call now conceptual art that just blows away after you take all those chop-cropped grainy enigmatic pictures of it. Then you hang up the pictures in some long skinny esoteric gallery somewhere, and the thing that's blown away is never seen or read by anyone. It's like a translation by someone who doesn't speak either language. I hate that stuff and have never had any regard for it. Myself I think and think about an arrangement of words, which is not the same as writing them down. But the chessboard and the chess pieces we made on the beach that day, and left them there on the sand, what would you call that stuff? We agreed to call it a real good time.

We got back to the gate and turned to look at the western sky. It was a whitish yellow color above a now-visible horizon line. The sea was a shimmery purplish blue near the shore, graying out farther on to a pale green lustrous disappearing smoothness. The Indian paintbrush glowed neon on the meadow, and the lupine blurred into the brownish ripples of grass.

"Gimme a hit from your pint," Peach said. Without a word I fished out my bottle and handed it to her. Norma looked on real calm and sort of amused, I think. When Peach handed it back I drank too. In a way I was surprised, but in another way it was almost like I was getting a reward for our day. Superfluous, right? I didn't turn down the drink though.

Just before we parted, Norma asked Peach to come on over for some leftover lasagna, but Peach said no she had to do something else. Norma told me later that the something else was to put on her long jade earrings and drink brandy at the Harbor Lounge with Lincoln Cartwright. Now that's a piece of gossip.

Being Her

"We seem to be at an impasse here," Victor said. Too right, thought Hawk. Victor continued, "What I'd like you to do—this is an exercise you may find useful—is be each other. Connie, I'd like you to pretend you're Hawk, and tell Hawk, who's meanwhile pretending he's Connie, all the complaints you have about her. And vice versa."

This is such bullshit, Hawk thought, but I can play their silly game. He got up from his chair. "Then we have to change places," he said.

"That's very good," Victor said, "You've got the idea."

Connie and Hawk exchanged chairs. They both looked at Victor.

"Okay. Don't forget to breathe. Connie, why don't you begin?"

"Do you mean me or do you mean Hawk pretending he's me?"

"I mean Hawk pretending he's you."

Hawk cleared his throat. He looked into the corner of the room, where a very large-leafed monstera staked out a slightly excessive territory. "How shall I start?"

"Tell me why you and Hawk first decided to come here."

"Well, I was concerned about Hawk's drinking." That was good. He was doing good. There was silence in the room. Hawk wished he could smoke.

"Can I smoke?"

"Yes, you can smoke," Victor said. The silence continued

and spread as Hawk smoked, but he felt better with a cigarette in his hand. Except for the vigorous, even intrusive monstera, which seemed to occupy the entire corner, the dim room was sad. Dark-paneled walls supported a couple of paintings that looked like little kids' scribbles. A big desk was piled with manila folders and little bits of yellow paper. An answering machine clicked loudly to itself as it secretly answered a call. Hawk was glad Victor had turned off the phone.

"Connie?" Victor prompted Hawk. Hawk went on quickly. "Spence is rude to me and it makes me crazy. I mean, I know he's a normal teenager, I know all teenagers are aliens on this planet and for arcane reasons of their own refuse to conform to the rules of social conduct. He eats like an animal." Hawk stopped. The cadences of Connie's speech were pouring out of his throat and he felt a little frightened.

Tears immediately began to flow from Connie's eyes. "Connie doesn't know how to stand up for herself when Spence is so ratty," she wept. Hawk could barely hear her.

"We're not talking about your kids here," Victor said, "We're talking about you."

"Well, and Hawk's drinking." Hawk put his hand out, palm up, in the signal of stop that meant he had said enough.

Victor turned his head. He said to Connie, "Hawk, how does that make you feel?"

"It makes me feel frustrated. I want to put an end to it. I want to drink. I want to get away from their bickering. I don't care if he takes out the trash or not."

"If Spence doesn't take out the trash, who does?"

"Well, she does. She pretty much does everything."

Victor turned to Hawk. "Connie?"

"I do take out the trash. But Hawk brings home a lot of money. A *lot.*" Hawk paused. Connie sat slouched over, her legs apart, her elbows on her knees, her face in her hands. She was staring at the floor. Hawk looked at his wife, at her pulled-back hair and her thin long nose. She used to be so pretty, he thought. Why is she wearing that ratty T-shirt?

"I used to be pretty," he blurted out.

Victor leaned forward very slightly. "Yes," he said softly in an encouraging voice, "go ahead."

"I don't feel sexy. I don't feel, you know, attractive." Hawk was so surprised to hear these words roll right out of his mouth that he shut his lips tight. He could feel his teeth click. Connie started to cry again.

"Go on," Victor urged.

Hawk hesitated. Oh, what the fuck, he thought. "I used to have this green slip," he said, "this green silk slip. Hawk . . . Hawk loved it. He used to put his hands all over me when I was wearing that slip."

"What happened to that slip, Connie?" Victor's voice was soft, compelling.

"I don't know." Hawk stood up. "Jesus!" he said, "is this working? Why are we talking about that fucking slip? I don't like this." He scudded a little from one foot to another and abruptly sat down again. "I really don't like this."

A steady stream of tears slipped out of Connie's eyes, which were now red and puffy. "I don't like this either," she whispered, and blew her nose.

Victor leaned back in his chair. "What's happening now?" he asked.

"We're getting a little too close," Hawk said. "I don't want to be with Connie anymore." He stopped. Something was not quite right. "I mean," he said slowly, "I don't want to be Connie anymore."

Victor spoke very slowly and very clearly. "You're getting too close, and you don't want to be with Connie. Is that right?"

I've gone into another zone, Hawk thought. All I can do now is run it out. "Yeah," he said. He cleared his throat. This was really hard. He couldn't look at either Connie or

Victor. "Yeah, that's right."

The silence in the room was now terrible. Connie had stopped sniffling. Hawk took a quick peek at her. She was sitting up, her arms folded loosely. She had a tight, concentrated look that Hawk recognized with despair. She was on it now, she was going to argue, she was going to cause him a lot of pain. He was going to have to have a beer pretty soon.

"Okay," Connie spoke. "Okay, okay, okay."

"Okay what?"

"Just... okay. I don't want to do this anymore either. Let's just end it. This is a good time to end it."

What was she saying? "What do you mean?" he said. Why was she being such a bitch?

"Oh, god, Hawk. You know what I mean." Connie frowned at him and looked at Victor. "Now what do we do?" she asked. "Do we call the lawyers? Does Hawk go stay in a motel? What?"

"Wait a minute," Hawk said. "Why do we have to do anything right now?"

"Because we never do. Because if we don't do something now, we'll just go on with ... it's got to be now. It's got to be right now. Victor?"

"I'm going to suggest that you work out the details in your sessions here. We can do some of it today. Connie, did you mean that you want Hawk to actually leave the house today?"

"Yes, I do. The sooner the better."

"Geez," Hawk moaned.

"I want Hawk to leave me the car," Connie said. Victor answered her. Hawk could not hear what he said. He watched their heads turned toward each other, their mouths opening and closing.

Hawk wanted a drink. He wanted several drinks. He thought of a cold beer, waiting for him somewhere. Victor was asking him something, but he couldn't hear the words through the cold wet glass.

The Dream of Ten Normas

EVEN IN THE BEST of times, meaning when Norma was there, Bailey's house was neither spacious nor light. But this afternoon, with Norma gone a year, heaps of derelict objects loomed and shadowed the rooms, bisected by slender pathways kicked out of little walls of newspapers. Rain was threatening, and a murky, somber, blotchy light came through the smeared windows from the dark sky.

Bailey was wearing the same clothes he'd put on two days ago, a T-shirt with wide suspenders holding up scruffy L.L.Bean corduroy trousers. This outfit, crumpled and stained, creased like corrugated hide when Bailey shifted in his chair. He roughly cleared a horizontal surface, about a foot square, on top of two or three books among the many scattered on the long table. Onto this small void he moved ashtray, cigarettes, lighter, soda pop, Elmore Leonard. He slouched in the chair and watched the cats gather at the bowl he'd just filled with crunchy dry cat food. He was listening to Charlie Mingus.

He calculated with despair and disbelief how many hours he had before Norma walked in the door. Twenty-two hours. He'd have to rest or sleep at least eight of those. Then he'd have to eat a few meals, say two, that's two more hours. That left twelve. He looked around. Couldn't be done. Think it over. Figure it out. She hadn't given him a lot of choice.

He found himself looking at a glass construction that Hawk had made. Sometimes Bailey thought he saw independent movement, regular as breathing, within the thin ranks of glass panes, which were arranged so as to confuse one's sense of opacity. He frowned at this familiar unfathomable object. Its thick layer of dust gave it the look of plastic. He ought to give it a wipe, shine it up.

When Bailey had first quit drinking, six months earlier, Hawk came over every day. Hawk had also driven him home from the detox center. They'd listened to jazz, washed the dishes, swept the floor. The glass sculpture had been cleaned. Then Hawk didn't show up one day, and dirty dishes rapidly accumulated. The next day Hawk came over and, after some small talk, cleaned up in the kitchen and even made Bailey's bed. But then he'd absented himself again for several days. Bailey didn't feel like getting it together on his own. Hawk resumed his visits, every few days now, but no longer offered to help. They drank soda pop and discussed Lester Young while the stacks of trash grew.

Bailey sagged. He listened to the tape in his head playing back last month's conversation with Norma.

Jack, honey, I don't want to spend my weekends cleaning up.

Sure, Norma. Makes sense.

Jack, listen. When I come next month I'm going to sleep over at Connie's. I'll go out to eat with you, and we can walk on the beach, but I won't sleep here or spend time here. Jack?

That's a no-slack position.

Yes, it is, honey.

Rain pattered on the roof and on the ground. Each drop sounded separate and distinct. It seemed to Bailey that one more lurch toward order, clarity, organization, space, light, vision, would be appropriate. Even admirable. He didn't want to think that those possibilities, upon which he somehow depended, were closed to him. Clean sheets, he thought, walking down the hall to the bedroom. But when he got there he stopped, paralyzed, overwhelmed by the gargantuan nature of the job before him. The bed rose like an island upon which filthy sheets, spotted with ashes and soda pop stains, churned and writhed. Piles of books served as bedside tables, balancing on their terraced surfaces a motley collection of political buttons, hash pipes, underwear, ashtrays, coffee cups, and tier upon tier of empty pop bottles, all sticky to the touch.

Say he divided up the housework into six parts: the bathroom, the bedrooms, the kitchen, the living-dining room, and trash removal. That would be a little over three hours for each part. Twenty hours. Nineteen, now. There was no way. Fat chance. Impossible. But he'd have to start. He couldn't really have Norma sleeping somewhere else, could he. No. She wouldn't do it, really, but she'd threatened. Her threat was proof that she had some serious feelings about the state of decay into which the house had fallen since she no longer lived there. She was living in the city, attending the classy medical school there. After twenty-five years as an R. N., she'd applied and been accepted and was now training to be a sort of super nurse, a diagnostic and technical specialist. The advanced degree would get her big bucks. More autonomy. More respect. Bailey uneasily contemplated all these rewards. More mobility. He'd visited Norma in her little studio apartment in the city, twice. It was a pretty room, with windows that opened out to the street, and a bathroom with a surprising sunken tub. Comfortable. Also immaculate.

Bailey sat on his bed, legs stretched toward the curls and waves of bedclothes. A narrow path surrounded the bed. Thrown on the other side of the path were piles of books, records, videotapes, shoes. Rugs, clothing, flotsam and jetsam, sleeves and socks of debris, covered the floor. A TV on a straight-back chair faced the bed. The walls were an erratic palimpsest of photos and clippings. Bailey rolled a cigarette and lit it with a disposable Bic. The rain suddenly increased in volume, taking on a deafening quality, and the sheer quantity of raindrops shook Bailey so that he trembled and the lighter went out. Heh. He cackled at himself. A little nap was what he needed. Clearly.

When he woke up it was very dark. He was still tired but had a sense of time having passed. It was time to begin, he knew. Gotta be now. Time was running out. He regretted for the hundredth time that he'd never had the sustained and focused practice that, he was now uneasily and morosely aware, might be necessary. Norma's attempts to set schedules, assign tasks, cover the maintenance in a planned and easy way, had been of course sabotaged by his drinking. If only he hadn't been drinking all the time, if only Norma hadn't been such a pill about his drinking, if only she'd been more of a pill and forced him somehow to confront the discomfort and extra work caused by his, let's face it, deliberate tolerance for chaos. If only he'd had these very realizations yesterday. When there was still time to clean the house.

Start in the kitchen, he thought. He stumbled down the hall. Gotta start somewhere. He leaned against the refrigerator, and tiny plastic magnets jabbed him in the spine. The dish drainer was stacked with clean dishes, but dirty ones occupied all the available counter space, nested inside each other within filthy pots in the double sink, their congealed leftovers hardened into cement on the stove, and were even heaped on the floor, close to the sink, waiting their turn. Occupying a lane of space between the cupboards and the floor was a row of brown paper supermarket bags overflowing with unrecycled trash. Sour-smelling rotted lettuce mingled with soda pop bottles and tuna fish cans. In the few feet of floor space roughly cleared near the dining area were four or five begrimed and crusty cat dishes, from which Chalky the house cat ate accompanied by her two cronies, the gray stripy one and the fluffy one-eyed black one, from the world outside.

Bailey sat down at the dining table. He saw again with a familiar fatigue that it was heaped with books and letters, some of them dating back several months, mysterious small plastic objects, grimy glasses, ashes, dirt, Hawk's dusty sculpture. He looked over the surface of the table until he spotted a couple of objects that he recognized and wanted. They were his rolling tobacco and his papers. He pinched wispy clumps of Bugler out of the sack and rolled a cigarette in his little machine. Then he lit it and smoked it. Fifteen hours. Oh, god.

He thought maybe he should call Hawk after all. If he had a flat tire in the rain he'd call Hawk. Maybe he could call someone else, though. Bailey leaned out of his chair sideways, then rose, creaking, to his feet. He thumbed out his little phone book, copied from Norma's big one before she left. His son's name, the older son who lived in Saint Helena, caught his attention, and a phone number as well. Saint Helena was three hours away. He leafed through his book. Clearly this was going to take some thought. Yes. He'd better think it over. Horizontally, for preference. Back to bed.

Bailey stretched out his arms, placed his hands under his pillow, under his head. Think about it. Figure it out. Ah, god, Norma. What you've brought on me. And not even a drink to fuzz it out. Figure it out. It's like the ospreys I see at the beach. Are they the same pair all the time. How can I learn to recognize them. How can I know what Norma will recognize as an effort. The bathroom, probably. Ugh.

Bailey's eyelids felt unbearably heavy. Think it over.

His eyes crashed shut like Venetian blinds.

He was watching from the tower room, which he didn't remember as having been there before. A sleek white van pulled up in front of the house. The back doors swung open and Norma marched down the ramp in her nurse's uniform, white Reeboks on her steady feet. Behind her came her identical twin. Then another Norma. Then another. Bailey's heart lifted. He was saved. The Normas, of whom there were by now ten, stepped competently into the house. They silently and cheerfully dispatched themselves two to a room, and pulled cleaning tools out of the air.

As they efficiently deployed themselves and began scrubbing, Bailey noticed their uniforms were dirty or smeared. No, they weren't dirty or smeared: there were large shadowy flowers printed on the fabric. No, the flowers weren't printed on the fabric: they *made* the fabric, big floppy-petaled flowers of a linen-like texture. They were faintly colored in transparent tints of brown, mauve, gray, pink.

Bailey sat on his bed as two Normas cleaned the room around him. One picked up all the dirty clothes and put them into a white plastic garbage bag. The other Norma picked up all the books and records and packed them neatly into a very tall bookcase Bailey had never noticed before.

Miscellaneous objects remaining on the floor were quickly sorted by both Normas, who put some into drawers and cupboards and tossed others into a black plastic garbage bag. Then the floor was swept, then it was mopped. Another black garbage bag was filled. The Normas gathered up the crumpled blanket, one on each side. They tipped Bailey right off the bed onto the floor, which was now smooth and clean, quite comfortable really. They stripped the bed and put all the linens into a white plastic bag. They turned the mattress over. From the very bottom of the linen closet, which Bailey had thought was totally empty, they pulled out a fluffy mattress pad, and flattened a clean pale blue fitted sheet over it. Another sheet, absolutely flat and horizontal, then a couple of warm, weightless comforters, downy and immaculate. Sheet folded back, pillows of a loft and billowiness that surprised Bailey, the whole composition crisped and cornered in a way Bailey could only remember from magazine advertisements.

From his place on the floor he watched the two Normas take away the plastic garbage bags. He followed them.

One of them took the white bag to Bailey's little utilities porch, where she rapidly emptied the bag and sorted its contents. There were two immense heaps of clothes and linens on the floor, one white and one colored. The washer was churning away. One of the Normas was removing towels from the dryer and folding them precisely in thirds, as he knew she liked them. Bailey watched a Norma carry two black plastic garbage bags out of the house. He looked out of the window. The van that the Normas had arrived in had been replaced by a big yellow scavenger's vehicle. BAILEY'S TRASH it read on the side in bold black letters. Norma threw her two black bags into the hopper at the back of the truck, where they were immediately ground up with a horrible screechy noise. Another Norma marched out with two more black bags, and the disposal procedure was repeated. All that trash out of his house? Bailey was impressed.

When all the floors were spotless and smooth, the Normas smartly smoothed the scrub tops of their still-crisp flowery nurse uniforms. Carrying their brooms and mops, they filed out to the waiting van, which had somehow reappeared, and without so much as a wave or a nod went away.

Bailey rose from the freshly made bed on which he was again reclining. He glided down the hall. The floor was no longer sticky. In the kitchen everything shone. The stove positively gleamed. The refrigerator, when he peered inside, smelled fresh. He saw lasagna in cling wrap, grapes, German beer, a pristine cube of butter, all neatly filed next to others of their kind. A fresh-baked pie was cooling on the drain board. Mr. Coffee's pot was full. Bailey poured himself a cup. Delicious. He cut a slice of pie and carried his snack to the dining table, which now had a long, shiny surface. A pot of pink tulips quivered almost musically on the table. Their leaves were stiff with tender green. Hawk's sculpture passed rays of sun through its panes into a hundred angled prismatic beams. As Bailey stared at the meticulously reflected shards of light, they melted and fell away and he awoke. "Shit, shit," he groaned. A familiar sour smell made him sneeze. He closed his eyes tight, not moving a muscle, but another sneeze overtook him and he swung his legs out of bed.

It was time to make a start. Past time. Good intentions should count for something. The dream faded patchily as he slowly began to pick up dirty clothes from the bedroom floor and toss them into one corner. He tugged sheets off the bed, moaning with a terrible sorrow he hadn't till then been aware of. He started a load of laundry. His back creaked, his stomach boiled, his mouth called out for coffee and pie. He'd never finish. Why was he doing this at all? Futile. He made up the bed with a set of clean sheets miraculously found in the bottom shelf of the otherwise empty linen closet. How had he known to look there? He opened the windows. It was still raining, now in slow, transparent drizzly veils. The sky was very slightly brighter. The room looked distinctly better than it had before. I'm making progress, he thought, amazed and puzzled. Minimally cheered, he stacked books neatly along the wall. Better still.

Bailey made a pot of coffee, shaking his head at the kitchen's squalid mess. Mr. Coffee sputtered and spat, and Bailey had to start over, cleaning out the plastic slide-in container that was choked with a hardened clay of old coffee grounds and a fungoid filter. I can't do this kind of work without coffee, he thought, and I can't get coffee without this kind of work. Classic. Like everything else. Sunk in gloom, he emptied the dish drainer. Finally, enough fragrant dark liquid was dripped through so that he could pour himself a cup. Delicious. Ahh. He took gulps of coffee while he washed dishes and refilled the drainer. Then he poured another cup and emptied the most visible ashtrays. Had he made a dent? Not really. He put clean dishes away, piled newspapers near the door. As he worked his dream came back to him in soft uneven rags. He knew he'd never make it, but somewhere inside him a crew of competent personnel knew what to do and how to do it. Maybe a little Diz would help. Bailey put on a record, lit a cigarette, drank more coffee. He began to hum along with "I waited for you" as he carried load after load of trash out to the garbage can. The rain had stopped.

Bailey washed more dishes. He swept the floor for the first time since Hawk had helped him, and was doing a fourth and maybe final load of dishes when Norma got out of her car and walked toward the house.

Bailey, at the sink, was watching the overcast mottled sky, which now had a faint, pale shimmery sheen, a portent of sunshine. He hurried to the door. Norma was carrying a bag of groceries and a pot of tulips, and Bailey, who had seen her car pull up through the window where he was watching the sky, opened the front door to greet her, his heart beating fast from coffee and dreams.

Leaving Town

"I DON'T KNOW," CONNIE SAYS. "He might hang on for a couple more days but he might not." She's calling from the hospital in the city where her father is dying. She's just gotten the doctor's report. It's 10 a.m. Hawk hangs up and right away starts washing dishes and calculating times. He can't leave town until 4:00 at the earliest. Okay. That gives him about six hours plus some leeway. Okay. The kitchen is clean. He sits for a minute at the table, drinking coffee.

First he calls the high school. He speaks with the assistant principal, who will personally take a note to Spence, who will then meet Hawk at Azevedo's Chevron at 3:30 sharp. Then he calls Bailey, who volunteers to come over every day and feed Spence's dog, Frito, and, if Frito appears lonely, to take him home. Hawk tells Bailey to write down the phone number of Connie's dad's house, where they'll be staying, and of the hospital as well. As soon as he gets off the phone he starts a load of laundry. While the washer is churning he makes four sandwiches with the leftover chicken and grabs all the apples and bananas from the fruit bowl, and packs them all up together. When the laundry is done, he picks out clean socks and underwear for Spence, clean socks and underwear for himself. He packs these in a duffel. He's pretty sure Spence took his jacket to school.

Hawk walks around the house, picking up newspapers and shoes, throwing away junk mail and empty beer bottles. He checks the clock. It's a little after noon and the house is shaped up. He walks out the backdoor and across the yard to his studio. He makes sure everything is turned off in there. Then he locks the door and enters the one beside it into his shop. He looks sadly at the oak cabinets, all sanded and with their first coat of Varathane drying. "Shit," he says, "shit, shit, shit." He locks the shop door, too, on his way out.

"Mrs. LeClair?" Hawk is on the phone again. "I won't be able to get those cabinets to you till Monday at the earliest. I feel real bad about this, but we've got a family emergency. Did you hear about Connie's dad, down in the city? He's in the hospital, very low." Hawk hates giving excuses but there's nothing for it. Ordinarily Mrs. LeClair is kind of a harsh-voiced, skeptical lady, but when she hears about Connie's father she gets real nice. Her own dad died last year, she tells Hawk. He calls Bailey again. "I guess you realize I won't be at practice tonight," he says.

"I guess I do," Bailey confirms. They talk for a few minutes about the new drummer, who they agree is going to work out fine. There is a fraught pause. "Tell Connie," Bailey hesitates, "you know, I'm right here."

Hawk leans over to rub a spot of hardened something off his jeans. "Hey," he says, "I'll call you."

When he gets off the phone, he fishes out an old pack of cigarettes from the junk drawer in the kitchen and lights one. It's about a year old but it tastes great. He feels a little dizzy as he smokes it, and sits down at the table with the very last cup of coffee in the pot. This is how it's gonna be, he thinks: smoking cigarettes and taking care of business, that's the day. It's now 2:30. Hawk takes a quick shower. He packs his shaving things and his sketchpad and his mystery novel. He puts everything in the truck. The lunch, in a brown paper bag, is on the seat. He spends a few minutes with Frito, telling him what will happen. Frito is calm. It's a gray, heavy day, and he just licks Hawk's hand and shifts to a more comfortable position on the porch swing. Hawk waves to him from the truck but isn't sure if Frito sees him.

At Azevedo's Chevron there's a message. "Spence called, his starter is out again, pick him up near the bleachers." While he's pumping gas, Hawk asks Grayson, the mechanic, if he can get his hands on a VW starter in the next couple of days.

"Call Ukiah this afternoon," Grayson says, "have it over here tomorrow."

Hawk drives over to the high school. Spence is sitting in the bleachers with a couple kids Hawk doesn't know. He's got his senior jacket on. He runs down when he spots Hawk's truck.

"Dad," he says, his head through the window, "I got here okay this morning, but then, after school, nothin', same old nothin'." Hawk and Spence pull out the tow bar and the chains and attach Spence's VW bug to the truck. They pull the bug back to the Chevron. "Did you talk to Mom?" Spence wants to know.

"She's holding up," Hawk tells him. "But she'll be a lot happier when we get down there." At the station they unhitch the Volkswagen and stow the tow bar. Spence gives Grayson the keys. Grayson waves them on and they drive off.

"There's some sandwiches here," Hawk points them out.

"I'm not too hungry right now," Spence says. "Okay if I smoke in your truck?" Hawk takes one of Spence's cigarettes and they both smoke. Hawk is silent as he thinks about the house, the studio, the shop, his car, Spence's car, food, money, Frito. Spence turns on the radio, looks sideways at Hawk, then snaps it off.

Hawk looks at his watch. It's a quarter to five. They've just crossed the county line. "Okay," he says to Spence, "let's do it."

Lizard Love

Jean-Luc Lizárd, captain of the Startank *Enterprise,* twitched on his smooth brown branch. His filmy white belly and neck pulsed, and his spidery fingers and toes gripped his perch. One beady eye turned in its swiveling socket, and a silent order was transmitted to his second in command, Madonna, and maybe to his ensign, Godzilla, as well.

Sitting on her son's bed, Connie watched his lizards through the glass wall of the tank. Spence's room was as tidy as she'd ever seen it, the blue-and-white-striped bedspread pulled up over a minimally wrinkled blanket and almost covering his shapeless old pillow. He'd picked up his dirty clothes before he left for camp, at her and Hawk's urging, to be sure, and now, heaped together in a basket, they emitted a faint grubby smell. She'd do his laundry, and of course tend the lizards, but leave everything else untouched. Her daughter's room, on the other hand, would need clean linens, Connie supposed, and vacuuming too. Hannah was due soon—well, in a few days. She hadn't been specific. She'd said only that she was driving cross-country from her college to spend part of the summer with them and part with a friend down south. Driving across the country. Thank god they'd insisted on a Volvo, she and Hawk.

After they'd taken Spence to the bus early in the morning, Hawk drank half a bottle of gin and drove off in his truck. It wasn't the first time and it wouldn't be the last, but it was unprecedented that they hadn't had a fight or even a bump.

What pushed him to it this time, she figured, might have been Spence's surly departure, his long, rather patronizing lecture to his parents on lizard care, and his refusal to take out the trash one more time. Hawk hadn't, she now recalled, given her his usual fraught look during Spence's nastiness, the look that meant, "Hannah was almost as bad as this," or "We got through it with Hannah, we'll get through it with Spence."

It was hard not to think about Hawk. She turned her attention to the *Enterprise.* The captain was now apparently dozing. Delicately, Madonna crept toward him and onto him. The two lizards rested, Madonna's front paws balanced on the captain's head.

Connie watched them, fascinated. She'd come into Spence's room to care for them as he'd taught her to do. She knew how to mist the inside of the tank, how to throw in several crickets at a time, how to make sure the hot pad and lamp were on. Spence's phone calls from the high school, particularly in the spring when he was running hurdles every day, had frequently put her in charge, made the lizards for a few hours effectively hers. She was by now practiced in caring for green anoles, *Anolis carolinensis.*

Spence had bought a lot of crickets the day before he'd left. "There's enough to last while I'm gone, Mom." The spray bottle was full. He'd been touchingly anxious, but she knew he trusted her to take care of the three anoles, who, even as she peered closely into the tank, retreated rapidly to the top branches of the arboreal lattice Spence had constructed. Nervous about Hawk's absence, and sneezing repeatedly, Connie was distracted and charmed. She had to have these darlings where she could see them. On top of the TV? By her bed? What if she put them in the kitchen? Yes. It was a simple matter to unplug the wires. Two trips were necessary to collect the paraphernalia and life-support gear. Finally, she staggered from Spence's room carrying the heavy tank.

She set it down on the long table where the family commonly ate, so that she could look at the three minuscule reptiles while she recovered from her cold.

That night, when she woke to pee, the light from the *Enterprise* glowed from the dark kitchen; it comforted her, and she made a quick side trip to greet its inhabitants. "Sleep tight, gang," she told them. In the morning she smiled to see them as she filled Mr. Coffee. "Good morning, gang." She swallowed a handful of vitamin C and generic decongestant, and called Hawk's crony Jack Bailey.

"Hawk's over here," Bailey said, "drinking and watching football on TV."

"Did he say what his plans are?" Connie was nearly in tears. The conversation with Bailey confirmed she'd again been abandoned.

Bailey offered a soft, comforting laugh. "Not really," he said, "probably the usual. I expect he'll start missing his own bed by tomorrow or the next day. Just like always."

"Thanks, Jack. If there's any change—?"

"You know I'll give you a call, Connie."

She knew he would, too, if he thought of it. She was relieved Hawk was still alive and not crashed in his truck over the side of the highway onto the rocks below. But the phone call also reminded her that Hawk was still drinking, and his simple survival wasn't enough. She wanted apologies. She wanted to forgive him. She wanted reconciliation. Two days went by during which she nursed her cold and tended the lizards. She could feel her loving indignation fading away. Ancient ferns and limbic intuitive nervous systems filled her stuffy head. She sweated and melted into the warm, humid jungle behind the glass walls of the Startank *Enterprise.* She just wanted Hawk back. Desolate, she fell rapt into Spence's tiny prehistoric world, where miniature dinosaurs leaped and lumbered, blinked and devoured crickets. Hannah was due soon, any day now. Then Spence would be home again too. Then school would start, and she wouldn't have much time to commune with or stare at or whatever it was she was doing with the lizards.

Spence's dog, Frito, tolerated the *Enterprise.* Frito considered lizards the enthusiasm of the moment, was Hawk's opinion, while he, Frito, was the long-term bonded animal companion. In Connie's view, Frito wasn't too aware of the lizards, they were just little moving images behind glass, similar to the TV screen, which he similarly shunned. Now, as she watched the tiny beasts, motionless except for the silky throb of their diminutive ribs moving in and out, she thought again how alien they were. You couldn't relate to them on the same level as with a dog. Frito, for example, who lay at her feet with his head on her sheepskin slippers, had an oddball quasi-Airedale cuddly quality, which the reptiles conspicuously lacked. They, on the other hand, had the allure of the non-mammalian world and the opulence of the miniature. They were ambiguous, mysterious, other.

The kitchen/dining room in Connie and Hawk's house was long and narrow. The sink faced Hawk's workshop out back, and at the other end of the room the big table stood by a window. Outside were the porch, the front yard, and the road into town. It was on the table, where Connie also prepared classwork, that the *Enterprise* had been placed. This was already a densely occupied corner. The toaster was on a shelf overlooking the table, next to the salt and pepper. Shelves below held letters from Hannah, an answering machine, a jar of pens and scissors and X-Acto knives with their blades stuck into corks. Family photos were taped to the walls. Connie sat down with a cup of tea into which she'd put a shot of brandy for her cold. She stared at the lizards, and they stared at her. The captain at this moment was nubby brown, stretched out on a branch of exactly the same color. Madonna lay on a flat rock directly below the light, glowing an eerie idiosyncratic green. Godzilla was green, too, nearly invisible, poised on a long sword-like leaf of gleaming dracaena.

Connie's cold, which had developed full-blown the minute Hawk drove away drunk, had made her sweaty and listless. Her nose was red and her eyes were pink. Her hair was pulled back, fastened carelessly with a rubber band, and her face had a pale pasty sheen. She wore a ragged once-red sweatshirt and khaki pants that her son Spence had last semester discarded. Her expression was very slightly that of Susan Sarandon rubbing lemon on her arms in the movie *Atlantic City:* abstracted, calm, taking time out from all the shit. As she gazed, her lips slightly parted, her head resting in her hands, the captain ran quickly down his branch and with a snap ate an ambling cricket. Connie breathed slowly. Godzilla too breathed slowly, and moved, almost reluctantly, to Madonna and walked over her until he covered her. Then he lay his head down on top of hers and appeared to sleep.

Connie admired the meticulous way her otherwise inattentive son had set up the life-support system of the *Enterprise.* Inside, a little jungle grew. Dracaena, pothos, and blue-eyed grass were rooted in the moist potting soil and sphagnum that layered the bottom. On the carefully latched screened top a lamp was taped. This lamp, and the heating pad under the tank, kept the animals warm. Branches were artfully arranged, and the lizards liked to roam or sleep on the tops of these. Flat rocks under the lamp were favored basking spots. Spence had been explicit about the dispensing of crickets. These lively little fellows jumped and lolled around their own screened box, which held a moist sponge and a heap of cornmeal for their insect sustenance. So far as Connie could see, the system permitted Spence to be a kind of god, and also an observer of alien life forms.

There was no doubt that they were beautiful, all of them, the brilliant green reptiles with their impossible elegant threadlike tails, the restless insects, the lavishly blooming grass, the branches, the shreds of feathery sphagnum.

Connie drank tea and ate oranges, cried when she thought about Hawk, took antihistamines, and watched the lizards. She was surprised to find the small animals so compelling. How big a brain did they have, after all? How much complexity were they capable of? For example, they were by no means always green. They turned brown sometimes, sometimes pebbly, sometimes smooth, and seemingly on a whim. Spence had said they changed color to thermoregulate, becoming darker when they were cold and lighter when warm. But what if it's an art form, Connie thought. Maybe it's their way, or one of their ways, of expressing themselves. Did they express themselves? Did they interact? Godzilla lay motionless for hours, on top of or beneath Madonna. At other times he ignored her. The captain was a loner most of the time, but sometimes he too crouched or reclined next to or overlapping Godzilla. "Lizard love," Spence told Connie, pointing to a drowsing pair.

The week slowly dragged on. Periodically, Connie dropped a scoop of agitated crickets into the *Enterprise*. Although she hated the idea of live food, she loved to watch the hunt. The lizards were fast, but they sometimes missed. When this happened they paused, as though dazed and gathering their wits, and tried again. The crickets randomly skittered about the tank, but, Connie wondered, despite their senseless movements, did they deserve to be eaten alive? Yet that was how it was. Cruelty and surprise were conditions of life.

Connie slowly made a list of things to do, and another list of items to buy at the big market in town. From time to time she rose from her chair, and with Frito padding behind her, his paw-nails clicking softly on the floor, she made up the bed in Hannah's room, did a load of laundry, washed her teacup. She continued to postpone the shopping. The house was still. Outside, birds chirped away in the daytime, frogs croaked at night. Down the road a chain saw whined its irritating plaint. Frito went outside and barked at crows and then came back in and slurped water from his dish. Mostly he kept his head on Connie's slipper. Connie followed the excruciatingly slow adventures of Godzilla, Madonna, and Captain Lizárd. She tried to read. She snapped off the TV it seemed more times than she turned it on. She was waiting for Hannah. She was waiting for Hawk. Soon ten days would have passed since Spence's departure, and she would be waiting for him too. Food was getting low.

Her temperature was still up. She was tired of being sick. She was restless sleeping alone in the big bed. She rolled the covers around her, and as she did, she miserably remembered all the other times Hawk had gone binge drinking and she'd wrapped herself in blankets and stared into the dark and waited for the sound of his truck. She thought of herself and Hawk fixing dinner together, moving in a kind of choreographed routine, she chopping vegetables, Hawk adding seasonings, first she then he washing the few accumulated dishes. She pictured the kids sitting at the table with their homework spread before them, tidier than they'd ever been in reality, waiting dreamily for their parents to assemble the salad, the roast chicken, the broccoli, into a meal for which they would soon be told to set the table. She imagined the family eating dinner. Maybe the platters on the table would hold a heap of living crickets, their antennae twitching, their wings quivering. Maybe the family would be mama lizard, papa lizard, and the teenage lizards. She examined the *Enterprise.* The captain silently crunched a struggling cricket in his pink-lined mouth. Maybe she ought to get herself a snack right now.

Connie sat down sometime later with a tuna sandwich, the ingredients of which she'd foraged from a sharply diminishing larder. Fortunately, she'd had mayonnaise and an onion, but since there was no bread, the tuna had been stuffed into a frozen pita hastily microwaved into softness. There was no fresh food left, not a rib of celery, not a leaf of lettuce. Only one orange occupied the basket on top of the refrigerator, which was normally full of them. Connie loved oranges and ate at least one or two a day. She knew she'd soon have to go out to shop. Her long list of food items to buy included bread, milk, potatoes, eggs. If she put off shopping till tomorrow there'd be nothing to eat except her last orange. She stowed her teacup in the sink and resumed her vigil at the *Enterprise*. From time to time she sprayed the inside of the tank with water.

She'd only bathed once, and felt her body to be covered by a gritty envelope of sweat and isolation. She knew she smelled of sickness, but in fact she was feeling a little better. Imperceptibly, the light had changed. She looked out the window. It was a mauve summer dusk with dark blue night coming on across the sky. In the dim room only Godzilla was bright among the branches. Madonna and the captain were murky brown. Godzilla had eaten two crickets that day. Now he lay stretched out on his favorite branch. His eyes were closed tight, and he glowed a neon green in the light from Spence's special fluorescent lamp. Connie stared at his tiny black spot, a feature she thought might be analogous to the human ear since it was in approximately the same location on his head. She thought she remembered Spence telling her that the spot was in fact something completely else. She couldn't remember what.

Headlights bounced through the window and the glass walls of the *Enterprise*. Madonna jumped and so did Connie. A car was pulling up, a car that Connie, her heart beating fast, saw was big, a station wagon, yes, a big Volvo station wagon, Hannah's car. Hannah! No food in the house! A grubby, demoralized mother! Connie rose and went to the door, her sheepskin slippers flapping. Frito raced after her and began to bark in a special anticipatory way. Soon Hannah rushed in and they fell into each other's arms. Wrapped in her daughter's hug, Connie to her own surprise and embarrassment began to cry. They held each other tight. Connie was an inch or so shorter than her child, and as she felt Hannah's muscular arms, belly, breasts, smooth cheek, she wanted to stay forever in this embrace. Frito was barking in a frenzied welcoming manner, and the women turned to look down at him. Connie blew her nose as Hannah squatted to stroke the adoring dog, who tried to climb into her lap. A shadowy figure left the car, came up the walk, and stood on the porch. Connie realized she hadn't said a word of greeting or asked Hannah about her trip.

"Mom, this is Jason," Hannah introduced the tall bearded person who had advanced to the front door. Connie smiled and held out her hand. She noticed that Jason had a mandala-like tattoo on his forearm. "Is it okay if he stays for a few days until we go down to LA.?"

Connie knew this was a rhetorical question. "Yes, of course." There would be few intimate, comforting moments, that was clear. She wiped her face and touched her hair in a vague way meant to indicate an attempt at smoothing it.

"Where's Dad? What's this tank on the table? What's in it?"

"These are Spence's lizards," Connie began.

"Lizards? Cool! Jason, look at this marvelous little setup my cool brother did! Isn't this gorgeous? Where is Spence, Mom? Why is his stuff on the kitchen table?"

"Spence went to track camp. He won't be back until Tuesday." Connie stared at the two young people. They were grubby too, but unlike her they looked taut and rosy with health. They seemed to be bursting out of their clothes while one shocked glance in the mirror told her that she had shrunken beneath her own. She was still wearing Spence's sweatshirt and ancient rusty khaki pants. Her sheepskin slippers were ragged and smelled exactly like Frito.

Hannah and Jason, who were now looking closely into the tank, had usurped her place at the kitchen table. Frito's tail was wagging and he was panting, his tongue out. He had already made friends with Jason, whose pats he was receiving happily. Connie had no food to offer, no pleasant appearance to impress or reassure, and no explanations as to why Hawk was gone and what she had been doing. Her tears began to fall again.

She pulled the curtains tight on both windows. Stepping over Hannah's backpack and duffel, she paused in the doorway. Her daughter's face was bright and rapt. Excited, she pointed out to her friend features of the *Enterprise* and its inhabitants, features that Connie had already observed and pondered. Frito, by now on Jason's lap, was also looking at the *Enterprise* with a new interest. Connie watched the two humans, the dog, and the three green anoles. The six creatures were grouped together in the glow from the tank's fluorescent light. Connie, standing alone in the dimmest part of the kitchen, realized that her cold was gone, that she was hungry, and that maybe Hawk had this time left her for good.

Bailey in Loco Parentis

CONNIE AND HAWK WERE back together again, and Jack Bailey was relieved. Hawk's misery and confusion during the separation had an unsettling effect on Bailey. Crony pressed into the role of confidant, not unfamiliar but not comfortable either, Bailey had remained calm and supportive but was secretly impatient. In the last year, while Hawk and Connie battled to the point of split three times, Bailey thought of himself as biding his time. Now the biding was over, and he was sitting in his car, smoking a cigarette, in front of his house, waiting to take Hawk's son home.

He turned on the car radio, which was tuned to the local jazz station. He squinted at the moist, bright morning fog. Cold. His cap was wedged in the visor and he put it on. Better. Just then Spence came through the front door carrying a box full of stereo equipment. Bailey got out of the car and together they stowed the box in the back seat, padded by more of Spence's belongings: laundry bag, clothes, backpack, quilt, and another box containing running shoes, clock radio, and pillow.

"That's it," Spence spoke with restrained cheer.

"You want to drive?"

"Yeah." Spence quickly slid into the driver's seat and, without looking at Bailey, turned the key. His face was pink with pleasure. Seventeen years old, Bailey thought, they gotta drive or die. "Okay, let's go."

"You got your jacket?" Bailey remembered asking his own

boys, now grown and living elsewhere, that same question about a million times.

"Yeah," Spence said, "it's in the back seat." He reversed out of the driveway.

Bailey was looking forward to being alone, maybe not even thinking about dinner for a few days. Frequently he'd had dinner with Spence and Hawk, either at their house or at the Pacific Inn. There was never a suggestion that they eat at Bailey's, which during Norma's absence had acquired a bachelor status somehow irrelevant or inappropriate to meals. Hawk liked to cook a spicy prawn concoction served over rice, which Spence particularly loved. Bailey was happy to eat Hawk's good food when he could. At his own place Bailey prepared pasta with cheese on it, or he and Spence made sandwiches. It was good practice, he knew. Norma would be back in a few months, for good, and Bailey had welcomed Spence, if not the situation that brought him, welcomed the opportunity to relearn the tricks of cohabitation, like eating a meal at dinnertime. Still, a little time alone was never a burden.

Spence, who was finishing up his senior year in high school, had been at Bailey's since the latest, and definitely worst, breakup. Since their reconciliation Connie and Hawk had come over several times, both separately and together, to invite Spence back home. Spence made a point of telling Bailey he was of two minds. On one hand, he said, he was comfortable right there at Bailey's. Bailey stayed up late playing jazz records and assigned no chores. He was amused to see how this schedule suited Spence, who'd quickly fallen into the habit of a nap after running hurdles. When he woke up he showered, ate with Bailey, and hung out while he did his homework. Bailey didn't think this routine could do him any harm. He looked okay, didn't get sick, and kept his grades up. Except for summer camp, this was probably the first time Spence had lived away from home. He'd applied for admission to all nine UC campuses. A year from now, from this very minute, he'd be maybe lounging in a dorm in Riverside or Santa Barbara, a totally different town. It would then be a big deal to see his folks.

On the other hand, "It's true I miss my room," he'd told Bailey. He'd set up his stereo and other paraphernalia in the room once occupied by Bailey's sons. "And Frito." It had been decided that Frito would stay with Hawk. The dog was loyal, but easily confused. "And both my folks are good cooks. What do you think, Jack?" Bailey had shrugged and nodded, meaning anything Spence wanted to do was okay with him.

Bailey was comfortable, even without Norma, but he knew that Spence, whose house was orderly, was homesick. Connie's kitchen smelled of oranges. A basket on the refrigerator always held at least a couple and frequently a dozen. Oranges were a kind of staple at Spence's house. Connie brought them home in ten-pound plastic sacks. Sometimes four or five would be consumed in an evening, as Connie lay on the living room floor, weeping at a video of *Fanny and Alexander,* or *My Life as a Dog,* or another of the Scandinavian movies she loved. She'd remove part of the peel and slowly suck out the juice and pulp. Meanwhile, Bailey, an easy visitor with near family status, would sit in the kitchen with Spence and Hawk. Hawk slowly sipped his one permitted beer; Spence alternated sections of orange with bowls of Cheerios; Frito sprawled at Spence's feet. Bailey himself often put away a couple of oranges from time to time while he and Spence and Hawk played Scrabble or Gin Rummy. Spence won at cards, and the men groaned with pride. At Bailey's house, there were no games, no snacks, and certainly no oranges. During his first week there, Spence had brought over a few. Bailey felt uneasy seeing the round, glowing fruit on his dusty refrigerator but he ate them anyway.

Now Spence drove slowly down to Main Street, coming to a complete stop and deftly shifting gears at each corner. Just before Main they passed the junior high school, where Connie taught math and art. Bailey glanced sideways at Spence, who was looking straight ahead at the road.

Connie had moved into town during this latest split. That was a first. She'd found lodging in a house occupied by two colleagues, walking distance from Harbor Point Junior High. She'd also, naturally, taken her van, which, for the few months he'd been driving, Spence had borrowed at every opportunity. Bailey and Hawk had plenty of nostalgic talk about Spence's driving, which had reminded them of Bailey's kids' first cars, which in turn set them off onto their own teenage driving experiences.

Spence made a right at Main. "How long's she been gone, Jack?" he asked. "Norma," he explained.

"In her third year," Bailey said.

"Geez, that long?"

"Oh, yeah."

"You and Norma ever split up? Before now, I mean. I mean, I know you're not split up now. It's not the same." Spence was embarrassed, Bailey could tell. Of course he knew Bailey was living alone only temporarily, knew Norma was in the city studying at the medical school. This was pretty personal talk.

"No," Bailey allowed as how it was not the same. "When she's through school she's coming back. That's what she said, anyway. I tend to believe her."

"Heh, heh," Spence acknowledged Bailey's little joke. He stopped at a red light. "Well, how long is it going to take her to finish up? Get her degree?"

"Another half year at least."

"My dad missed my mom," Spence blurted out, "while she was gone. I guess you must miss Norma." At the green light he smoothly accelerated.

"Oh, yeah. All the time. You must've missed your mom too."

"Well, yeah, but I see her in town. For lunch and all that. Course we couldn't drive in together like we used to. She used to let me drive, you know."

"Yeah?"

"Practically all the time. Her car needs work real bad. You know?"

"Yeah?"

"Oh, yeah. The brakes are bad. There's a terrible rattle, I think it's maybe in the transaxle." Spence reddened as he uttered big-time sacred auto jargon.

"You know, me and Norma did split up a couple times." Bailey delivered this extremely intimate remark as quietly as he could. He looked out the window, so that Spence was free to disregard it if he chose.

"Really?" Spence was too interested to observe Bailey's courtesy constraints.

"Oh, yeah. Before you were born. Even before Hannah was born." Bailey knew the time before Spence's older sister existed was the Dark Ages, but still. He thought of Hannah, now at school back east. Then his thoughts took him to Spence, who would be in school next year. Yesterday, Bailey had watched Spence meticulously dusting with a damp paper towel the panes of his dad's glass sculpture, which occupied a space on Bailey's table bounded by a pile of books, a row of empty soda pop bottles, and a pot of once-pink tulips, whose mushy dead stems now flopped over the dry soil like the dormant fleshy tentacles of a dozing alien.

Bailey had enjoyed his own sons. They were all grown-up, they were men. Spence must've remembered when they lived at home, shared the room that he'd just vacated. They would've been old to Spence, big, hanging out with a raucous, intimidating group of teenagers, never ever mixing with the adoring kids. Now Spence was big, taller than Bailey for sure; and the delicate squalling infant Hannah had grown into a pre-law Ivy League beauty. Bailey shook his head in wonder.

Spence turned inland on North Point Road and concentrated on his driving. Bailey was grateful. He didn't want to answer any more questions or disclose any more history. A quick glance told him the boy was anxious but feeling good. Bailey felt more and more relieved that Spence was going back to his parents where he belonged. Coastal cypress clawed the sky. The sun slipped suddenly out from its scrim of overcast gray, and within a couple of minutes Bailey was warm. He removed his cap and threw it in the back seat. Next to him Spence rolled down the window as he drove. When they pulled up in front of the house, Bailey saw right away that Hawk's truck was there but that Connie's van was not. Hawk was standing on the front porch. He looked pretty spiffy, a clean shirt tucked into neat khaki trousers, his hair freshly combed. He held up his hand in a formal gesture that could have meant welcome but could just as well have meant stop. Frito flew down the front steps, barking happily, and rushed over to Bailey's car. Bailey got out and began to walk toward the house, Spence close behind him, and Frito close behind Spence. Bailey stopped. Something was wrong. "Hey," he said. Spence and Frito passed him on the path. Bailey stood where he was, uncertain.

"Come on, Jack," Spence said. Bailey shook his head and turned away, frowning. With a glance at his dad, Spence followed. "What is it, Jack?" he asked Bailey. Bailey walked to the car and got in. He lit a cigarette. Spence looked over at his dad on the porch.

"Hey, Bailey," Hawk called out, "I'd like the company."

Spence was halfway back up the path, Frito following.

"Where's Mom?" Bailey wished he couldn't hear every word so clear.

"Ah, god," Hawk said, "It's over, Spence. She's left for good. She's left us." He started to cry. Bailey had seen Hawk cry only one other time. That was a few hours after Hannah was born, and Hawk, who'd been in the delivery room, woke Bailey up at 6:00 a.m. to describe the birth. As he told how Hannah had come out of Connie's body, how one outrageously tiny perfect hand had clutched the doctor's finger, he wept. Bailey's throat had felt lumpy, and his eyes had stung, whether from the early hour or from his friend's revelation he hadn't known.

Spence moved toward his dad, then stopped as though encountering a wall of terrible revulsion. He looked at Bailey, who was sitting in the car smoking and watching his two friends. Then he looked back at his dad, who was standing on the steps crying. He turned again toward Bailey. Bailey lovingly gestured to Spence, then wished he hadn't.

No Blame

Ellie bent down to kiss her mother. "Miriam still didn't call me," Dora said. Ellie opened her mouth to respond but Dora had already changed the subject. "Eleanor, sweetheart, I have a real treat for you today. Can you guess what it is?"

"Chopped liver," Ellie said. Dora shook her head. "Eggplant? Matzo balls?"

Dora was triumphant. "No, you can't guess!" The gaze from her filmy eyes seemed to pull her entire head forward on the drooping neck that emerged from between the shrunken shoulders. Her face had a thousand lines cutting deeply into the soft pink skin upon which geometrically defined areas were incised among the masses of wrinkles. She wore diamonds screwed into her ears.

By now Ellie was actually getting a little hungry. "Cookies?"

"Yes! I felt good yesterday! It wasn't too hot! I made cookies for you, sweetheart. But you must take some with you for my darling Rose." Ellie greedily ate a few of the wonderful cookies Dora now brought to her on a plate. How did she do it? And why couldn't Ellie or Rose recreate these unique cookies? What did she put in them, anyway? They had copied out the recipe a hundred times, but when they baked up the buttery dough the crumbling results were disappointing. Not thin enough, not crisp enough. Ellie's ex-husband, Richard, an experienced scholar of Dora's cookies, said of one particularly close batch, "There's a certain core tenderness that's lacking here, Ellie. Sorry." However it was done, Ellie was glad to eat them now. She put on water for tea and set out the blue and white cups.

"Mama, remember, I brought my fortune-telling book today."

"I'm waiting for your cousin Miriam to call, the *momzer,* she's been in town for three days and not a word."

"Mama, remember we talked on the phone yesterday? You said it might be fun?" Did she remember that conversation? Did she understand what it meant?

"Who needs a fortune? Life goes on. I'm going to die, and that'll be it. You'll live, and Rose, bless her heart, will live. Now you know what it is, you have a daughter of your own."

"Mama, you said—"

"Sure! I remember! Did you bring your Chinese book?" Dora spoke in a low, sweet voice. Occasionally, when she had not spoken aloud for some time, her voice was cracked and strained. She cleared her throat frequently, with a little "Ahem!" sound.

"Okay, Mama, now first you have to ask your question."

"Go ahead, darling."

"No, no. You have to ask a question."

"What question?"

"Any question you want."

"I don't want to ask a question. I thought you were going to tell my fortune."

Ellie said clearly, looking directly at Dora, "I'm not going to tell your fortune. The book is going to tell your fortune. But first, you have to ask a question."

"Okay. I'll ask about you. I'll ask if you're going to get married again."

"Mama, you can't ask about someone else. Ask about yourself."

"What can I ask, sweetheart? What can I want to know?"

"Well, you could ask if Miriam will call you. In fact, Mama, you can ask about your relationship with Miriam. You can say something like—"

"Can I ask a secret thing?"

"Can you—?"

"Do I have to say it out loud?"

"No. You can ask a secret thing." Ellie was disturbed. She got up and poured boiling water into the teapot. She brought it to the kitchen table where they sat.

"I'll ask a secret thing. There, I asked."

God, Ellie thought, how can I read her the answer if I don't know the question? Ah, well, does it matter? It's only to amuse her.

"Okay, Mama. Now take these three coins in your hand. You have to throw them six times. Every time you throw them, I'm going to make a special mark on the paper, and when there's six marks, we can look up your fortune in the back of the book, here, see?"

"Ah, too complicated for me, sweetheart."

"I'll take care of it, Mama. You just throw the coins."

"Are these Chinese coins?"

"Yes, Mama. Chinese."

"Okay, there."

"Okay, two yins and a yang, that's a broken line..."

Dora threw the coins gently, hardly bothering to jangle them in her crooked arthritic fingers. However, the fifth throw produced a moving line.

"That's good?" Dora poured tea, holding the pot with both hands.

"Well, it's more interesting. Once more now. Okay, let's see, you have 47 changing into 40." Ellie turned the pages of the black-covered *I Ching*. "47. Oppression, Exhaustion." She swiftly scanned the words of the oracle. She thought, god this was a bad idea. Now what do I do? I'll just do my best. "Okay, Mama, listen. Success! No blame! Mama, are you listening?"

"Yes, my darling."

"When one has something to say, it is not believed."

"What?"

Ellie read the sentence again. Dora smiled. "Sure," she said, "It's always that way."

Ellie went on, reading those sentences she thought might have significance for Dora. "He who lets his spirit be broken by exhaustion has no success. But if adversity only bends a man—"

"If adversity what?"

"Bends, Mama, bends. If adversity only bends a man, it creates power in him. At this time there is nothing you can do but acquiesce in your fate." Ellie stopped reading. She sucked air through her teeth. Would such words bring bad luck? She gulped a little hot tea. "Remain true to yourself, this alone is superior to all external fate."

"That's very nice."

"And here's your moving line."

"What does it mean, the moving line."

"Well, it means you get two fortunes. The first one, the one we're reading now, is about the present time. The second one is what will happen in the future."

"Ah. A little extra."

"That's right. That's right, Mama. A little extra. Okay, your moving line says, Maintain your composure until things take a turn for the better."

"There's no turn for the better at my age."

"We don't know that. How can you know that?"

"You're right, darling. Of course. So that's my second fortune?"

"No, that's still part of the first fortune. I'll read the second one now."

Ellie sipped tea. She turned the pages back and brightened a little at hexagram #40. "Deliverance, Mama. Listen. The difficulties are being resolved. Tensions and complications begin to be eased. Don't push on farther than is necessary. Clear the air, pass over mistakes, forgive misdeeds—"

"What? Sweetheart, read that again."

"Clear the air. Pass over mistakes. Forgive misdeeds. Wash everything clean."

"That's very interesting. That's really marvelous advice, darling."

"Does that mean something important to you, Mama?" Ellie hoped Dora would now reveal her question.

"Yes. Yes, it does. Forgive misdeeds. Ah. Well, why not?"

Ellie held her mother's mysterious hand, a twiggy, limp claw draped in a crumpled silky leafy substance. Why not, she thought. Ah, god. Why not?

After Leo Died

"SWEETHEART, COME IN." DORA'S sweet voice was querulous today, and hesitant. "Renata?" she asked uncertainly.

"Renata's parking the car. It's me, Ellie. Eleanor." Ellie came into the room and bent down to hug her mother.

"Yes, my darling, Eleanor, of course." Dora was sitting quietly on the couch, her hands comforting each other, stroking, rubbing. Ellie sat down close to her mother. Dora seemed very small. *I'm the grownup,* Ellie thought. As though she'd heard Ellie's thought, Dora frowned and imperceptibly moved away. *She's confused,* Ellie thought, *she's forgetting who I am. Don't take it personally,* she repeated her sister's mantra, *it's only chemicals in the brain.*

She could hear her sister Renata and Renata's daughter Julie arguing as they came up the stairs to the porch. "Okay, now," Ellie could hear Renata say, right outside the door, "just come in to say hello. Please be back in *one hour,* Julie. Don't be late this time."

"I can't be late, Mom," Julie said coldly. "You know I have to pick up the kids at four." They paused at the door. "Hi, Grandma." Julie smiled.

Dora peered at them. She pushed herself up and rose, teetering a little. Ellie, as surreptitiously as she could, nudged the walker with her foot toward her mother, who ignored it. "Renata, sweetheart, I have coffeecake for you," Dora said, hugging her elder daughter. She turned to her granddaughter Julie. "And my darling Eleanor," she said. Behind her, on the couch, Ellie felt resentment rising in her throat and jealousy flooding behind her eyes. *Why didn't she recognize me?* She knew there was almost certainly no coffeecake. Tiny Dora embraced tall Julie. "Got a new boyfriend, darling?" Dora's arm was around Julie's waist. "You look beautiful, Eleanor. Beautiful. You must have a new boyfriend. Ah, it's wonderful to be young."

"It's Julie, Grandma."

"Eleanor?"

"No, Grandma. I'm Julie. Renata's daughter."

"Renata?"

"Sure, Grandma. Renata," Julie gave in. Ellie and Renata exchanged a complex look, compounded of misery, hilarity, and relief.

"Renata, sweetheart. You look wonderful. Beautiful."

"How about you?" Julie asked her grandmother. "You got any boyfriends?"

Dora laughed heartily, holding her chest. She turned to face Renata and Ellie, who were now sitting side by side. "Ah, that Julie," she said, "that Julie, she listens with a hundred ears." Her two daughters burst into delighted laughter. Dora turned again to Julie, whom, it was now apparent, she had finally recognized. "Sit, darling. Sit. You're too tall for me. You look beautiful. Life is just beginning for you. Tell the woman to bring us a 7-Up."

"The woman?" Julie looked around wildly.

"Liliana. I'll do it." Ellie went into the kitchen. Liliana stood leaning against the sink, smoking a cigarette. A few dishes were stacked in the drainer. The stove was immaculate. The floor gleamed. Two clean place mats topped by place settings waited on the table for dinnertime. There was no trace of the previous meal. A small radio very softly played popular songs in Spanish. "Hi, Liliana, how's it going today?"

"Not too bad today. She little confused but she finally

ate lunch. Tuna fish sandwich she didn't want it. Cucumber, tomato, it didn't look good to her. From the freezer I took the Lean Cuisine." Liliana smiled triumphantly. "Six minutes in the microwave! Six minutes, Ellie! She ate the whole thing. Sirloin tips and rice. Then she lie down on the couch till you come."

"Good work, Liliana." Ellie opened the refrigerator and took out a couple of cans of 7-Up. "Sirloin tips and rice, huh? You better lay in some more of those."

Liliana shot Ellie an equivocal look of pride and amusement. She opened the freezer and pointed. Inside were a dozen boxes of various Lean Cuisine meals. "I fix the fresh food," she shook her head, "every day I fix the fresh. Because I like it. You know? But if she don't eat the fresh, I got the Lean Cuisine."

"Ah, Liliana. What would we do without you?"

"She starve, that's what."

When Leo died, Dora had refused to believe it. "He went to the bank," she explained out loud, sitting up in bed at 1:00 a.m. After a restless and fitful doze, she arose at 6:00 a.m., muzzy and groaning with pain. Liliana helped her to shuffle blindly to the kitchen table. There she drank a cup of decaf, which perked her right up. "Leo is just taking a shower," she told Liliana reassuringly. Sometimes she called out, "Leo! Leo! Come, your coffee's getting cold!" Much of the time she forgot him, as she did everyone and everything. Her hands caressed each other as old episodes were replayed in her diminished brain. The first thing she saw or apprehended took the brunt of these ghostly, rewired emotions, which now made up her most immediate experience. If she was eating bacon, which she loved, when a spasm of, say, aggrieved anger passed through her, she spat it out. "Pah! You call this crisp!" Liliana rolled her eyes.

About once a week Dora planned a little anniversary

dinner for herself and Leo. "Fifty years," she exclaimed to Liliana; or, sometimes, "Sixty-five years! What do you make of that!" Her arthritic old hands shuffled a couple of old photographs. "Cook a nice piece of fish, Liliana, with a baked potato. Leo loves baked potatoes." She dropped the photos. "Oh, Liliana, where's the present I bought him? What did I buy, Liliana? Remind me, darling."

"Silk underwear." Liliana had her own private jokes.

"He won't get anything else like that, will he." Dora sniffed with snobbish excitement. Liliana, who had slowly finished up the dishes, stripped off her rubber gloves and lit a cigarette. "Oh, Liliana! Better put it out before Leo catches you!" And the anniversary dinner was forgotten for another few days.

She continued to make excuses for Leo's absence. "I think she knows," Liliana told Ellie and Renata after Julie left, "but she don't admit." They looked through the front window at Dora. She had pushed her walker out onto the porch to call for Leo who, she claimed, was watering the lawn.

Ellie walked out and stood beside her mother. "Come in for tea," she said. "Liliana's making tea."

"Ah, he'll come in when he's finished," Dora replied, and then looked up, frowning, at her daughter. "Stand up straight. You didn't like the eggplant?"

Ellie admired the way Liliana and Dora made themselves understood to each other. Her mother had been erratically deaf for years. She grasped what was said to her if certain requirements were fulfilled: (1) if the person was well known to her, and spoke slowly and clearly; (2) if she wanted to hear what was being said; and (3) if she was lucid enough at the moment to find any remark interesting. Otherwise she winged it, and conversations with her were like trips to the Land of Oz.

Several times each day, Dora accused Liliana of stealing.

"You took my watch," she hissed.

"You're wearing it," Liliana calmly pointed out.

"Ha! I got it back, didn't I?"

Dora was feeble, but not too feeble to shop. The two women had ventured out to the market nearly every day for the last year. Liliana drove, a distance of about a mile, in Leo's old Buick. Dora masterfully decoded the items on her unintelligible list. Liliana paid the checker.

"He won't let me hold the money, he lets the woman hold it," Dora confided to the bag boy. "Leo. He says I lose it." She peered up at the tall skinny kid and said, enunciating clearly, "But I don't lose it. I hide it."

Liliana saw the boy look sideways at the checker. "Shit," he whispered. "Now what?"

Ellie and Renata were sitting at Ellie's small kitchen table. They were drinking a sludgy mixture of coffee and cocoa powder.

"She'll be depressed and disoriented," Ellie said.

"Yeah? Give me a little more milk. What is she like now?"

"That doesn't make it right."

"God, this is like a conversation with myself. Could we have a little common purpose here, please? A united front? More milk?"

"You're right." Ellie pulled milk out of the refrigerator and handed it to her sister. "I'm just trying to think. *Think.* Is there a way she could still stay at home?"

"Yeah, if we could afford another person, a backup person, like Liliana. Liliana isn't young anymore, she can't do it. The whole thing, I mean."

"I know you're right," Ellie repeated.

"Or, of course, she could live with you."

"With me? Where?"

"She could live here." Renata waved her hand, indicating Ellie's peeling paint. "Here, in your house. We could sell her house. There'd be enough money for Liliana and two other people."

"But it's my house. Where would I live?"

"You could live here, with her, in your house."

"With her, and Liliana? And the other person? Why can't she live with you? Your house is big, much bigger than mine."

"I have a family."

"And I don't?"

"Well, just Rose." Renata got up and began to mix herself another cup of bogus mocha. "And she's only home for a couple of weeks here and a couple of weeks there," she went on. "Once they go to college they never really come home again."

"Julie came home."

"That's different. Anyway, how long do you think Mama can hang on?" Renata sipped from her cup.

"Renata, you're veering. I have a family, and you have a family. Maybe it would be good for Mama to live with a family. She might have a richer social life. She might feel more, you know, cared for. Anyway, how long are Julie and the kids going to stay? Maybe she'll get back together with the unappreciated poet."

The sisters exchanged a sarcastic smile. "She says never," Renata said.

"Yes, but it could happen. I hope she doesn't, but you never know. Or she could move away on her own, or with a new person. They might be leaving any minute."

"She wants to wait until both kids are in kindergarten."

"When's that, next year?"

"What if it is? We love having them with us. Anyway, there's not enough room. As it is, the kids are sharing a room."

"Oh, *you* don't have enough room, but *I* have enough room? One bedroom for me, and the other one for Mama and Liliana and the backup person?"

"All right, Ellie. You don't want her and I don't want her. She's our mother and we love her but she's demented and she's nearly blind and deaf, and frail, and we haven't got the energy and we haven't got the money. *It's not required.* The Oakland Home for Jewish Parents is right over the hill, we've gone to look at it a million times, and it's a perfectly okay place."

"If it's perfectly okay, why do I feel awful? Why are we arguing about which of us is the most deprived and least able to take care of her? The truth is she always loved you best."

"Ellie."

The sound of her own name, enunciated in a warning tone by her older sister, made Ellie close her eyes. "Mama should be dead," she said. "She's lived too long." Before her father died, she'd felt merely worried about her mother, who was old, after all, and unsteady on her feet. After Leo was gone, the same line of thought then led to a more realistic assessment, and Dora's stooped posture, memory lapses, changes of subject, tremors, fatigue, all came together suddenly. *You're not my mom,* Ellie had thought, *I want my mom.* The discovery that Dora was a kind of replicant, or husk of the person Ellie still treated her as, was terrible. *My mom is gone, my mom is gone. My mom as I knew her to be my mom is gone,* she repeated over and over in a litany that she perceived to be as frightening as the situation. "I mean," she went on, "how many people in the world have parents in their nineties?" This was a question she and Renata had asked each other a hundred times.

"Millions," Renata said. "Penicillin. Good nutrition. Lack of stress."

"My god, we're almost elderly ourselves. It's just not fair to have to take care of her. We're almost ready to be taken care of ourselves."

"Speak for yourself." Renata was sensitive about being older than Ellie.

"I miss her," Ellie said. "This person is not my real mom."

"Remember her voice? Remember what a low sweet voice she used to have? It's so strange to hear her now, her voice is all cracking and, you know, old."

"Everything she says irritates me and repels me. She's not my mom, is why." Two tears rolled from Ellie's eyes. "This person is some kind of faded leftover of my real mom. I feel sorry for her. I have, you know, a certain amount of good will toward her. I don't want her to suffer or be in pain or be bewildered or hurt. But *I can't relate to her,* this old, bent-over woman, as she really is. Whatever that might be. What's left in there, in that flour-sack body, tottering across the kitchen to peer mistakenly at what she's cooking?"

"Or thinks she's cooking."

"Rubber bands in the salad." The sisters smiled a familiar ironic smile.

"Thank god for Liliana," Renata sighed.

"I mean, what's left? Some kind of food-giving instinct, but what can it mean? Is it conscious? What's in her head when her old, dull eyes look across the room and glaze out? Is she back in her past, does she remember *her* sweet-smelling mommy, does she want to go home and be taken care of and be safe forever in *her* mommy's arms? Help me, Mama, help me with this. This is too hard to do without you." Ellie began to sob. Renata put her arms around her sister. "Help me, Renata. I can't do this. I don't know how to do this."

It was Ellie's day to visit alone. She walked up the crumbling cement stairs. At the top was a driveway big enough for two vehicles. Dora would not permit visitors to park next to Leo's

Buick, not even in the rain, not even late at night. "What if there's an emergency?" she said, "What if the drugstore needs to deliver?" Her daughters were impressed that Dora could still spin out hypotheticals, and wanted to encourage the continuation of this kind of thinking. Hence they each dutifully climbed the stairs twice a week.

Over her shoulder Ellie carried her purse, with a bag of chocolatey coffee candies in it, and a glossy magazine for Liliana. She let herself in with her own key. Dora never heard the doorbell, and sometimes Liliana didn't hear it either. She was as immaculate and cautious with Dora as ever, but twice Ellie had come to find a stack of mail on the tiny porch. She didn't mention this to Renata, who often worried out loud about Liliana's bad knees. Today, however, the porch was bare. It had even been recently swept. "Mama?" She put down her purse. "Dora?" She walked through the front living room and into the hall. "Liliana?"

"We're in the bathroom," came Liliana's voice.

"Just a minute, darling, I'm in the bathroom." *Oh, good,* Ellie thought, *she's rational today, she's aware, it's one of her good days.* Ellie knew that one day, one of Dora's bad days, something would happen, and Dora wouldn't know, and it would kill her. Liliana would run out to the drugstore, the stove would explode, there would be a fire, Dora would fall, there would be some kind of old person's accident. When the phone was not answered, Ellie and Renata simply persisted and kept on calling. So far, there had always been an answer eventually.

Now Dora shuffled her walker over to sit on the couch. "Do you want some chopped liver, darling?" she asked. Ellie looked at Liliana, startled. Liliana shook her head.

"No, thanks. Have one of these." Ellie offered her mother a candy. Dora took it and put it in her mouth.

"I'd like a cup of tea, darling," she said in a quavering voice.

"I make it," Liliana said and went into the kitchen.

"Do you have any candy today?" Dora took another piece from Ellie and ate it thoughtfully. Then she suddenly began to speak. "He goes to bed early. I'm all alone here. I get so bored I want to scream. If I lie down to read, I'll probably fall asleep myself. When I wake up I sometimes hear his TV going in his room."

Ellie felt tears well up as Dora remembered when she could still hear the TV, long ago, when Leo was still alive. "He listens to the educational station," Dora said. Her voice was strong now, and unbearably sweet. "He'll be watching a movie about starvation in Angola or the bombing of Dresden. Then if I get up, for some ice cream or to make myself a sandwich, I'll see his light go on suddenly under his door, and I know he'll be reading one of those magazines about foreign affairs. It's almost like we're waking each other up, all the time, to make sure we're both still alive."

"Oh, Mama," Ellie said.

"One time I was napping on the couch about ten p.m. and something woke me up. I couldn't hear it but I knew it was a strange noise. I knew it was Leo falling, before I even put on my glasses and got off the couch. He was lying half inside the bathroom and half out, on his side, and he was breathing like a person breathing under water." Ellie recognized the story of her father's death. She'd never before heard her mother tell it so serenely, so coherently. "I called the ambulance right away, before I did anything else, and I put some towels under his head and covered him up with his flannel robe. Then I put my hand on his heart, and I could feel it beating. Leo, Leo, can you hear me, sweetheart? I said to him. I tried to make my voice low and calm. He opened his eyes a tiny slit. 'Call doctor,' he whispered, 'heart attack.' I did already, Leo, I told him. I already called the doctor. I took care of everything." Dora's voice cracked. "Then when the ambulance came, it seemed right away, couldn't have been more than fifteen minutes, I called the doctor's exchange and told them to tell the doctor to meet us at the hospital because Leo had had a heart attack."

"That was smart, Mama. You took care of everything."

"I'm very resourceful in an emergency."

"You certainly are, Mama. You always have been."

"At the time, I didn't know what really happened," Dora sighed, "if he'd really had a heart attack. Of course later it turned out that he had, and then he had that open-heart surgery. Remember when we waited in the hospital? And then he was gone." Dora smiled. Her blurred eyes were luminous in her old powdery crumpled face. She peered at Ellie with cheerful, unquestioning love. "But we're still here, sweetheart."

"Yes, we are, Mama."

"What, you're crying? Don't cry, darling. You'll find yourself another boyfriend. You're still young."

The Feather in Data's Wing

I WAS HOLDING THE letter from Herron while Lieutenant LaForge, on the TV screen, rerouted the dilithium power source. He was aided by the android Commander Data. Neither suspected that Commander Riker and Counselor Troy were having an assignation in a vertical access tunnel.

I'd run home from the deli with goat cheese and a six-pack of Anchor Steam, grabbed my mail, including Herron's letter, and panted up the two flights of stairs to my apartment. Immediately I pressed the remote. Captain Picard's voice told me the star date, and I knew I hadn't missed anything. A secret subspace message came in for Riker, and everyone on the bridge was curious about its contents, but too professional to ask.

During the commercial I lay where I was and finished the letter from Herron. I'd been waiting over two years for this letter, ever since he'd left town. He'd promised to write even as I screamed, "Liar! Traitor!" in a hysterical rage. Later, in a calmer, more considered rage, I found myself curious to hear from him. Then I sort of forgot about him for weeks at a time. My thesis proposal got accepted. I got a job teaching freshman composition. I heard from friends at Wisconsin that Herron had found a new girlfriend. But he'd promised, after all, to write. What would his first email say? *I've thought about you every day,* he wrote in my fantasy. That was satisfactory. *My life deteriorated as soon as I left you.* That was better. His imaginary email conveniently didn't mention that I'd screamed and begged him not to go. Now, two years later, it was clear that email was way too spontaneous for Herron, the sneaky strategist.

When the Cardassians had slunk back to their own quadrant, and Picard had made his mild concluding joke, the episode was over. I reread Herron's letter until I heard a knock on my door. It was the old guy from upstairs. I let him in. Harrison Metz was his name. He lived in the apartment above me. As it was Friday night, we had a date for dinner.

I always looked forward to these nights, which were ostensibly focused on dubious Chinese food; but Herron's letter had arrived like an earthquake or an avalanche or a sudden attack by the pitiless Borg, and I couldn't get it out of my mind. Before Herron had left for Wisconsin two years before, I'd thought we were just two English majors in love, promising academics with the added bonus of a rent-controlled apartment. What could be more wonderful? But if it was all so wonderful, why had he kept important secrets? He didn't tell me he'd applied for a TransArts Graduate Fellowship, and written to Maslin, the Conrad expert at Wisconsin. He didn't tell me he'd been accepted. These things take months, he could have told me any time, but I never knew. A week before he left, however, he couldn't put it off any longer.

"I was afraid to tell you. I was afraid you'd make a scene. I was afraid of a terrible fight," he said.

I tried not to cry, but tears pushed out of my eyes. We made love before he left. "I love you," we whispered while in each other's arms. Then Herron finished packing and we had our terrible fight and he took a cab to the airport. He'd already sent on his books in four big cartons. This is a good time to move, I thought, but where would I ever get a rent-controlled apartment in the fall of the year?

I decided instead to redecorate. First I sold the few scraps Herron had left behind, and his electric juicer too. I tossed his hiking boots and his mustard-colored necktie into the free box for the homeless. I smashed his favorite mug and threw away the fragments. I was pleased to discover that my expenses didn't increase too much. Herron had liked to eat out, he'd liked to go to jazz clubs, he'd liked to drink Scotch whiskey. I was frugal by temperament. Every day I picked up a sandwich from the deli on my way home from the library. I began watching television. My dissertation outline, which had been tentatively planned as a study of alienation as reflected in popular culture, was suddenly approved when I narrowed down the topic to a study of alienation as reflected in *Star Trek: The Next Generation.*

I moved the table so that it angled out from the kitchen area in a way I thought would separate food from relaxation. In fact it only made each activity inconveniently related to the other, but never mind. I also bought a couch, a folding futon. The two young men who delivered it put it together, making a lot of noise and playing rap music very loud on the radio they brought with them.

The futon boys had been overheard by Harrison Metz, whom I still thought of as "the old guy upstairs." I didn't actually know him to talk to, but we recognized each other. We respectfully and politely nodded to each other in the library or on the steps of our apartment building. This was the Berkeley way: not to intrude, but to let someone know you acknowledge their existence. That way, if they ever wrote a book, you could say, *Oh yeah, I knew him.*

So the old guy, Metz, had come down the stairs and for the first time was standing at my open door. "Need any help?" he said.

"Thanks, no," I answered. There was an awkward moment, the first of many to come. A sideways look was exchanged.

When the new couch was assembled, the futon boys took away the old, frayed one. They bumped down the stairs with it. Good riddance, I thought. I felt all clean and virtuous and as though I were starting over. Herron had been gone a month.

After I declined his help with the couch, Metz sort of rocked back and forth from one foot to the other in slow motion, a nervous habit I associated with his uncertain teaching style. I'd been a student of his, in the same freshman comp class I was presently teaching. His teeth had metal fillings, sure sign of an older generation. His smile pulled his beard apart. He was the same height as me, and as old as my parents, but his stretchy smile was sweet. He'd given me an A.

Now, as he rocked, he said he'd seen my roommate leave. He actually used the word "roommate."

"Yeah," I said, "He went to Wisconsin. Big-time prestigious fellowship."

Metz nodded. "I heard about it in the department," he said. Oh, so everyone had known but me. I was the one who was left in shock, cleaning up after Herron's departure, the apartment bleak.

"What, everyone knew?" Asking this stupid question made me feel stupid.

"Well," Metz faltered, "it's an important fellowship. I tried out for it once." Clearly there were many things he hadn't achieved. He dressed like he was still a teaching assistant, in a jacket that was all rumpled in the back, and Dockers. He had a kind of untended look. You could tell he lived alone. He'd been old for a teaching assistant even when I was a freshman. Now I was the teaching assistant, and he was one of those lecturers who're renewed every year by a miracle but never get promoted and never move on. Needless to say they do not publish.

A few days later, I was watching that episode where Counselor Troy tries to help Worf but he resists and refuses. He always does that. This was one of the phenomena my thesis would definitely explore. In fact, once interpreted and explained, it was actually one of the main points of my thesis: that the aliens have no greater affinities with one another than they have with actual humans from earth. When my doorbell rang it startled me because it was such a rare event. I was even more surprised when I opened the door to see Metz. He had a foil-covered dish in his hand.

"I made an awful lot of lasagna," he said, "and I don't know what to do with it all."

"Freeze it," I suggested. Worf was talking about the lonely way of the warrior. The camera was focusing on his special curvy Klingon sword.

"I thought you'd like to have some." Metz saw I was wavering. "Actually, I wanted to invite you up to have some with me," he went on, "but the cooking process got messy." I was en rapport with the Klingon mind, still human enough to wonder how to accept the food politely but also dying for Metz to go. He could see my TV was on. He probably thought I was watching for fun. It was embarrassing in a way. "But I see you're, uh, busy," he said. "I'll just leave the lasagna. Maybe we'll get a chance to talk another time." He handed the dish to me.

"Thanks," I said, and he was gone up the stairs.

Metz and I had the best apartments in the building, the ones in the northeast corner. Beautiful light, but never too hot. Actually, his apartment was the better one, being on the top floor, but mine wasn't bad. He was the tenant above me, and he was very quiet. I was very quiet too. He played a lot of Mozart, but not too loud, and anyway I liked Mozart.

After he left I rewound the tape and replayed the scene between Troy and Worf a couple of times, taking notes directly into the computer. Meanwhile I ate the lasagna, which was maybe a little too spicy. Through my window the sky got dark. Worf declined Troy's help but agreed to receive it if he ever *really* needed it. I thought I'd wash out Metz's dish and return it that very evening, thereby impressing him.

"Come in," he said. He'd either lied about how messy his place was or he'd cleaned it up since he'd talked with me. He had a real desk, with a plant on it. Gee, a plant, I thought. I should get a plant. Even Captain Picard has a tank of fish. Metz also had a real chair with a real footstool. This wasn't messy, I thought, this was how grownups lived. But then I got confused, because it wasn't how my parents lived. They were grownups too, but Metz was more like me, an academic in an apartment. This was definitely a localized distortion in the space-time continuum.

"I brought back your dish," I said, offering it through the door.

"Come in, come in," he repeated. "Sit down. Do you want some tea?"

"Sure." I sat. He heated the water, opened a box of Persian Sunset tea bags, dropped one into a cup, poured water over it. "The lasagna was really good," I said.

It wasn't easy talking with Metz. There were awkward silences and arrhythmias in our conversations. Maybe after a long acquaintance such hesitancies are overcome naturally, or just disappear. In any case, when Metz and I talked it was like a slow mutual stutter. Topics, even sentences, were begun but developed into random and alarming pauses. I was helpless as whole ideas fell into fragments and disintegrated. I didn't know how to talk to him so that he would respond less elliptically, or how to answer him more smoothly and directly. When we accidentally looked straight at each other, it was as though our eyes opened wide and we immediately looked away. Too much eye contact was disconcerting, unseemly.

One of my favorite episodes in *Star Trek: The Next Generation* was about the android Commander Data. Data had a dream, which we, the fans, knew meant a malfunction, probably in his positronic memory circuit. In an exhaustive attempt to analyze his "dream," he painted pictures of the images. One of the images was a large, black crow-like bird, which later turned out to be a symbol of Data himself. In the dream, the bird variously perched on his desk or flew in through his window. Data painted a picture of the bird, then a close-up picture of the bird. Then he painted a picture of the bird's wing, and finally a picture of a feather in the bird's wing.

That's how I wanted my conversations with Metz to be. I was always wanting to get into things with him, deeper into things. But we never managed to zero in on the point. We never quite indicated what the point was. We seemed always to be on the edges of each other's thoughts but never actually in them.

The Friday night following the lasagna was when we first started going out for terrible Chinese food. Metz asked me at the restaurant if Herron was my boyfriend. I supposed it was his being middle-aged that gave him the social permission to ask me such a personal question.

"Not any more," I said, and then, because I was curious about what he might ask next, I added, "He dumped me." I waited for his next question but there was no next question. "What about you?" I said, hoping to elicit a few intimacies. I had the definite feeling that he was attracted to me, in spite of my youth and what might be presumed to be my naiveté and callowness.

"Oh, I– I'm a kind of loner," he offered a brief scratchy laugh, "as you may have noticed." I was suddenly too embarrassed to pursue this evanescent topic further, and in any case our food arrived. We were sitting at the corner table at Main Chow, eating won-ton soup. This soup was the best dish we ever ate there. It had plump balls of minced pork and ginger, and thrown in the thick chicken broth like an afterthought was a heap of Chinese greens. It kept us going back hopefully week after week.

I would willingly have poured out my heart to Metz but it was clear he didn't want to get personal. Herron had been like that too. In other ways Metz was different. When I spoke with him about my work, he did not, for example, try to take it over with his own. "That's just like in Conrad," Herron had invariably said, and gone on to tell me why, and my point was lost. Metz, instead, nodded, or he said, "Oh, I see." However, these brief punctuations had the same result as Herron's analyses: they inhibited me.

To change the subject, I began to tell Metz about my thesis. He said he'd never thought the theme of alienation could be applied to actual extraterrestrial aliens. This was a comment I'd heard way too many times. At first it had boded well for my dissertation, that I was actually working on something new. Then it boded ill, a simplistic joke.

"There's so much overt alienation in American culture," I told him, "disaffected youth in the inner city, for example." Metz laughed, a slightly abrasive sound. Was he laughing because he thought I didn't know anything about disaffected youth? I *was* disaffected youth. It's true, though, that I didn't know anything about the inner city. "Hundred-dollar sneakers," I went on, proving that I cruised the TV news. "It's a kind of alienation without alienation. But on *Star Trek: The Next Generation* you have aliens who *admit* they're aliens. They *call themselves* aliens." Everyone I knew seemed alien to me, I didn't say to Metz. "The humans from Earth, who are the power structure of the Federation, are the standard of normality. They're very tolerant toward the aliens, and even have love affairs with the ones who aren't too bizarrely different."

"Interesting," said Metz. I was dying to continue, to tell him the entire rationale of my thesis, even to read him the first few chapters aloud. He stared at my right ear in an attentive sort of way but I wasn't sure what it meant. I felt dumb and young again, and I was absolutely unable to sustain silence.

"Next time let's try the Szechuan eggplant," I blurted out, pointing at the menu, and then I froze. What had I done? How could I have arrogantly assumed he'd want to go out for dinner with me again? But he was nodding.

He took the menu from me and said, "Or the scallops with snow peas." Did this mean he was counting on my company again? Next Friday night? Oh, how I hoped this was true.

I think one of the reasons I chose *Star Trek: The Next Generation* for my thesis topic was that it was on every night. It became my regular habit to recline on the couch, sandwich du jour in hand, and watch the adventures of the *Enterprise* crew. After the program I'd go over the notes I'd written in my special thesis notebook, sometimes transcribing whole paragraphs into the computer. My daily tape of *Star Trek: The Next Generation* was the last thing I watched before bedtime. After a year this ritual came to have a soporific effect, and I experienced even the most tense and fearsome confrontations as soothing.

Picard and the other officers became more and more the focus of my day. Who else did I have to hang out with? In the morning I turned on my computer and did finicky line editing for a thesis editing service. I turned twisted garbled academic dialect into pure and lucid thoughts. The people who wrote theses, myself excluded, were astonishingly illiterate. For a couple of hours a day I received quite a lot of money. Not everyone could do this kind of skilled work, for which a precise eye was required. Also, three times a week I taught the section of freshman English that Metz had taught five years ago. The freshmen could barely read, let alone write a two-page paper. It was my futile task to teach them to read and write. The job had benefits unrelated to literacy, however: my status as a teaching assistant obligated the graduate division to waive my tuition. In the late afternoon I was usually in the library looking up boring pop-culture references. The editing was boring and the teaching was boring. Sometimes I could hardly believe how boring my life was. This problem vanished when Picard diplomatically finessed the Romulans out of yet another potentially explosive battle for control of the quadrant. I cheered him on, chewing an egg-salad sandwich and drinking dark beer from the bottle.

Counselor Deanna Troy spent all her time helping others, but she was taken for granted, and lonely. She began to get bitter and resent her fellow officers, as she saw them receive praise and commendations for their rare excesses of merit, while she daily toiled to maintain their self-esteem and sense of honor. I knew exactly how she felt. I, Reba, cleaned up incomprehensible prose and pointed out to young adults the difference between subject and object. Where was my reward? I wanted something romantic in my life. The ponytailed young man at the grocery store deli took me out for coffee—on his break, to be sure—and we seemed to have a rapport. He made excellent sandwiches, and I told him so. *This is going well,* I thought as we talked about jazz and the possibility of an excursion to a blues club in Oakland. But then it didn't happen.

"In *Star Trek: The Next Generation*," I later told Metz, "it's clear that the aliens are the aliens and the humans are the humans. The humans maintain the power. They may have conflicts, even battles, with the Cardassians and the Ferengi and the dreaded Borg, the worst guys in the whole universe, but they never actually lose. And the guys they have battles with, this part is very interesting, are enough like them to be called *humanoid.* When they're sensing life forms *down on the planet,* which is something they're always doing from the safety and comfort of their big starship, they often say, 'Sensor indicates humanoid life forms, Captain.' In fact, they rarely communicate with intelligent *non-humanoid* life forms, although you would think that there must be a zillion kinds in the galaxy out there. And when they do, when they *do* communicate with plasma life forms or shape-changing life forms or crystalline life forms, these life forms almost invariably take human, or humanoid, embodiment. So the aliens are enough like us to communicate, cooperate, or engage in hostilities. But they're always alien. They come from other planets in other star systems. Their starships run on different principles. Their cultures are strange and even offensive. They're always, irrevocably, alien."

Metz was listening closely. I love when people do that.

Metz was like me, I thought, a born listener, moderate and regular in his habits. Metz was abstemious. Metz took me seriously. Also, Metz was a normal size. He was a little short and maybe a little overweight, but that was probably normal for an old guy. He didn't look in bad shape, though, and I'd seen him ride his bike to and from campus several times a week. Whereas Herron was abnormally tall, way over six feet, and noticeable in any context because of his extreme skinniness. I'd always been repelled by skinny men, and at first was by Herron, too, until we went to bed together. Then I liked his thinness, and even found it sexy. I was ashamed of this, but what could I do? I'd supposed he was so abnormally thin because he drank whiskey and snorted cocaine every time he got the chance, which, on a student income, was not often.

I was rereading Herron's letter when Metz showed up at my door. I was still agitated. I accidentally ripped a jagged piece off the envelope. *Dear Reba, I've missed you,* the letter began. It was a warm early evening in May when this occurred, a Friday. My tacit arrangement with Metz—not that we ever spoke out loud of anything resembling an actual date—was to meet on Fridays and walk over to the funky Chinese place around the corner. We were eating our way through the menu, hoping to find something as good as won-ton soup. So far we'd discovered the potstickers were okay, but potstickers were okay everywhere, really. It was nearly 8:00 p.m. and I knew I should get ready for dinner but I was poleaxed, stopped in my tracks by Herron's letter. I wanted to study it sentence by sentence, word by word, there and then. I was immobilized by Herron's same old convoluted phrasings. First he said he missed me, and then right away he said he'd had two publications. Fortunately, happily, I'd somehow missed seeing them. Then blah blah blah the department and blah blah blah his dissertation committee and blah blah blah Conrad Conrad Conrad; but he also wrote, *There's so much I want to tell you,* and *I feel guilty for the way I treated you,* and *There are some things that seem flat without your presence.* Before he signed it he wrote by hand, *Please write to me.*

I hated his letter. It was smug while pretending to be diffident, and brought back to me the aura of the real Herron. I'd gradually replaced him with an idealized Herron, brilliant and charming, a Herron whom I'd tragically loved and lost. The real Herron, displayed coldly in his letter, was still the same old chickenshit hypocrite I'd begged not to leave even as he was struggling out the door with the biggest suitcase in the Western world.

I especially hated that the letter diverted my attention from Metz. Something was happening with Metz. I couldn't have called it intimacy, but it was something, well, it was an increased familiarity, a kind of comradeship almost. I thought about holding his hand. I wanted to touch him. I began to think that such a step, for I viewed it as a very big step indeed, was possible. In fact, before Herron's letter arrived, I'd planned to touch Metz very soon. I'd been thinking about it constantly.

I was shocked by Herron's letter, my heart beat fast, but I welcomed it. My growing attachment to Metz, which baffled and obsessed me, had something in its way, something like a piece of crust in the throat, something preventing me from going further. The something was Herron, and I'd known it.

Later that evening, while Metz and I were eating rubbery Szechuan prawns, it came to me how kind he was. Keeping me company. Listening to my dissertation problems. And how interesting he was, how mysterious, with his elliptical comments on my theories, and his stuttering, precise academic encouragement. Gratefully, impulsively, I put my hand on his arm. A prawn fell from his chopsticks. He chased the prawn as it slipped away again and again. It was the first time we'd touched. He looked at the prawn, not at me. My face was hot.

"Oh," I said, "I'm so distracted." This came out like an acknowledgment of crazed behavior, though I'd meant it as an apology. Metz retrieved the prawn and replaced it in the dish. He picked out a sticky piece of onion and ate it. I had to tell him. "I got a letter from Herron." I knew the minute I said it that a mention of Herron could easily contaminate or even abort the tenuous sweet formal rapport I had with Metz.

"You've heard from him?" Metz sipped lukewarm tea from a cup half full of dregs.

"He wants me to write," I began, "but I can't think of any friendly words." Tears came to my eyes as I remembered how I'd been wronged. "You don't want to hear this," I said, but I looked at him with hope. Maybe he did want to hear it. I waited for him to say so.

"Maybe you don't want to write friendly words," Metz

said finally, in a new, distant, aloof voice. His very posture indicated the topic was distasteful to him.

"What?"

"Maybe all you want to write is unfriendly words. The tea is cold. Are you finished? Let's go."

We paid, leaving a too-large tip as usual, and slowly began to walk the four blocks to our apartment house. I couldn't leave it alone. "What do you mean?" I pressed him.

He stopped, rocked back and forth, made two ambiguous arm gestures, looked away, looked down. "This seems to me an opportunity." He took a few steps. "You told me you never got a chance to tell him how hurt you were. No, you said he never gave you a chance. You argued about the suddenness of his leaving, isn't that right?"

"Right," I muttered. Had I told him all these things? When had I told him all these things?

"Maybe he's giving you a chance now."

"He's asking for it. Is that what you mean?"

"Well..."

"Are you saying I should write all my rage and hurt? Isn't that, like, retaliation? Can I justify the principle of retaliation?" Metz is a reasonable man, I thought, I should spend more time listening to Metz.

"You could also write a pleasant, friendly letter. That would surely imply that everything is okay."

"Everything is not okay. He dumped me and broke my heart and he's an asshole."

"Well. You could choose not to answer his letter."

"I believe that would be cowardly. I believe I could force *him* to choose not to answer *my* letter."

Metz laughed his raspy laugh. Then, picking up on my distress or maybe humiliation, he nodded. "So he can't win. There's nothing he can do to make you think well of him."

I didn't want to think of myself as vindictive. I wanted to do mean acts, but I didn't want to be a mean person. But

Metz had elicited something I hadn't wanted to look at. I definitely wanted to win. I wanted Herron to lose. If I didn't answer the letter, I would lose by cowardice. If I answered it and was nice, I would lose by lying. But if I answered it and was ratty, I would win by honesty, as I chose to interpret Metz's advice. And if Herron then didn't answer, he would confirm my win with his own cowardice and hypocrisy. As Lt. LaForge would say, the distortion field was fluctuating. Meanwhile I was beginning to feel uneasy with Metz, as almost always happened if we spent more than a couple of hours together. Our emotional schedule required that we part soon.

The letter from Herron lay on the table, obstructing my life. I determined to get Herron out of my memory, out of my mind, out of my conversation with Metz. I'd write Herron's fucking letter and Herron would be finished. And I could then follow up the intimate exchange I'd had with Metz. I could enlarge on it, enhance it, look more and more closely and deeply at it. The feather in Data's wing.

"You're right, you're right," I told Metz. I was jittery because of the still-exciting topic of Herron. "Okay, listen, good night, I'll see you, take care," I babbled, unable to stop myself from filling the uneasy charged space between us.

"Good night," he said, and walked up the stairs to his classier, lighter, cleaner, altogether more attractive apartment above me.

Heartened by Metz's remarks over the Szechuan prawns, I wrote the letter to Herron. My opinion of Conrad had evolved, I wrote, and I'd now come to think of him as a racist advocate of crude colonial machismo. I knew the word crude would make Herron wince. *I wouldn't take his aesthetic so seriously if I were you,* I added nastily. This was an oblique response to his query about how I was getting along with my alienation. It took me several concentrated days to compose the letter. It was snide. It was sarcastic. I told him I'd be willing to write to him if he thought he could accept a few conditions. I said I didn't want to hear about his stupid students or his arrogant colleagues until we'd acknowledged and discussed what had happened between us. *If that sounds reasonable to you,* I wrote, *I think we can write. If not, not.* I knew it wouldn't sound reasonable to him.

I printed out the letter and read it over. I was thrilled to imagine I might devastate Herron as he'd devastated me. I walked out to the mailbox that very night, high on revenge and closure. On the way back I thought about knocking on Metz's door, to tell him what I'd done. Surely he'd congratulate me, smile directly at me. What was I thinking? Get a grip, Reba. He'd be appalled.

During the next few days I didn't see Metz. I watched one episode of *Star Trek: The Next Generatio*n over and over, the one in which Worf falls in love with a brilliant and beautiful Klingon woman and makes love to her in a particularly sexy and poignant scene. What they do is, they smell, and then bite, each other's hands. That really got to me. Then, when he discovers she's half Romulan, Worf dumps her.

I made several pages of notes on this episode. Did Worf reject Kaylah because of his own intransigence, his inability to widen his areas of attachment? Or was it really, as he claimed, an issue of Klingon honor, a refusal to betray his empire by a connection with his traditional enemy?

I was ready for Metz now, I felt. I was perfectly free. There were no entanglements in my life. Perhaps we could advance to the next level of conversation. I was eager for this to happen, and looked for him on the stairs and in the halls of the department.

On Friday, I remembered that we'd made no date for Chinese food at Main Chow. The topic of Herron had so preoccupied me, and Metz too, apparently, that we'd forgotten to discuss the next item on the menu. I was afraid to call him on the phone. I thought that would break our traditional mode of contact in a way that would be, simply, too harsh for him. I set my VCR and walked upstairs to his apartment. I put my ear against the door. Nothing. I knocked, and then I rang the bell. No response. He wasn't home. Or was home and pretending he wasn't home. Whichever it was, it was clear we weren't eating together. I couldn't concentrate on *Star Trek: The Next Generation* that night. I slurped yogurt out of the carton. Finally I wrote him a note.

Hey, Metz, I wrote, *I missed you tonight (Friday). I was kind of looking forward to the stewed tofu. How about next Friday for sure?*

Reba.

I slipped the note under his door. I had to assume he assented to its invitation. On Monday as I was hauling my book bag up the stairs I heard his footsteps below me, and I stopped and looked down.

"Hey, Metz."

"This isn't your usual hour, is it?" By that question I knew he was avoiding me. My skin got extremely prickly. Core breach was imminent.

"No, I worked late." I waited until he caught up with me and we walked up the second flight together. Then we were on my floor. I turned toward my apartment. He began to walk up the next flight.

"Well, see you," he said.

What had happened? Maybe nothing, I told myself frantically, maybe he was just busy. I was covered all over with a sweaty film. I couldn't think. What had I done wrong? Before we'd always talked about *Star Trek: The Next Generation* and my thesis and my section of composition and my editing job. We'd gossiped a little about people in the department. But at our last dinner we'd begun to get personal. Was I so young that he assumed I was narcissistic and self-obsessed? In fact I *was* narcissistic and self-obsessed, but so were many adults. I knew this from literature. Was he bored with or even offended by what he maybe perceived as my ephemeral problems? I was humiliated that apparently I'd told him so much over the months, and he'd actually remembered it. Sending off the letter to Herron had filled me with a new kind of power, though, and I now felt I could never again go another moment in my life without saying what I felt.

"Did you get my note about Friday?" I called out to Metz. "Shall we try the tofu?"

"Uh, I can't this Friday," he said, "Maybe another time."

It was time for an emergency core shutdown. My heart thudded against my chest, bang, bang; I thought it would crash right through like the disgusting creature in the movie *Alien*.

I played that night's *Star Trek: The Next Generation* tape. The entire crew had gone for three days without sleep as they simultaneously repaired the impulse engines, damaged to near ruin, and battled the intelligent slime molds who insinuated themselves into dark corners to reproduce. Yuck. Probably it wasn't other people who were the aliens, I thought. Probably it wasn't Herron, Metz, the guy at the deli I never went to a jazz club with. Probably it was me. I wanted to love Metz, because we seemed alike. But how are people alike, after all? How are aliens alike? For that matter, how are they alien? Worf was proud and shy, Deanna Troy was empathically sensitive, Data yearned to experience the unconscious. I was the alien, all right. I got ready for bed. Finally the engines were good as new, and the slime had been floodlit to extinction. Picard dismissed his weary officers and turned on some Mozart. Soon he was dozing. Worf, Riker, LaForge and the rest were also stacking serious Zs. Commander Data the android, who had no need for sleep, was on the bridge, calm and confident. My eyes closed. Data would pilot the ship, I knew.

Have Sex, Eat Mosquitoes, and Die

SUKIE WAS COOKING DINNER for Philip. The chicken, with its layers of sliced onion and its honey-mustard sauce, was simmering in a medium oven, and the freshly washed salad greens were crisping in the refrigerator, wrapped in paper towels. Sukie measured out brown rice, barley, and wheat berries, and stirred the grains into boiling water. She turned the gas down very low and put a lid on the rice pot. Then she sipped from her wineglass and lit a cigarette. She leaned against the counter. The sink was full of dirty dishes. There was plenty of time to shower and change. She thought about her green silk shirt.

Patrick loped into the kitchen, shoelaces protruding like spaghetti from his high-topped sneakers, which were inscribed with what looked like ancient runes. His hair was stringy and strangely ruffled in the back. His jeans were a disgusting collage of ripped patches, and he was wearing parts of three shirts. He looked pinker and weedier than usual. He didn't smell too great either. "Hi, Mom, what's for dinner?"

"My god, you're a day early." Sukie smiled at her son. "I thought you were going to be in Mendocino all weekend."

Patrick was staring into the open refrigerator. "Is Perrier all we've got?" he asked, "Isn't there any of that fruit Koala?"

"Patrick, why didn't you call?"

Patrick opened a bottle of Perrier and chugged it leaning against the open refrigerator door. He tossed the empty bottle neatly into the plastic wastebasket, and threw another full bottle through the kitchen door. Sukie lunged for it, but it was caught by a grubby hand that shot suddenly out of a gauzy pleated sleeve. Patrick meanwhile was peeling a banana. "I got a ride," he said. "Mom, this is Sabina. It's her dad's van we came back in. That smells good. What is it?"

"How do you do, Sabina?"

"Hi." The girl in the gauzy blouse had practically no hair. However, possibly to compensate, she had several earrings in each ear. They seemed to have been chosen randomly, or perhaps there was a semiotic significance to their arrangement. She had a pale, flattish face and pale round eyes of an amorphous smoky color. She's really quite beautiful, Sukie thought. To her knowledge, and of course as the mother of a teenager, she was privy to essentially nothing, Patrick had never before manifested any interest in a girl. Now, however, he tenderly handed the peeled banana to Sabina.

"Patrick," Sukie said carefully, "I've made rather complicated plans for dinner. I'm cooking for a guest."

"Old Philip, huh? Old Philip coming over?"

"Yes, but that's not the point. The point is that I didn't plan for you. As you can see, there's a chicken in the oven."

"Awww." Patrick's disappointment came out in a squawk. "So what are we going to eat? My mom's cooking *meat* for Philip," Patrick said to Sabina, who had advanced as far as the kitchen door and was standing there with one foot resting on the inner part of her other knee. She looked like a shorebird wearing Levi's. She was staring at the refrigerator door, upon which Sukie had stuck various clippings from the newspaper. "He's this lawyer who always wears neckties," Patrick went on.

"Patrick, please," Sukie was exasperated.

Patrick ignored her. "He's got this Beemer with a burglar alarm, and this car is, like, always really *clean*."

"I'm not a vegetarian," Sukie explained to Sabina.

"Meat-eaters are made out of meat," Sabina said.

Jesus, thought Sukie, what does that mean? "Why don't you guys go out?" she suggested. But what if they didn't want to leave? She couldn't *make* them leave. Could she make them leave? "Hey, how about going out for pizza? Vegetarian pizza?" Sukie dumped her purse out on the dining room table, which was already set with two tall candles. "Here," she pressed money into Patrick's hand, "here's twenty, twenty-five, twenty-six dollars. Go to a movie too. Come home late."

Patrick stuffed the money in his pocket. "Hey. Thanks. *All right.* But listen, Mom? This would all be a whole lot easier if you let me use the car. And, you know, safer too."

It's all tradeoffs, thought Sukie. "Sure," she said, handing Patrick the keys, "Here. Go. Have a good time."

"You mean *right now?*"

"Yes! Now! Go! Take the car! Take the money! Go!"

Patrick started laughing. Sabina stood wide-eyed in the doorway. Patrick grabbed Sabina's hand. "What do you think?" he asked her, "Shall we go out now and listen to music later?"

Sukie held her breath, hoping they were very, very hungry, and waited for Sabina's answer.

I was so juiced about Sabina coming over, Sabina is totally awesome, but my mom was cooking dinner for old Philip. The dinner smelled great but it had chicken in it. Consequently we couldn't eat it. My mom was not in a great mood when she met Sabina, because she didn't know we were coming.

Thing was, we just got there and all. I could tell Sabina didn't feel good about being sort of shoved out the door. My mom was, like, hassling me about making phone calls and letting her know.

"I didn't know you were coming," she said. I mean, did she think I was going to spend the rest of my life in Mendocino?

Meanwhile, Sabina was standing there all polite and, like, it's nice to meet you, Mrs. Akulian. My mom, you could tell, thought Sabina was weird.

Yeah, like Sabina's weird, right? Like old Philip, Philip wears these outstandingly anchorman neckties, like Philip *isn't* weird. Philip isn't weird and Sabina's weird. My mom's values, it's like, whoa, suddenly its 1970.

Anyway, I sort of guilt-tripped my mom about dinner and all, and consequently she gave us money to go out. And then she gave me the car keys. Cool!

I was hoping my mom would make a good impression on Sabina and have, you know, great stuff for us to eat and, like, leave us alone. There was nothing to eat except fruit and soda pop. There were no chips, none of those crunchy Italian biscotti cookies. Sabina was super-cool though. She didn't even seem to mind. Sabina is awesome.

Watching Patrick and his mom interact is a trip. His mom is all uptight because she has a date with some lawyer dude, and Patrick is all joking around and cool. He knows I have a joint in my pocket. We were planning to go up to his room and listen to Galen Doom and The Dregs.

Patrick is all, hey, Mom, you didn't fix any food for me. Patrick's mom is all, like, whoa, you've got to get out because of this date I've got. She gives us hell of money for pizza. Then she and Patrick sort of argue for a while and she gives him the car keys. Patrick's mom is all, like, you've got to cut out *now.* Patrick is like, *Mom,* we're gonna hear some music, and she's like, *now,* Patrick.

There's these clippings from the newspaper tacked up on the refrigerator. One is a cartoon with Clinton in it. One is an announcement of an art show. And another one is a headline, it's really cool, it says, HAVE SEX, EAT MOSQUITOES, AND DIE. Patrick's mom is drinking wine and smoking cigarettes, which is really gross and uncool, but it's all warm and steamy in the kitchen and she knows we don't want to leave because it's not exactly, like, fun or anything, but, you know, it's kind of nice.

Height

PATRICK AKULIAN'S SISTER COLETTE was a freshman at Cal, and there were some things about Colette living away from home that Patrick didn't like. For instance, with Colette around, no one had ever noticed him. He'd pretty much been able to come and go as he pleased. Also, it didn't seem fair that Colette had actually gotten away and he hadn't. He was essentially stuck until he left for college, assuming he got into college. And what if his parents changed their minds by that time, or got poor, and no longer felt their offspring automatically deserved a subsidized higher education? Then he'd probably have to live in his same grubby room forever, and get a job bagging groceries at Slaveway.

It had been a big relief to Patrick when, right after Colette moved into the dorm, his dad had left home too. The continual tension and terrible bickering between his mom and dad had ceased as if by magic. But the house seemed forlorn and excessive with only himself and Sukie in it. Patrick's interactions with his mother were usually confined to question-and-answer sessions about food and laundry and, more recently, the use of her car. On his sixteenth birthday, Patrick had acquired a driver's license, and sometimes felt his whole life was spent waiting to drive. The minutes and occasional hours spent actually driving were times of transformative tallness, power, control. Certainly he had felt that way before Nina. After Nina, his enthusiasm for driving his mom's Subaru did not wane, but it moved over, made room, for this huge new presence in his life. He had no idea of trying to define in any way his feelings for Nina and the vast space she occupied in his thoughts, vaster than smoking dope or selling dope or talking about dope, vaster than driving. He no longer craved to own his mother's car. Merely to drive it was now enough. This in itself was a change. Patrick was definitely conscious of everything having changed. There was then, the whole of his life including his driver's license and his parents' separation, and there was now, the comparatively thin but fraught two months since he'd become aware of Nina for the first time. Not actually for the first time, of course, not really; he'd known her forever, she'd been a big kid when he was a little kid, she was the daughter of his mom's best friend Nola.

Patrick's mom, Sukie, and his dad, Greene, had gone to college, in some unthinkably ancient time, with all their same close friends that they had now—Nola, Judith, Tony, Joel, Philip. Patrick thought this was unutterably oppressive and incestuous. The only one of these people he could tolerate was Joel. Well, and Nola wasn't too bad. But Philip! How seriously boring could you be? Patrick had never understood how his dad could be partners with Philip, although recently he'd observed that since Philip was dull, and Greene was flamboyant, they were probably a very well-balanced law firm. Since his mom and dad had split up, though, or separated, or starting living apart—whatever—Sukie had been "dating" Philip. God. It was repellent beyond belief. Anyway, the two attorneys had been coining it, although the big bucks had rarely been passed on to Patrick. Now it was too late, because Greene had quit the partnership and was presently working for another lawyer, for less money. He still gave Colette a huge allowance, though. "When you get into Cal, buddy, you'll have the same," Greene had said pointedly. Patrick's grades were okay, but he hoped he wouldn't end up at Cal. He hoped he'd get into the State University at Arcata, too far away for his folks to visit except by very special appointment, or even to a college in another state. That would be the best, probably. He might have the flash to go to Cal, but the truth was he didn't want to. He didn't want to stick around, like Colette, talking to his mom on the phone all the time, and having to be in the physical presence of his dad. On the other hand, if he stayed in Berkeley, he'd get to see Colette, and that meant he'd get to see Nina. That would be good. That part, if it came to pass, would be fine.

As children he and Colette and Nina had played together until the girls realized how little and useless he was. They were nine and twelve at the time, he was seven. Nina had never emerged from the background of his life, where people other than himself dimmed out and disappeared. Now she was real, probably the realest presence he knew or could imagine knowing. After his sudden awareness of Nina, there had even been a slight but noticeable improvement in his schoolwork. It seemed his whole life, which, he saw now, had been devoted to refuting and avoiding his father and his father's repellent rebarbative mode of life, his whole life had brightened and expanded to accommodate the fact of Nina, and also the fact that he was a certified driver.

This day, however, Patrick was not driving. From Berkeley High to the UC Paleontology Department was a distance of about a mile. After roll was called in his compulsory Phys Ed class—running laps and volleyball—Patrick left the athletic field, changed clothes in the locker room, and removed himself from the school, which was in any case an "open campus." He tied his Converse high-tops neatly. Then he ran a couple of blocks, dodging the crowds of shoppers, panhandlers, business people, and tourists, on Shattuck Avenue. He cut up Allston Way to Oxford and entered the UC campus. Alternately walking and jogging, he took a circuitous route north and east, past Nutrition, Biology, Psychology, the Moffit Library, the Doe Library, the T buildings, and Computer Sciences. He swung left over to the terrace of Engineering, where he purchased a bag of chips and a bottle of water at the café. He consumed these while sitting semi-dangerously on the parapet of the terrace. He then rounded the corner of the old Architecture building and climbed the hill to the patio of Earth Sciences. The strangely out-of-scale statue of a saber-toothed tiger guarded the space, which was, as usual, empty. Patrick entered the building.

Immediately he took the stairs, two at a time, to an upper floor. He slouched through the hall, his face cast down and sideways toward the wall, just in case. All went well; he was unobserved. He paused before an open door from which desultory chatter and laughter wafted, and stealthily looked inside. He was in luck: there sat Nina, her thick red-gold braid gleaming in the light from the west window. She sat facing away from Patrick, by another stroke of good fortune, talking with a small group of her colleagues.

Before Nina, Patrick and his best friend, Spit Hatada, had spent every day after school getting high or cruising Telegraph Avenue near the University campus. They had browsed the record stores, spent their allowances in the Games Arcade, and drunk Italian sodas at the outdoor cafés. Of course Patrick never participated in sports or clubs or any other high school "activities."

When Colette, as a new freshman, started UC Berkeley, Patrick and Spit had spied on her often. They'd followed her to her dorm; they'd loitered outside The Gap while she shopped, and around the corner from the café where she drank her latte. Soon the boys began to see her with Nina, who had just begun graduate studies in paleontology, a subject that Patrick, at that time, knew nothing about, not even how to pronounce the word. Then Colette had left the dorm, and she and Nina rented a little house together in Emeryville. After Patrick saw them embracing at Annie's party, he no longer wanted to share his surveillance with Spit. When he went up onto the campus, he went alone, surreptitiously seeking out a glimpse of the two young women and then retreating almost immediately to drop some quarters at the Games Arcade.

Patrick knew the campus area well from his constant forays with Spit. He knew where the campus bookstore was, with its lame and embarrassing yet somehow enticing sweatshirts that screamed UC BERKELEY across the front. He knew where the scattered on-campus delis and snack bars and coffee shops were, and he had frequented them all. He and Spit had hacked into the Unix computer, tapping away at monitors supposedly reserved for registered students only. He knew how to use the campus library and how to call out from campus phones. He also well knew where the Paleontology Department was.

This department occupied three floors of the ten-floor Earth Sciences building on the north side of campus, the area Patrick had heard students refer to as "the dark side of the moon." He had visited the department several times in the past two months, reconnoitering the hallways and staring in wonder at the displays behind glass of fossils and bones and calcified curly stems like feathers. He had scrutinized the notices on the various bulletin boards, familiarized himself with the geographical layout of the department, and read the names by every door behind which a professor or lab technician or administrative staff member lurked. In his invisible manifestation, that of a slouching, weedy, long-haired white boy, he had found the coffee room where the graduate students gathered, and the communal office where a select few of these students, those who were employed as TAs and RAs, shared a few broken-down desks and lamps. Most important, he knew where these same students and their friends met for coffee (Enrico's) and for pizza and beer (LaVal's). Patrick had scouted out all these sites and locations in the two months since his revelation of Nina. In this way he had compiled a map, not detailed, but accurate enough for his purposes, of Nina's movements and whereabouts throughout the day. This enabled him to search her out and look at her whenever he felt like it, which was almost always. However, he was constrained by school and by the fact that at night, which was when his mom most readily lent him her car, Nina and Colette, he had discovered, mostly hung out at home with the blinds drawn. He had been in their cottage a few times as a visitor, and had a good picture of the interior, but no idea what they did when they were alone. Just as well, he often thought.

Outside Nina's office, Patrick flattened himself against the wall of the corridor. On one hand, he thought he'd die if Nina spotted him. She'd be all friendly and mature. "Oh, Patrick," she'd say, puzzled and surprised, "what brings you around here?" "Uh, nothin'," he'd mutter, and spring out of the building, through North Gate, to the pizza parlor where he'd rapidly throw down all his money for a double-cheese slice and a coke. Then he'd die, speechless, lovestruck, paralyzed.

On the other hand, nothing would please and electrify him more than to be noticed. "Hi, Patrick," Nina's thrilling, slightly hoarse voice would be so calm that he'd himself relax and return her affectionate smile. "You're just in time for coffee," she'd say. They'd walk slowly down the hall....

Patrick had recently shot up to nearly six feet, and he was fully, keenly, definitely aware that he was actually taller than the very tall Nina. His dad was the same height as his mom—not too tall—and Patrick noticed how much better he felt about Greene now that he was the taller. He was disoriented by his new height, though, and had desperately improvised a loose-kneed gait, more a lope than a walk, just to get his huge feet out of the way. Patrick was fair like his mom, with long, narrow green eyes like hers, and a pink sunburned nose that had the same long straight shape as hers. But his mouth was full, like his dad's, over his loathsome, rebarbative braces, and sometimes, when he was wearing his baseball cap, he caught a glimpse of himself in a window and was shocked at the resemblance to his dad around his mouth and jaw. Colette had that same mouth, and Greene's black hair and black eyes, but her inflections and mannerisms were like Sukie's. Patrick, contemplating these odd similarities, thought maybe he should pay more attention in biology when genetics was presented. Maybe his dad wasn't even his dad. That would be good.

It was almost amazing and funny how much Nina looked like both her mom and her dad. Patrick could easily discern features of both Nola and Tony in Nina's face. She had the nearsighted turquoise de Vos eyes, the color of swimming pools, big and dreamy behind her glasses. Her mouth was Nola's mouth, curvy at the corners, very pink, the upper lip turned up a little. Nina was muscled and sturdy. She had round, bouncy breasts and a slim waist and strong confident legs. She had thick red hair like sunshine, usually pulled back into a careless braid. She was, Patrick thought, totally perfect and totally beautiful. Especially now that he was taller than she was. How glad he was to be nearly seventeen, and tall, and a licensed driver. His life would begin soon, soon. He was almost ready. First, senior year, then graduation. High school was an incarceration as far as he was concerned, and as far as his friend, Spit Hatada, was concerned too.

...Yes, he and Nina would walk slowly down the hall and out through North Gate, two tall, fair people standing out from the crowd by their tallness and fairness and by the radiance that was streaming from them, and they'd go to one of the cafés on North Side. Patrick was not too crazy about coffee, but of course he knew how to order a decaf cap, which was more or less drinkable and definitely respectable.

Naturally, a lot of bad things could happen, too, things other than Nina spotting him. Repellent things, rebarbative things. Nina could be meeting Colette. Sharp-eyed Colette could catch sight of Patrick. Then she'd tell their mom. Patrick shuddered. The thought of his parents, especially his dad, but definitely his mom too, knowing anything about his real life, was alarming and made his mouth feel dry. What was it about his family that was so impossible and intolerable?

Everyone he knew was all so related. This was gross, in a terrible way. For one thing, it meant that everyone knew everything, or, if they didn't know it, they had access to knowing it, and would probably overhear it or in some other way absorb it, even if they didn't want to know it. In just this way Patrick himself had learned things about his parents and his parents' friends that he would definitely rather not know. He certainly hadn't wanted to know that Nina and his sister Colette were lovers. That had been disgusting. It wasn't disgusting now, because he was more used to it, plus his mom and Nina's mom Nola seemed to find it just too, too charming and fascinating, so this once-riveting piece of information had lost its original irresistible, glamorous, awful quality. Also, before he first learned of their connection, Nina had meant nothing to him. She was just the cousin-like big girl he and Colette had played with when they were children.

In fact, Patrick had been the first to know: he'd seen them together at a party, the two of them, sitting on the bed in Annie Zeff's bedroom. He remembered it very clearly, sitting in the dark, facing each other, their profiles slightly illuminated by the light from downstairs. He had tramped up the stairs, Joel behind him, looking for a private place to smoke a joint. When he saw the two young women, their arms loosely around each other, he had instantly known what their relationship was. He'd been paralyzed for only a moment, then turned and stumbled rapidly back down the stairs, pushing Joel before him, repeating in an urgent croak, "No, not here." That picture, Nina and Colette face to face in the dark bedroom, had burned a hole in his brain for months. Naturally he had told no one.

Now, of course, everyone knew. First, Sukie's other best friend, Judith, had found out, he didn't know how, then Nina's mom, then his own mom, and they were all so delighted. They thought the girls made such a cute couple, all politically correct and, frankly, totally rebarbative. And then it wasn't shocking anymore, his sister Colette lovers with his mom's best friend's daughter Nina, and it all became familiar and cozy in a way that Patrick normally detested and was completely repelled by. It was at that point that he'd first noticed Nina as an actual, if exalted and supreme, person.

That afternoon, an ordinary afternoon, Patrick had entered his house through the back door, and was searching out a pre-dinner snack. He had just come from the Student Union, where he'd hoped to spy on his sister. He'd had no luck, and that had made him hungry. Patrick sometimes hung out at the bookstore, browsing through comic books, *Star Trek* merchandise, and sex magazines. He might look just a little retro at Berkeley High, where sparkling bleached white sweatshirts were this year's fashion, and athletic shoes with comets of gleaming reflection, and intricately shaved and combed hair. But here on the Cal campus he absolutely faded into the huge population. He looked more or less like the other university students, maybe a little grubbier, and could definitely pass for a freshman. He liked the Student Union. No one ever spoke to him or bothered him in any way. There was one store devoted solely to computers and new exciting software, another with chocolate and other gorgeous candy, still another with small high-tech electronic gear like watches and calculators and cell phones. The lights were bright, he was in a mall filled with people just a little older than he, and with products that he coveted. He had been about to buy a sugar cone filled with banana frozen yogurt and topped with chocolate chips, but found he had no money. This had made him even hungrier, and he'd rushed up the hill to his house.

As Patrick foraged in the kitchen, he had become aware of voices in the living room. His mother and father were fighting. What else was new? But what was his dad doing here anyway? He couldn't avoid hearing their weary discourse.

"I've only been out of this house a few months, and look what's happened."

"What? What's happened that's so much worse than when you were here?"

"Well, look at Colette. Look at your car." It was true that Patrick, in his first few weeks of licensed driving, had pranged the passenger side of the Subaru. Sukie, uncharacteristically, had not been upset. Maybe—probably—she had been preoccupied with other things. The car had not yet been fixed.

"What do you mean, look at Colette?"

"Living with a woman—"

"Living with Nina, Greene. Not 'a woman.' And what if she were 'a woman'? What would that mean?"

"Nothing. Nothing. It's just that I see signs of deterioration in both the kids. They're sullen. They've changed."

"Yeah, they've changed. They're less fearful."

"Patrick's grades—"

"Patrick's grades are just fine, and you know it. I don't know what it is you're trying to say. You're trying to badmouth your own kids to get yourself off some kind of new imaginary hook. Christ, Greene, that's low. It's not new, but it's low. And you've been drinking. I can smell it."

"Ah, god, Sukie, you've got to get off my back, you know, you really do." Greene's voice was in a high, whiny register, the tone he used for put-upon complaints to his family, as opposed to the low, seductive tone he used for strangers and clients.

"Who started this?" Sukie's voice was in her staccato accusatory mode, as opposed to the soft, distracted, martyred loving tone that she typically used talking to Patrick and Colette.

Patrick then remembered it was Greene's "visitation day," and he had forgotten about it again. He had just decided to sneak into his room—but how? how?—and turn on Galen Doom and The Dregs really loud. He certainly didn't want to focus his parents' attention on him, which might well happen if he entered the living room while they were in the awkward throes of a hostile stuttering standoff. He pulled a fresh carton of milk from the refrigerator. Maybe he'd left his window open, and could quietly climb through it, as he had done many times before. He scooped a handful of Froot Loops out of the box and ate them. Good. He scooped out some more. The back door opened and Colette and Nina came into the kitchen.

"Hi, Pat, 'sup?" Patrick rolled his eyes toward the living room to indicate the ongoing argument. "Oh, god." Colette dropped her pack on the kitchen table. "Bad timing." It was clear the combatants hadn't heard the girls come in. Sukie and Greene continued back and forth exhaustedly, as though they had many times rehearsed this dispute and, against their will, had to go through it again and again until it was just right. Their monotonic voices faded in and out. "Well," Colette went on, "I don't have to get that coat. I can wear my leather jacket. Let's get out of here, Nina."

Instead of moving to the door, Nina had looked at Patrick. "How are you, Patrick?"

Patrick shrugged. He jerked his thumb toward the living room. "Okay. Under the circumstances."

"Do you want to come with us?"

"Where are you going?"

Before Nina could answer, Colette broke in. "He can't come with us! We're just going to meet some friends, Pat, you wouldn't be interested."

Nina had kept her gaze fixed on Patrick. "You might not be interested in our friends, Patrick, but we could all leave together, and we could drop you somewhere. This doesn't seem like the most felicitous place to be right now."

"What does 'felicitous' mean?"

"Happy."

"Too right."

Colette had been impatient. "Let's go. I don't want to stand here and listen to this. I only came to get my coat."

Patrick tossed the empty carton into the trash. A perfect throw. "Nah, I think I'll hang out here. It's my night to have dinner with Dad." *I think I'll try to sneak into my room somehow and roll a joint* was what he didn't say. The young women had then left. Later, Patrick remembered the quality of Nina's attention, which had been focused intensely on him. He replayed the interchange until he could remember all the words. He also perfectly recalled Nina's solicitous voice, her totally beautiful face, and her wonderfulness. He remembered these things the next day, too, and the day after that.

Soon it became apparent to him that this memory had a rosy, glowing, overwhelming significance, and that this seemingly casual encounter had changed him inside and had also changed the texture of the world.

Life became less irritating because he had this new immense thrilling secret to think about. In this way he was able to avoid most repellent thoughts, especially about his dad, a miracle in itself. Patrick always tried not to think about his dad. He was disgusted and embarrassed by Greene. He had previously used the music of The Dregs to blot him out. This was hard, because his father was as dazzling and dimensional as a movie star. His glossy black hair fell perfectly over his brow, his dark eyes gleamed, and his vigorous black mustache fairly thrust itself out above his even white teeth. In a crisp white shirt Greene shone as though in a spotlight. Even in his sweat-darkened, aged CAL sweatshirt, he looked like an incognito king pursued by paparazzi. But he delivered no solemn, hopeful pronouncements. Every word that came from his arrogant mouth was threatening, sarcastic, and demanding, or wheedling and fretful. When people laughed at his dumb jokes or permitted themselves to be flattered and touched by Greene, Patrick could hardly stand it. His dad made him despise and distrust all grownups. Well, almost all. Joel was okay, of course, and Nola was okay too. Her voice was sweet and interested, and she looked at him in a serious and respectful way. His dad, on the other hand, spoke to him, really spoke to him, only when they were in the car together.

Since his folks had broken up, Patrick sometimes was forced by circumstance to be in the car while Greene drove him out to a really dumb restaurant, which he'd never done when they lived together. While driving, Greene asked interesting questions. These questions, though intimate, were sort of impersonal; they could have been asked, Patrick thought, of anyone. "Do you remember anything about being a baby?" Greene asked, "No? What if you did? Pretend you remember. What would you remember?"

Greene was always interested in Patrick's replies, and Patrick was too. He surprised himself as he came up with sappy little cartoon scenarios. He and his dad laughed as Patrick said, "I'd remember Colette reading bedtime stories to the dog, that old dog we had, Rotifer, remember old Rotifer?" "Yeah, that sounds right," Greene said. Patrick thought of those conversations as though he'd made them up too, as though they were what he'd come up with if he pretended he remembered talking to his dad.

Now, as Patrick peeked around the edge of the door into the office of the teaching assistants, he saw them initiate a certain amount of group activity. They were picking up their books, they were slamming drawers into their desks, they were tying their shoelaces, they were walking out into the hall. Oh god. Patrick forgot his happy fantasy of coffee with Nina, and began loping back toward the main office. A door swung open in front of him, nearly smashing him in the face, and twenty or more students bounced out. The hour had struck, class was ending, was over, new classes were beginning. Patrick stumbled into the crowd of young people, whose dress and posture were practically identical to his own. He disappeared into the crowd, became one of the crowd.

Looking back as he slowed down, his hands thrust into his jeans pockets, he saw Nina and three other assistants talking together, gesticulating and walking more slowly than the crowd he was with. His ardor pulled him away from the other students and he ducked into another empty room whose door was fortuitously open. Nina and her friends passed him. After a minute he exited. They were down the hall, far ahead of him. Sticking close to the wall, he followed. He kept behind them as they walked toward the main exit and down the steps and up the cement path that led to the border of the campus. It looked like they were going over to one of the cafés, and Patrick began to feel very pleased with himself. He could probably follow them right into the café, once they had sat down with their cappuccinos, and he could order something and sit behind Nina and sort of study her if he wanted. He could memorize the plaid shirt she wore over her T-shirt, he could try to read the titles of the books she carried under her arm. He could also cautiously check out her companions. He could think of all the reasons why that guy with the earring was wimpy or stupid or rebarbative. For one thing, the guy looked a little bit like Philip. Poor guy.

Philip was—Philip was too—something. Patrick wished he knew more words. Perhaps he should learn a few more words. How glad he had been to learn "repellent"; how appropriate, how apt, how useful it had been. "Repellent" had served him well. Philip was repellent. But the other characteristics of Philip, though he might not know what they were, were definitely excessive, and must always be modified by "too." Patrick knew that Philip used to "date" Judith, who in turn used to be married to Joel, back in the olden days when Patrick was such a little kid he could barely remember it. How disgusting, how awful, how totally repellent the old folks were. And Joel and Tony de Vos were brothers, and Tony was Nina's father. Tony was in Burundi now, or was it Angola? Patrick could never remember. Nina often wore gold and ivory hoop earrings which, she'd once told Patrick, her dad had sent her from Ethiopia. Patrick knew, he had somehow absorbed this information, that Tony, the elder brother, was handsomer and more distinguished than Joel. Patrick didn't know Tony too well because he was never around, whereas

Joel was really, except for Spit, his only friend. Definitely his only adult friend. And now Joel had accrued an additional importance because he was Nina's uncle.

Joel lived up north, in Mendocino, a coastal village Patrick privately thought was just too artsy and craftsy for words, and filled with disgusting, fat, white, slug-like tourists as well. However, Joel's cabin was a useful sanctuary for Patrick, who liked to get away from his parents' house, especially now that Colette, his one sort-of ally, no longer lived there, and from his school. A four-hour bus trip was paradise compared to a weekend in the stupid city of Berkeley. Also, Joel was Patrick's partner in the dope business: Joel was the grower, on a scale that seemed to Patrick way too small, and Patrick was the dealer. In addition to these marvelous advantages that Joel's friendship held for Patrick, his geographical distance and his position as the source of Patrick's pocket money and weed, Joel also was sometimes interesting to listen to. He'd given Patrick a zillion pieces of good advice about how to cut school, how to get decent grades without studying, and how to get his father, Greene Akulian, with whom Joel had a rocky history of conflict, off his back. On the other hand, Joel was not very affectionate or warm. He had his own life, as he'd often told Patrick, and was neither ready nor inclined to take on a parental role.

Patrick was content in Joel's cabin, curled in his sleeping bag near the wood stove, listening to old blues records, genuine LPs, or sometimes to eerie, incredibly calming Gregorian chants, or other soporific music by Couperin and duPres. At home he listened to Galen Doom and other heavy metal bands, but not up at Joel's.

Patrick liked the way Joel sort of didn't take Greene seriously, and he liked the way Joel lived all alone, far away from the other friends, but he didn't like the way Joel absolutely loved and defended Philip. "Its okay," Joel told him, "we don't have to like all the same people, you know." Patrick understood that, though he wasn't happy about it. Just about the only thing about Joel that he couldn't understand was why Joel didn't have TV in his cabin. They often argued about TV, and Patrick found himself becoming quite eloquent in its defense.

Patrick reasoned that if people had chemical receptors in their brains, very precise receptors, for powerful flattening drugs, then they probably had similar receptors for TV, which also made you feel good and as though you'd figured something out. Patrick liked programs about complicated grownups talking about how complicated they were. These scenes gave him a dreamy thoughtless warm feeling. The adults on TV were smoother and more loving than his parents and their friends. They stood up for themselves better, and they were more forgiving too. This was very satisfying because in real life his parents were in another galaxy. He didn't understand them at all, and he never would. They and their friends behaved in a way intelligible to Patrick only through his fascination with his favorite characters on the tube. He knew that these characters, unlike the actors who played them, or unlike himself, were fictional, made up from words on paper. Nevertheless he thought about them, and even consulted them to extract useful information about real people he actually interacted with. Patrick loved a couple of these characters. He didn't put it quite that way to himself. To himself, and in his arguments with Joel, he said he was learning a lot from watching TV. Joel strongly disagreed. Joel was disgusted: "Look at your shoes. You were made to buy those particular shoes. That's all those programs do," said Joel. "That's all."

While thinking about Nina's uncle Joel, Patrick was following Nina out of the Earth Sciences building. Just then Nina hugged the guy with the earring, and wheeled around in another direction entirely, toward Psychology. Keeping a discreet distance, Patrick followed her.

She strode through the cloister at Tolman Hall and turned into the plaza of the small café. Little tables were bolted to the pavement here, each one with four stools, also bolted down. Patrick stopped abruptly when he saw his sister, Colette, sitting at one of the tables, a book open before her, a pen in her hand. She closed her book when she saw Nina. Patrick hung back and turned slightly so that his face was not visible. He moved to a kiosk stapled over with notices about concerts and seminars and apartments to share. He pretended to be intently reading the leaflets, his back turned to his sister and Nina. Slowly, very slowly, he moved around the kiosk, his shoulders announcing that he was deep in concentration. As he paced, the young women came into view again, and he allowed himself to look at them. They were talking and gesturing. Nina looked almost directly toward him, and pointed toward the place he had just been. Colette stopped smiling. They continued to talk, more earnestly now. Patrick's stomach ran cold. They had seen him. Hadn't they? But what if they had? What would it mean? He could have legitimate business on the Cal campus, couldn't he? For instance, he could have come to get an application for admittance. What a great excuse. His dad would be impressed. But no, they'd never believe that. Colette had at least some sense of his distaste for Cal and for Berkeley and for anyplace his parents resided. She'd suspect—what? Something, something that Patrick couldn't bear to think about.

They hadn't seen him, at least they hadn't looked directly at him, at least he hadn't seen them looking directly at him. This was a good thing. Of course he didn't want Nina to know he had followed her. That would have been truly rebarbative and awful. But what would be worse, much, much worse, was for Colette to know he had followed Nina.

Oh god, what if they had seen him after all? It wasn't just a matter of Colette and Nina. After Colette told Sukie, which she was bound to do, Sukie would tell Nola. Sukie would probably also tell Philip, since she was seeing him fairly regularly now. Yuck. How foul. How repellent. They would all talk about him and his infatuation. Well, fuck them all. Except that he and Nina were related along with the rest of them. Well, not related exactly. No, not related. Something, but not related.

Now Nina and Colette were definitely looking right at him, at his actual face. Oh god. They'd seen him, they were waving, smiling, gesturing for him to join them. Panicked, Patrick stood immobile. He'd have to make something up, some kind of excuse. Could he get away with the admissions application story? No, because why would he be checking this out a whole year before he had to? What if he said he often came up to the campus just to hang out? Would they believe him? It was sort of true, it used to be true. Unfortunately, it didn't sound true. But he couldn't come up with anything else right now. It would have to do. It was his only story, however lame, and he was sticking to it.

Of all the things he'd ever done in his life, walking over to Nina and Colette was probably the hardest. Getting up, going to school, sitting through calculus, which he was somehow passing, sitting restlessly through the occasional dinner when his father took him and Colette out to some awful restaurant, these weren't the same kind of thing, but they had the same severity of obligation, the same compelling force. Of course they were totally incompatible categories. Not the same at all. Walking over to his sister and her lover, who was his own secret lover, was not comparable to anything else. But just like those other terrible unavoidable demands, he wished he didn't have to do it. But he had to. He hitched up his jeans and removed his baseball cap. He passed a hand over his longish lank pale hair and took a spastic step in the direction of the young women. He put his baseball cap back on and tried to smile and stand up straight, both at the same time. Then he hesitantly walked forward.

Substance

Joel de Vos was driving south, to the city, for reasons both personal and professional. The ocean mist, softened by the late-morning sun, hung about the car. As it dissipated, clarity brightened his resolve: yes, today, surely it would be possible, even easy, to stay straight. No more getting stoned. Today was the day. Clean up, and start writing the book. This was Joel's official and also secret agenda, the dual purpose of this trip. Below him, to his right, past the edge of the narrow coastal road, the sea glittered in the pockets of its purple swells, then dulled out to a thick band of grayish green near the horizon.

Joel rolled the window down. He sniffed. His authorial tasks would be covered in long, pleasant, separate sessions with his friends Lenny Rubin and Philip Stern. His more personal obligation was the result of an urgent distress call from his ex-wife, Judith Alba, a call to which he was not, strictly speaking, compelled to respond. His self-image, however, was at stake. He wanted to think of himself, especially now, as a decent person, a compassionate person, one who would never hesitate to help someone out of an emotional jam, particularly someone whose gratitude and high opinion he craved as much as Judith's. It wasn't easy to grab or otherwise manipulate Judith's admiration. It was an inexplicable fall of good luck that she'd called him for help during her recent heartbreak. The latest boyfriend had dumped her, as most of them mysteriously did, as Joel himself had done twenty years ago for reasons he had never understood. This time, Judith claimed on the phone, she'd been sure it was The Great Love of Her Life; this time she was absolutely devastated, and when The Great Love went back to his wife, Judith was a zombie. "They didn't even get along, they fought all the time!" Judith had sobbed indignantly into his ear. Joel, who knew the couple she was talking about, said nothing. He was willing to boost his stock in Judith's eyes, though, and quickly agreed to keep her company for a few days while she got used to the defector's absence. "You'll make it possible for me to go to work," she pleaded, "if I know I won't have to be alone at night."

Joel gathered from this remark that Judith had alienated her closest friends during her affair. She'd want to talk a lot, probably. Well, Judith's talk, even when obsessed and self-indulgent, was usually witty and malicious. She'd make him laugh. And during the day, while she was at work, he could discuss his book with Philip or Lenny.

Why, he wondered now for the hundredth time, why hadn't Philip and Judith stayed together? He'd never heard the details of their affair and breakup, which had occurred without his knowing. This could be his big chance, his only chance. Judith would be in a mood to talk; and then later he could quiz Philip while cautiously remarking to him on Judith's current state of mind. "She's making a good recovery," he'd mention casually. "Much better than when she split up with you. By the way, Philip," he'd then add, as offhandedly as possible, "I've never heard the whole story." He was pleased, he had to admit, that Philip and Lenny didn't like each other much. Joel liked to keep his associations, his lives, really, in distinct compartments, the membranes of which were permeable only by himself. How glad he was too that Lenny and Judith, though politely acquainted, were not friends.

Joel found he was looking forward to these two narratives, this Rashomon-like story, with immense anticipation. Automatically he passed the Navarro Bridge. He'd earlier thought he'd maybe drive down the coast, as it was a bright and beautiful day. The coast road was difficult and dangerous, with hairpin turns and sheer drops off the side of the road to sharp rocks a zillion feet below. He'd imagined driving the coastal route as a kind of rite of passage, and when he reached the city afterward he'd be, not exactly reborn, but certainly clean, shed of his urge to smoke marijuana. Well, too late now. Fate or habit had decided for him, and he'd driven right past the turnoff. Now he was firmly fixed on the easier, more direct, freeway route, at least a couple hours shorter. It would be good to get to the city as soon as possible; he saw that now. He was absolutely ready. He'd carefully packed a lot of clean clothes in his big suitcase, and he'd also trimmed his graying beard. His once-reddish hair was a little long and shaggy, perhaps, but he'd slicked it down with water and even slipped a comb into his pocket. His striped shirt was clean, and so were his jeans. All in all, he'd earlier decided, assessing his tall, neatly dressed figure in the mirror, he looked pretty tidy. Not too country. Not so country as usual, anyway.

Had Philip and Judith remained a couple, Joel mused as he drove on, they'd be quite rich. They might have bought a big house with a little guest cottage in the back, and who more likely to be warmly welcome there than that wonderful friend of both, Joel de Vos? Ah, but staying at Philip's house was always weird. He liked it better when Philip drove up to visit him. Although it wasn't often. And Philip was always so disapproving when he did come. Philip deplored all drugs, even marijuana, which, Joel had told him over and over, was about as drug-like as chocolate.

Anecdotal evidence didn't matter to Philip Stern. An

illegal substance, to his lawyer's mind, was an illegal substance. Philip's less scrupulous law partner defended drug dealers, and brought many, many thousands into the firm, but Philip himself would never touch such a case. He was so abstemious that his eyes actually sparkled when he had a glass of wine with dinner.

Philip would no doubt be solicitous and supportive when he learned Joel was giving up marijuana. Philip would take care of him. Philip would help him examine all the reasons he wanted to clean up. And he'd be with Philip a lot during the next few days. Familiar with his friend's crowded calendar, Joel had already arranged several blocks of time.

There was a common myth that pot was not addictive, but Joel well knew this was not true. In the past month, since the notion of quitting had seriously occurred to him, he'd tried, a couple of times, to simply pass the evening without his nightly joint. To his surprise, he hadn't, when it came down to it, wanted to abstain. Yet, in the daytime, as he sat working on the manuscript, pleased with his DSL for quick literature search or emergency email to Lenny, he often forgot what he was writing, and had to read over the previous sentence several times to make sense of it. That was frustrating and scary. Even worse was waking in the black, featureless night wrestling with his blanket, and the slow, slogging struggle to frame frantic questions: What's this? Where? Who am I? It was these incidents, and others, that had convinced him to try life without dope. At least until the book was done.

Judith's crisis couldn't have come at a better time for Joel. He'd be compelled to leave his house, his smoking buddies, his indolence. In the city he'd have an actual schedule, with Judith and Philip, who would distract him from the difficulties of quitting, and encourage him as well.

Joel piloted his Honda around the curving road. He was driving well today, he noticed gratefully, even though he could barely keep his mind on it. Truth was, he admitted, he could barely keep his mind on anything these days, barely get his mind around anything so solid as a thought. A thick woolly blanket, the comforter of marijuana, fuzzed out the line between him and his ideas, kept them at arm's length from each other. Yup, time to clean up. The mildness of the day, and the sweet thickness of the warm air, gave him confidence he could do it.

He'd quit before, several times, for periods of a couple of weeks to several months, but after such an interval his first encounter with marijuana always generated the toasted thought: god, this is great fucking stuff. When he'd previously cleaned up it had been because he wasn't getting high enough, or he was running out and didn't know how to get more. But this time he was losing his coordination. He misplaced important objects, like the scissors and his car keys. Dope was powerful shit. He was beginning to seriously wonder if he was an addict.

Last night, for example, lying on his couch with his eyes closed, he'd been listening to Arvo Part and watching the faces on his eyelids. When they'd first appeared he'd thought they were just your typical peyote or acid flashback. Next he figured these were all people he knew from past lives. Then he thought maybe he was tapping into the minds of everyone who had ever lived, in random disorder. Maybe he was telepathic, and was picking up images from a comic book artist like Stan Lee. Then he'd realized these were signals sent to him by aliens. He could only perceive them via particular marijuana receptors. Wherever they came from, he loved them. He courted them. He pondered their particularity. They certainly weren't people he'd known. Maybe they were faces he'd subliminally seen during the day, from his car perhaps, through windows of shops and cafés and other cars, seen without perception, almost without sentience. He tried to remember each one before it metamorphosed into another. But always it was too fast and the best he could do was a few words—"Fred Astaire" or "Indian with headband" or "fictional Aunt Sybil" or "old, wrinkly." They never actually looked him in the eye, come to think of it. They never spoke to him.

Most nights he lay on his couch and listened to tape after tape of chamber music on his small player. He contemplated, or tried to contemplate, ragged shadows of thought. Sometimes there was nothing there, no content. He felt ephemerally solid, buoyed and propped by the subtle intelligent music, the foam pillows beneath his head, cigarette smoke rasping his throat, mouth cancer for sure, the cup of herbal tea. Around him was reality, or at least tangibility. Substance. Within there was no sense of texture. Only experience. Ego, Freud would call it. The entity who perceived the outer world and clumsily responded to it. That the brain recognized and organized melodies and chords was already unbelievable.

Sometimes he wondered about the geography of being stoned. There was a recognizable space he entered, gray, cloudy, diffuse. He knew he was on the couch, but only sort of. It was a kind of neutral zone. No one flew in or out or across. Only something muttered at the border. Oh, the table was there, and the chair, and the lamp with its yellow selective light. And he was there too. Sort of. Was he alive? Yes, in a way. This conclusion cheered him. But wait, hey, where was he, actually, here and now, in the geography of California? A landmark lasered through his eyes and he realized that his hands on the wheel were steering his car toward the Cloverdale Café.

The Cloverdale Café had lousy cappuccino but it was a pleasant place for a pit stop. It had serviced Joel and his friends forever. The restroom was clean. The counter people were friendly. The pastries, while not particularly memorable or even tasty, were huge. Joel ordered a double cappuccino and a slice of lemon pie. He used the bathroom, then sat down at a table near the window, where he glanced at the local free alternative paper and gulped his coffee. The piecrust was soggy. He ate the lemon custard and left the remains, pasty and limp, on his plate. He felt a twinge of queasiness as he walked to the car. Once again behind the wheel, he returned to his previous line of thought.

Yes, his consciousness, his brain, or the generated blips in his brain, had rushed into the insubstantial and the imagined. But not entirely. He could still see real things. He remembered the strange little cactus in his window at home, with an impossibly spider-like red flower erupting from the tip of one of its fleshy angular protrusions. Hazy descriptive images flitted through his brain, perceived somehow as words, phrases, apposite connections. He could be a brilliant poet if he only wrote this stuff down. His poems would win the Nobel Prize. He'd be rich and famous and totally private. He'd never give interviews. Except to *The New Yorker.* The cactus was probably an extraterrestrial being. He'd been chosen as its host because he was receptive to it. And he was smart too, he hastily added. But he was declining, he knew. They—the aliens—had better hurry. He had fewer and fewer lucid hours. And even they weren't as sharp as they used to be.

Joel was at first uneasy cruising down 101, a big multilane freeway. He hadn't driven such a road in a couple of years. His hands were tight on the wheel, his eyes regularly scanned his mirrors. But by the time he reached Santa Rosa, he was driving with confidence, cockiness even. He maneuvered smoothly and patiently through the Santa Rosa crush. He still knew how to do this. Piece of cake. He wouldn't want to do it while stoned, of course.

Dope definitely altered one's state of being. It made it possible to be alone at night. Or with other humans at night. It made the night possible. He was looking forward to discussing these topics, in an impersonal, general way, of course, with Lenny.

Lenny Rubin, one of his two best friends in the world, had visited Joel the previous month. Since his visit Joel missed him terribly. Lenny had stayed four days, sleeping gape-mouthed on Joel's couch, setting the walls atremble with his snoring. They'd walked on the beach, shouted and argued, roared with laughter, discussed their projects, drunk many bottles of German and Mexican beer.

They were colleagues; their work connected them. They talked on the phone frequently, recommending books and reading paragraphs aloud. But this was the first time they'd, just the two of them, spent intensive time together—four days!—since college, since forever. Joel had loved it. Lenny was so easy to be with. With his white hair, stooped shoulders, and slightly belligerent posture, Lenny often looked combative. But with Joel he was always agreeable, always sweet. Whatever Joel suggested, Lenny said, "Okay, why not?" He'd asked Joel to proof his new article. Joel was touched, and promised to concentrate and do a good job. In gratitude for Lenny's confidence in him, he asked Lenny to look over the outline of his new book.

For several years Joel had been writing a book on juvenile drug users, which he conceived as the sequel to *Invisible Users: The Functional Consumption of Illegal Substances,* his first book. He was still living on the proceeds of *Invisible Users,* which had examined successful hard drug usage, "successful" meaning users who completely evaded the law enforcement system, and whose usage was only one part of their otherwise "normal" lives; and "hard" meaning heroin or cocaine. He had interviewed, and compiled statistics on, over a thousand middle-class adults, including health professionals, lawyers and judges, members of the military, teachers, scientists, winemakers, farmers, craftspeople, musicians, computer personnel, restaurateurs, and elected officials. He had for purposes of the study defined middle-class by two criteria: college educated and gainfully employed. Some of the users were recreational, some addictive. About a third were women. About a sixth had a history of alcohol abuse. And so on. Joel loved to cast and recast these data in his mind, as numerical proofs of hidden deviance.

Because the book was used as a text in graduate sociology classes all over the country, Joel had a modest income. Philip Stern regarded him with an edge of suspicion because he lived off money that came in the mail, Joel knew. But Philip was also a workaholic. Which he, Joel, clearly was not. Philip viewed persons with spare time as suspect.

Between Santa Rosa and San Rafael, driving on autopilot, Joel fell into a comparative reverie. If he quit smoking dope would he become like Philip? If he continued, would he be like Lenny? Each had his virtues, his unpleasant characteristics. If he were like Lenny, he'd have to teach lower-division classes, and maybe get to teach his specialty, "The History of Drug Policy," once a year or so to a handful of graduate students. Lenny was an assistant professor. He'd never gotten tenure because of his somewhat marginal area of expertise, which contradicted the research premise demanded by important government grants to the university. But he'd probably never be let go either. Students loved him. Even his freshman classes were crowded. Monomaniacal, a loner, Lenny was happy to squirrel up in his apartment, clicking emphatically away at his Mac. When a consultation job came his way and he found himself briefly rich, he bought gifts, thereby getting rid of the excess.

Joel found himself grinning at the thought, and again yearned for Lenny, simultaneously realizing that he'd ostensibly, no actually, promised to stay with Judith. At her house.

And Judith would expect him to be there when she came home from work, to walk out to one of her new favorite restaurants for a light supper of pizzetta or unagimaki or gazpacho, or maybe she would like to find him stirring a pot of fresh tomato-and-corn soup as she walked in the door, under her arm a crusty loaf of sourdough she'd picked up on the way home.

His vision of Judith's expectations began to seem more and more attractive as his thoughts turned to the finicky, time-consuming pre-dinner protestations of Philip Stern. "I'm not in the mood for Japanese," he'd say fretfully. "Maybe a salad," he'd say morosely. Both of them knew these verbal regrets were merely sops to Philip's paunch and reluctance to exercise. Both knew that wherever they ended up, however complicated the menu, Philip would locate a hamburger, or something disguised as one, or one disguised as something else, and order it, and eat it without paying attention. Philip, who was tall and balding, was in terrible shape and defensive about it. He had big sharp brown eyes behind his attorney's regulation gold-rimmed glasses. But his eyes softened with affection when he shifted to his confidential and intimate mode.

Judith's adventurous dinner habits were also preferable to Lenny's. Lenny usually had something in his refrigerator, something left over, something he'd made in economical bulk. The only problem was, his cheap nourishing plentiful meals weren't very good. His stew was flavorless, and seemed to contain more string beans than potato; his fruit salad perhaps should have been retired the day before. However, there was always plenty of beer at Lenny's, and usually marijuana too.

Ah, but that's what he'd vowed to try to avoid. Wasn't it? Judith's was certainly the happiest place to stay. Her couch folded out, as his men friends' couches did not, into a wonderfully comfortable futon. She dressed quietly in the morning, grabbed her briefcase, and was out the door, leaving only a faint trace of her perfume (its name was L'Something and it was sprayed from a narrow, severe bottle), and sometimes a note directing him to call her. Also, Judith was a stylish and attractive woman, definitely wonderful to look at, with her glossy black hair pinned back in a bun, and her silky jackets and skirts. Judith was the tapestry curator at the university library, and the large salary from her interesting career enabled her to rent the upper flat of a big house in the Claremont district. Joel loved Judith's house, and all the amenities available to him while he was there.

The last time he'd stayed with her—also between boyfriends, he recalled—she'd been in a great mood. "Good riddance!" she sang out, after discovering the old sweetie's black loafers in the kitchen and throwing them cheerfully into the trash. Then she'd told merciless hilarious stories about that person's character.

One night they'd adjourned to her deck, which, over a thick, hilly expanse of ivy, faced the street. All the exterior surfaces were deeply and permanently embedded in an ivy jungle, ancient and tenacious. Joel and Judith were sitting on the steps that led from the deck down into an apparently bottomless ocean of ivy. They were smoking cigarettes, an activity Judith did not permit indoors.

They gazed at the houses across the street. The facades were blotched and patchy with shadows thrust onto them by competing lights: the single orange street light down the block, the moon, the light from Judith's neighbor's carport. The house directly in front of them was bisected by a small flight of steps rising to a big white front door, gleaming here and there with reflected light. As Joel blew smoke, Judith pointed.

"See those shadows?" she said. Joel had followed her finger and stared across the street at the white door. Dark areas sketchily defined a somewhat blurry black-and-white image of two persons sitting side by side on the steps, their bodies melting into the floor. Joel and Judith were also sitting side by side, also on a flight of steps. The shadow figure at the left was a woman wearing a long white skirt. She sat up very straight, hands clasped around her knees. Joel couldn't see her face, but her dark hair was maybe pulled back from her brow, maybe in a kind of braid. He'd seen that hairdo somewhere. Where? The man, sitting intimately close, wore black stovepipe pants and a white shirt. His large head was bent nearly onto his chest in an attitude of grief or shame.

"Yeah," said Joel, "looks like a man and a woman. She has a long white dress on, see?"

"Frida and Diego," said Judith.

"What?"

"That's who they are, those shadow people. I've seen them before. I've named them Frida and Diego."

Joel put his hand on Judith's back and began gently rubbing her shoulders. He was connected to Judith by more than history, for sure. He felt very happy. Frida and Diego.

"From all accounts they didn't get along too well either," he said.

"By 'either,' I assume you're referring obliquely to you and me?" Judith was laughing. As they watched the shadows, Frida's legs began to move to and fro in a ghastly fashion. Joel was paralyzed. A faint cry was heard. His stomach turned cold. Suddenly the porch lights went on. A large gray cat stood where Frida's white skirt had been. Frida and Diego had vanished. The front door opened, a thin crack of dimness, and the cat scurried into it and was gone. The lights went off. Frida and Diego reappeared.

Eyes opened wide, Joel and Judith turned toward each other, their faces so close their noses almost touched, smiling in astonishment and perfect affinity.

"That's never happened before," Judith had whispered.

Joel sighed with pleasure at the memory. He was nearly in San Rafael. Should he stop for another coffee? No, he was close to the city now. He was lucky, he knew, to have had that shadow experience with Judith. Even one shared moonlit surveillance counted for a lot. How often did he get to prove the absolute reality of something indistinct? He had some really good memories, that was something. He wasn't entirely hopeless, thank god. He remembered standing on the beach with Lenny, their shoes getting wet, throwing stones into the waves. He remembered the icy weight of his toes.

He'd had plenty of drug-induced trouble experiencing his body. His existence, his consciousness, though still functioning elaborately through the sensory apparatus, was shrunken or vaporized into a baseball-sized miasma residing in his head, just in back of his eyes. He couldn't exactly feel the edges of his brain, but he knew it was there, its flashing synapses sparking across enzymatic gaps. Truly the material world was an illusion.

But maybe his moment-to-moment physical sensations were all there was of him. Maybe he was nothing more than the lurching urges to satisfy his thirst, his hunger, his nicotine addiction. Maybe those half-conscious jerky movements, and his contemplation of them, usually at some quite other time, were the sum total of his personhood. But these formulations too were probably dope induced, and therefore no doubt little verbal hallucinatory diversions.

There were so many arrangements, good ones, as Joel saw it, to get stoned. The best choice, he knew, he'd always known, was to smoke once or twice a week on a small euphoric or compensatory basis. Oh, how he wished he was capable of that! He had tried to refrain, tried to "save" getting high for weekends or social events. But his evening didn't seem complete, it didn't quite jell, his day wasn't "finished," without getting stoned. But getting high, apparently, was what was between him and coherent thought. Let's face it, he had trouble focusing. He couldn't concentrate. Not too good for someone who was supposedly writing a book.

He'd approached this book the same way he'd done the other one: first, about a year of organizing his ideas so that they followed logically one from the other. This became a rather detailed outline, with the references already Xeroxed, the conversations transcribed, the data graphed and tabled. Then another year to write the text. Joel prided himself on his lucid prose, which every reviewer (four altogether) remarked had the enviable characteristic of transforming complex dense ideas into statements of utter clarity, even quotability. But in the last month he'd done nothing more than stare at the outline of chapter 1, struggling to understand it. What does that mean, he'd asked himself repeatedly, what could I have had in mind? He'd written a couple of paragraphs, but they looked fatuous to him, obvious, even stupid. Worse, he just couldn't get his mind around what he'd actually meant. Had he meant that drug use was a particularly American phenomenon? That was one of his subheads, as clear as clear: "Drug Use Uniquely American," it read. Had he meant that Americans were hypersensitive and vigilant to pleasure and by extension to every "illegal" aspect of self-medication? But self-dosage with intoxicants went back to prehistory. Or didn't it matter either way? Did drug laws in the U.S. need to be presented in a larger historical context? Lenny had thought they did. Lenny would know what he meant. He'd ask Lenny to explain it to him.

The closer he got to the city the more he regretted his arrangement to spend time with Philip. At Philip's house, he knew, he'd have to step outside to smoke a cigarette. To smoke a joint he'd have to sit in his car, all windows closed, and emerge reeking—Philip would not hesitate to tell him—of the skunky residue left by marijuana on one's clothes and hair. He imagined Philip sniffing primly, Philip's disgusted looks, until Joel stepped into Philip's shower. But wait, he was no longer smoking dope. That had been decided already.

When he hung out with Lenny, on the other hand, he could smoke anything he wanted, even indoors, in Lenny's apartment. If he rolled a joint, Lenny would accept half of it with enjoyment. I consider it a hard drug, Lenny had many times murmured, staring intently into the lenses of his glasses. It would be good for the book, too, if he talked it over with Lenny. Lenny's field and Joel's were very close. Their positions on drug policy were indistinguishable. Lenny had read his first book in manuscript. He'd been an invaluable critic. Of course he knew the material as well as, better than, anyone.

But what was he thinking? Philip too had read Joel's book, and his questions, coming from a legally critical intelligence, often collapsed Joel's arguments. In consequence the rewritten sections were dramatically sharper, and more inescapably made the point. Philip often didn't understand the statistics, or statistical theories, that produced Joel's tables and charts: these, the strongest evidence in the book, had to be laboriously defended and explained. This exercise had given Joel a more meticulous overview of his conclusions.

He knew Philip would do a better job on his book. Lenny, however, was much, much easier to be around. Philip was particular. Lenny didn't have a lot of preferences.

"What do you want to do," Joel often asked his amiable friend. "Want cappuccino? Want to go to the bookstore? A movie? For a walk?"

"Sure. Okay," was Lenny's invariable response.

Philip, on the other hand, answered: "What movie? When? I'm not in the mood for caffeine. I need to take a little nap first. Let me check my calendar. I'm too tired, I don't feel well, I'm terribly overworked, how about in a half hour, tomorrow, next week?"

Joel laughed out loud, thinking of his finicky friend, whose success in his law practice and a series of ambiguous love affairs were both directly attributable to his caution. On the other hand, if Joel had a problem—like wanting to kick dope, for example—Philip was definitely the man to talk to. That is, if he wanted to talk. Philip asked hard revealing questions, the kinds of questions that made Joel's brain jog into insight and clarity. Philip had a way of framing things that Joel had somehow never thought of before. He also miraculously remembered every personal thing Joel had ever told him, and referred to old events and concerns when he asked his wonderful questions. Joel loved Philip's interrogations. If he didn't want to talk, however, Lenny was his man. Lenny would not only not ask questions, but would—you could tell by his demeanor—conveniently ignore your problem. Lenny's great asset as a friend was that he had no personal curiosity. Everyone should have one friend with that trait.

Judith, now, Judith was charming, Judith had great food, he had an intimate connection with Judith, but Judith made demands. Emotional demands involved complex responses, quick wits, and articulate conversation. Did he have those requirements?

Ah, god. He was exhausted already, just a few hours from his departure. Could he evade Judith's frontal emotional assault, just for tonight, and stay at Philip's? Approaching the Richmond Bridge, a wave of disorientation passed through him as he remembered how it was, sleeping at Philip's house. Philip's couch was comfortable, not too narrow, but Philip got up early and puttered around, in a noisy uncoordinated way, for a very long time. Then he took a long morning shower and a long morning shave. He turned on a noisy, sputtering Mr. Coffee, and his toaster made a strangled grinding sound. He fussed with the papers on his desk, which was in the small dining area hardly separated at all from the living room where Joel, uncomfortably roused by now and with a crushing full bladder, commonly slept. Philip loudly locked the door on his way out. His answering machine clicked constantly, recording important messages, which he would later retrieve from his office. By the time he was gone for good, Joel was miserably awake.

A weekday morning at Philip's house involved groggily and laboriously reading the note Philip had left, full of instructions about keys and lights and the purchase of frozen orange juice. How to disable the call waiting if he made a phone call, what time to call Philip to arrange dinner, where to put the mail, and so forth. It was all so complicated. If he turned back now, made a call to Judith pleading a sudden cold—she was sometimes paranoid about germs—rapidly unpacked, slapped together a sandwich and smoked a joint before taking an evening walk—if he did all these things now, now, he could sleep in his own bed and wake to slow familiar silence in the morning. But of course he couldn't smoke a joint, that was the point of this entire effort, and the whole plan fell away for lack of that one sweet hinge. He was going to the city, to Judith's, in fact, to clean up. That was the Real Reason. Let's not forget it.

Traffic was thick now, and Joel drove with more attention, shifting gears up and down, watching the lines of cars in his mirrors, cautiously changing lanes. Almost there now. He was pleased at how smoothly and expertly he was driving. He knew his way around in the city and felt confident he could drive just about anywhere without difficulty. He passed the exit that led to Philip's house, in a small, heavily gardened old money enclave near Oakland, where it was hard to park on the narrow winding street. There was easy parking in the back of Judith's house. If he went instead to Lenny's he'd stay on the freeway longer, emerging in the downtown area and slipping through side streets.

He drove on, not so steadily as before. In the midst of stop-and-go rush-hour traffic he had the urge to close his eyes and drive to wherever his hands and feet wanted him to go. Instead he drove off the freeway to a café located only a few blocks from Lenny's house. He was sweating as he locked the car and fed coins into the meter. In the café he picked up a copy of the free weekly and turned its pages while waiting for his cappuccino. He drank the delicious coffee in three gulps. He was suddenly very tired. His stomach burned and gurgled. It was later than he thought. If he were at home now, he'd be maybe walking on the beach. Looking out the café window, he saw the shiny roofs of cars, their hostile metallic colors. He walked to the pay phone outside the café and stared at the dial. Numbers shimmered in his brain. It was getting dark. Could he drive back up the coast in the dark? Judith was expecting him. What if he just stopped briefly at Lenny's, just to get high, just to take the edge off? He should definitely call someone. Whom should he call? He was in the city now. He could always clean up tomorrow. Joel tucked his rumpled shirt back in his pants and fished for a quarter in his pocket. As he dialed Lenny's number his fingers trembled just a little, and he couldn't remember ever having had a better, or even another, plan.

The Annals of Dentistry

MAYBE SHE WAS FINALLY too old for a love affair. Sybil Stern was gloomy as she maneuvered her Prius through early evening traffic. She was on her way to Walnut Creek, where the new boyfriend lived, to be fed a dinner cooked by his own aged hands. "I'll cook you snapper a la Ettinger," he'd said, planning ahead in a way Sybil recognized as kin, although her private judgment was that one should live for the moment. Between the phone call and the actual date, however, the ordinary unpredictabilities of life had intervened. Her best friend, Estelle, had left town, for one thing. She'd decamped with her two sons and granddaughter to an enviable hot-spring spa up north. Sybil, who had only one son and no grandchildren at all, was miffed. She and Estelle habitually took little trips together. Estelle had never gone off without her like that before. Sybil knew it wasn't personal, and that family reunions were entirely normal, but she couldn't help feeling rejected, discarded, and lonely. Estelle hadn't even met the new boyfriend yet.

Estelle's defection wasn't the only misfortune that had occurred after Austin's phone call. A number of Sybil's appliances had inexplicably, and simultaneously, ceased to function. The microwave oven was silent and dark, the blender had fallen apart in her hands, and the VCR blinked and emitted a grinding sound in lieu of playing or recording tapes. She was under siege. She could depend on nothing.

At seventy-two, Sybil made a point of keeping up. Her

son, Philip, an environmental lawyer, had long since mastered digital technology, and while Sybil loved his solicitous attention, she hated his condescension. She'd taken classes in running her computer, which she used to record transcripts and notes from her practice, and she resisted Philip's offers of help. When the microwave ceased to yield beeps, Sybil didn't need her own child to tell her it was well and truly dead. Later, she'd made a special trip to Costco to replace the broken items. As she set her new, better, state-of-the-art DVR so that it would record *A Murder of Quality* on PBS while she and Philip went out to dinner, she had to suppress an impulse to brag about how easy it was to program the new machine.

When Austin Ettinger, the new boyfriend, whom she'd seen a total of nine times now, invited her to his Walnut Creek condo for dinner, she accepted immediately. She'd been to his house for two afternoons of lovemaking in his big bed; but this very special invitation was for a home-cooked meal and to spend the night. It was a first.

Austin was a few years older than Sybil, the oldest man she'd ever been romantically involved with. She was glad and relieved to have an admirer after a long solitary interval. It meant she'd recovered from her previous love affair. She was tired of longing for that feckless blue-eyed Bruce, tired of deploring her longing, tired of anger at the deploring. She was severe on herself for having fallen in love with a manifest charmer, an avoider of intimacy. She knew she'd been driven by sexual deprivation, but she was bitter about her relinquishment of her cynic's margin, and ashamed of the wholehearted and greedy way she'd enthusiastically merged.

Sybil had a long, wrinkled, commanding face with silvery hair still blonde in streaks. Her once-remarked resemblance to Virginia Wolfe was no longer visible, but her posture was still that of a tall former beauty, imperious and elongated.

She now wore flat shoes for stability, and also, secretly, to minimize stiffness and pain in her hip. When she leaned on her customized cane, she sadly saw herself in the mirror as squat and hesitant. She never used the cane in public. This was only one of the many dilemmas concerning aging that she was forced to confront after breaking off the affair with Bruce. The men she knew had for some time neglected to routinely flirt with her. This was a great betrayal, and led her to notice their flaws. They talked all the time. They were gross and hairy. They were jerky, arrogant, inattentive drivers. They were obsessed with conspiracy theories. Better to value them at a distance, she thought, and shun them as potential intimates.

Austin took her by surprise. He was enough older than her other friends that at first she deferred to him. Then his sexual interest in her became apparent, and she was flattered. She began to look at him more carefully. Austin had an older man's erect sprightly walk, and the unstudied good manners of someone in their own generation. He had a naturally dour mouth but a frequent smile under his spiky white mustache. He was amiable, and he also asked personal questions. "How are relationships done these days," he questioned her. "How do two strangers like us get to a relationship? Do we make it up as we go along?" His perplexity was charming. "Yes, we do," she'd told him firmly.

Sybil wanted, as she explained to her best friend Estelle, to feel au courant. She was willing to move with the times, sexually *of course,* and in other ways as well. She might be unwilling to permit her son to explain digital electronics in a patronizing tone, but she definitely wanted to take advantage of the astounding new gadgets the twenty-first century had to offer. The best of these—better than her now-obsolete VCR, which had given her more sustained pleasure certainly than any man she'd ever known—were health benefits: cataract surgery and lens replacement; plastic hip sockets; and tooth implants.

Sybil felt she'd been waiting all her life for tooth implants. She'd long ago lost three upper molars and one lower. Of her remaining teeth, fully half had had root canals. In addition she had a bridge, several crowns, and innumerable fillings, inlays, and other restorations. Her mouth was an advertisement for her marvelous dentist, Dr. Beitner, and his specialist colleagues—the dental surgeon, the periodontist, the porcelain artist, the root-canal man, the thrice-a-year hygienist. Sybil always put herself out to charm these people, and on more than one occasion a mini-council of experts sat around her recumbent figure on their lunch hour, passing X-rays back and forth and scheduling the surgery appointment one minute after the taking of impressions. Indeed, Sybil had wondered about the possibility that her dental council regarded her as the perfect experimental subject, so eager was she to keep her teeth or the semblance of them.

All these thoughts jostled and crowded in Sybil's mind as she drove smoothly toward the freeway that would take her to Walnut Creek. To her disgust, she entered the onramp as one of a horde of rush-hour vehicles. How had she forgotten? That damned Austin, inviting her for 6:30! But no, it wasn't his fault; she should have known, should have planned. Replaying their telephone conversation, she heard herself say, "Shall I arrive at 6:30?" and Austin's answer, "Sure, Sybil honey." If she'd given the afternoon more thought, she could have spent it in the stress-free dark of the Walnut Creek Cineplex, watching George Clooney and sipping Diet Coke until, at 6:15, she could have combed her hair in the ladies' room, sprayed on a final squirt of Joy—Sybil was still partial to the perfumes of her young womanhood—and, utterly composed, found her way to Austin's condo.

Now, she thought crossly, she'd arrive all tense and cranky, much as she'd try her best to put on a smile and an attitude of relaxed anticipation as she rang Austin's doorbell. Worse were the trickles of sweat issuing from each armpit, ruining the extravagant dark green shirt that she'd bought for just this outing. She'd been eyeing it in her favorite boutique for weeks. She'd jumped at this excuse to own the sexy skin-like blouse, of a green so bluish, so blackish, that it reflected Sybil's memories of another shirt, the green silk shirt she'd worn when, shortly after having been certified to practice psychotherapy, she saw her very first unsupervised private patient. This memory was so satisfying that she'd wanted to recapture it tangibly; so satisfying that of course she'd wanted an event, not necessarily seminal, but at least important, to which to wear the memorable garment.

Finally arriving at Austin's, her blouse was not even admired. Although she hadn't exactly planned on a compliment, not getting one made her irritable. Then, Austin had the TV on, and was clearly mesmerized by it. He was watching news of a big fire in the dry October hills. It was out of control, the newscaster said. It was sweeping over the freeway she'd just driven, Austin told her.

"I didn't see any signs of it," Sybil said skeptically. She sat down on one of Austin's two matching damask chairs. Immediately she felt weak and frightened. The neighborhood of the fire, as shown on the TV, was where Estelle lived, and also Philip, and Philip's friend Judith, and—

"I'll have to make some phone calls," Sybil said. But when she stood up, her legs trembled, and she sank back again into the chair. Austin brought her a cordless phone to use, and she fumbled with it, punching the buttons randomly and impatiently.

"Here, honey, just press this—"

"I know how!" Sybil snapped. She felt like screaming with irritation and worry. By some miracle she reached Philip at his office, where he was working late, and gave him Austin's phone number. "The media are overreacting, mother, as is quite natural after the '91 firestorm." Philip was so authoritative. He said the media always exaggerate. He said the fire had never been really out of control. When Sybil hung up she felt stronger and definitely able to cope. As a sign of her readiness she accepted a glass of chilled white Zinfandel.

Austin wanted to get the latest bulletins, but Sybil, put out at the lack of admiration and attention she was getting, said she was hungry. She had to fight against sagging in her chair when the fish dish Austin was so proud of proved practically inedible. Well, it wasn't inedible, but it was pretty terrible. Covered with a snowfall of inappropriate Parmesan, which had turned to a pallid, sticky film in the oven, the snapper was tough and flavorless. Sybil politely chewed each mouthful, but really, she'd expected something juicy, slathered with the last tomatoes of the season, perhaps, and parsley, and a bit of onion. She was exhausted with the burden of her disappointment. Worst of all, while eating Austin's strange dessert of fruit salad, which pathetically combined fresh bananas and some unmistakably canned fruit she couldn't identify, and was topped with *walnuts* of all things, the plastic jacket of her first implanted tooth crumbled in her mouth. She spat out the pieces and looked in the mirror.

"Oh, shit," she wailed, "my tooth!" Austin, whose own false but well-fitting and expensive teeth Sybil had privately deemed acceptable, stood by in a pose of helpfulness. Sybil began to explain the surgery that had preceded by months the implanted peg that had preceded the visible tooth. "From bone graft to tooth," she continued, "one year!" It was too late to call Dr. Beitner.

Austin tried to console her with a cup of decaf and some misplaced pats. She shook him off and snapped open her purse. She searched agitatedly through the zipper pocket and pulled out a rubber-banded baggie. It contained one cigarette. She immediately lit it.

"Sybil!" Austin was shocked.

"This is *an emergency,* Austin. I always keep *one cigarette* for emergencies." Austin redirected her smoke with dramatic arm gestures. He opened a window, Sybil noticed, instead of scolding her about polluting his smoke-free house. However, he couldn't conceal his yawn. This clearly indicated to Sybil that he was bored with her tooth, or annoyed about her smoking, or possibly too tired to make love. Whatever. She didn't care, really. Austin was nothing. Getting to the dentist was everything.

Invited to stay the night, Sybil had packed a chic little duffel with her silk bathrobe and best toiletries. Now as Austin yawned and stretched she saw her careful packing as irrelevant. What she really wanted was to drive home to Berkeley, where she'd be geographically closer to Dr. Beitner. But she didn't want to offend Austin's perception, however misguided, of his own hospitality; and also her night vision wasn't good. Trying for a judicious compromise, she requested the use of Austin's guest bedroom. He graciously acquiesced. Sibyl thought he looked a little relieved.

The next morning Austin definitely did want to make love. But Sybil, who hadn't had a good night, had jumped out of the guest bed early and was already on the phone with Dr. Beitner's office. She was pleased and reassured to find she could be seen at 4:00 p.m. She could hardly wait.

"Let's go out to breakfast," she begged Austin.

"Sure, honey," he agreed. He took her to a restaurant he claimed was one of his favorites. The brewed coffee was awful and there was no espresso. Sybil drank tea. Defiantly, justifying it to herself as a result of her crumbled tooth, she ordered soft scrambled eggs, while Austin, digging in hungrily to his cholesterol-free unbuttered English muffin, looked on with tolerant disapproval. The TV was loud with news of the fire, and the waitress was distracted. Sybil's tea grew cold and she could not summon anyone to bring her hot water. When they left the restaurant, their waitress stood immobile at the window. The sky was a funny color. When Sybil saw the sky, and caught a throat-stabbing whiff of smoke, she understood that this might be another actual firestorm, destroying actual houses, killing actual people, and inconveniencing Sybil herself much less than it was wrecking the days and weeks and lives of others. When this realization came to her, she felt a little embarrassed. Other than conferring with Austin about the logistics of her return to Berkeley, and to the protective healing office of Dr. Beitner, she had not complained out loud, but now she felt as though she had. She was ashamed that she'd been unable to manifest, or even fake, a sense of perspective. After all, her implants would certainly get repaired, if not today then certainly tomorrow or Monday at the latest, whereas the fire was clearly in the category of a disaster, a civic emergency. She well knew she would feel better about herself, more compassionate and generous, not to mention competent, when she'd rushed from Dr. Beitner's office to the First Unitarian in Oakland, where she and her colleagues would gather to offer free trauma counseling to the fire victims. In the '91 firestorm they had all been heroes.

The radio in Austin's big Chrysler told them the fire had been contained. Sybil felt smug; she'd already known this; her son Philip had told her. However, the freeway and the Caldecott Tunnel were still closed. Two wildfires, in fact, had been burning, one on either side of the freeway, and a repeat of the '91 firestorm had been feared. Arson was suspected. No traffic was going to or from Oakland or Berkeley on 24 or even 880. Sybil was frantic. Her appointment was for 4:00 p.m. Only her implants mattered: they couldn't be put off; no fancy rescheduling could console her.

"I'll just have to take the long way around," she told Austin, once again at his table. She sipped pineapple juice. Austin had no tea, and his coffee was the same brand used by the restaurant where they'd had breakfast. She felt powdery and dry, like the air, like the October Indian summer waiting outside, surrounding her car like a mobile miasma. "There is a long way around, isn't there? Isn't there a way through the North Bay?"

"Six-eighty to 4," Austin said promptly, "through Hercules. Depending on traffic, it'll take you a couple hours at least. But it's only eleven now, honey. You've got plenty of time. Let's go to the movies."

"I don't go to the movies in the daytime," Sybil lied, "I want to see my dentist."

To Austin, possibilities proliferated. Sybil could see *his* dentist, whom he would call immediately. He himself would drive Sybil to Berkeley via Hercules. Then, when the roads were clear, they would come back together to Austin's for another evening, and Sybil could pick up her Toyota. Alternately, Sybil could ask Dr. Beitner himself to arrange an appointment with a dentist of his own choice in Austin's area.

Sybil looked in the mirror again and again. The little plastic pin erupted from her gum among her teeth like a skeleton claw in a row of gravestones. She stared at it, moving her lips up and down, fascinated by how sort of ostentatious it was, how unavoidable, how ugly, how egregious. Austin, that good soul, didn't seem to notice. Cheerfully, he made himself a fresh pot of his awful coffee; kissed Sybil with apparent enjoyment, just as though there were no conspicuous gap in her mouth; and hummed as he washed his spoon. No dark side to *him*. Sybil studied her mouth again.

"Or," Austin continued, clearly pleased with his ingenious solutions, "we could call the helicopter service. We could drive out to Dwight Field and take the copter to the Oakland Airport."

Sybil was tempted by the idea of this adventure. "How much would that cost?" she asked. Before he answered she recovered: "No, no. Don't be ridiculous, Austin. I'll take 680 to Hercules. As you yourself suggested. If it's faster than we think, I'll do a little shopping at the Hilltop Mall. I don't mind the trip; I've got a radio in my car, I'll listen to NPR," Sybil said virtuously. "And I'll get to my appointment in time." She began to pack up her belongings.

"Whatever you say, honey."

Sybil admired the man's good nature, a trait she lacked, but his constant affability was beginning to get on her nerves. "I'll go alone," she added emphatically. Thrusting her eyeglass case into her black nylon briefcase-style purse, she asked, "Have you seen my book?" She'd brought Proust with her, as she always did when sleeping away from her own house, hoping that on one occasion or another the deprived, boring, stripped nature of a strange location would overcome, or push into the fascination zone, the dense, elusive prose of Proust. So far this had not occurred, and Sybil had covered barely a hundred pages in the last couple of years. The only character she could remember was Marcel's mama.

"Here it is, honey. Can't I persuade you to stay?" Austin handed her the Proust, which she'd been using as a coaster for her juice glass. Sybil looked into his shrewd, sweet brown eyes, bisected by the line of his bifocals, and felt a little rush of affection and gratitude.

Four years ago, Sybil had agreed to see as many members of the Ettinger family as could gather themselves into her office at 4:00 p.m. on Thursday. Those who showed up were Donald Ettinger, a lawyer in his thirties who worked for PG&E; his wife, Pam; their two children aged nine and seven; Pam's mother; Pam's sister; and Donald's father, Austin Ettinger. Sybil's therapeutic method was neither orthodox nor radical. Rather, from a somewhat participatory position, she focused her sharp, practiced attention on the interactions of the group, looking for distinctions in courtesy, power, rhetoric, demeanor. Sometimes merely pointing out what she'd observed was enough for a dramatic redefinition of identity or relationship or both. Other times several meetings were necessary—although Sybil discouraged long-term therapy—before one or more of the family members experienced a shift in perception and began to behave differently. At this point, Sybil formally articulated and commented on the change taking place. She charged outrageously high fees, but, in the assessment of nearly all her former patients, earned every penny.

In the case of Donald Ettinger, who'd known he was homosexual at age twelve, but was only just coming out at thirty-eight, Sybil found her job was mainly to permit support for Donald's decision to take place and be heard. This support came from Donald's children—"I know my daddy loves me"—and father—"Be true to yourself, son, and go for some good times"—and the opposition came from wife, sister-in-law, and mother-in-law.

It was an interesting situation, particularly in hindsight, since three similarly conflicted families had come Sybil's way afterward. Also, that particular case had set into motion Sybil's uncomfortable journey on this afternoon four years later as she groaned at the bumper-to-bumper traffic on the freeway to Hercules, where she would essentially make a sort of U-turn and drive back to Berkeley. Sybil shifted her hip against the soft pillows with which her driver's seat was supplied. The case of Donald Ettinger was relevant now because, nearly four years later, Donald's father had left a message on Sybil's machine requesting that she call him back.

Sybil, who punctiliously treated former clients and their referrals with very high priority indeed, had called Austin back. To her pleasure and surprise, he asked her out.

"I never knew if you were married, or, or what," he said, "or maybe you are now? But I was kind of attracted to you. I liked your long skirt." He paused here to chuckle. "I'm a true geezer." Sybil laughed, and thought she'd take a chance, and agreed to meet for dinner. She'd tried but couldn't remember anything about him except that he loved his son. She wasn't sure she was ready for him to come to her house, just like that. She'd suggested her favorite, somewhat pricey, Thai restaurant. It was relatively quiet and shadowy, and the food was Frenchified and artfully presented.

When they had ordered, and Sybil was sipping her Sing Ha beer, she was annoyed to see Austin had asked for nothing to drink. Was he an ex-alcoholic? Although Sybil would never, never again permit herself to become involved with an alcoholic, she was almost equally wary of the new puritans, whose motto was "If it's fun it can't be good for you." This motto was pretty much the opposite of Sybil's.

Austin was not puritanical in bed, however. He worked hard to help her along to a throbbing, happy, noisy orgasm, and it was kind of him, because at his age erections were chancy and genital intercourse an occasional bonus. On the other hand, she'd been kind to him, too: she'd turned him on, and his panting, lusty gratitude was probably a fair exchange. Not that one thought of sex as an exchange, exactly, but she approved of fairness. Also, the fantasies she and Austin had traded, while lying naked in his king-sized bed amid a tangle of condoms, vibrators, silk scarves, and Astroglide, had been just that small degree of daring beyond what she'd previously disclosed to other lovers. With his frank, urgent, dirty talk, Austin had elicited a good deal of response from her erratic libido. But sex is only 80 percent in the mind—who said that?—and Austin's long, deep, attentive kisses accounted for the other 20 percent. Sybil, remembering their last afternoon together, stirred in the driver's seat. She hadn't wanted it last night, but now...

It was a long, slow, frustrating drive. The stop-and-go traffic was making her hip hurt. How glad she was the Prius had automatic transmission! Bored to tears with NPR's reprisal of the National Health Plan and frequent analyses of the ever-more-contained fire, Sybil switched to the classical music station and found herself wondering how to terminate the liaison with Austin. She was surprised to find herself thinking these thoughts. She'd expected to obsess about her teeth and the procedure to fix them, and the appointment later today at which it would be done. Also, she'd previously envisioned introducing Austin to Estelle, pictured her two friends liking each other—Estelle always liked Sybil's lovers, even when she politely deplored their effect on Sybil—and imagined the three of them out to dinner at the new, trendy Middle-Eastern restaurant on the bay. But no, this latter picture was all wrong, as Austin had specifically told her he didn't like restaurants where no bread was served. Did pita count as bread? The first time he'd mentioned this was during their first date at Sybil's favorite Thai restaurant. She thought his preference the tackiest she'd ever heard, but she certainly had her own food prejudices. She and Estelle liked to consider themselves original old-time Berkeley foodies; they'd been in the vanguard of those who bought their coffee at Peet's, their cheese and bread at The Cheese Board. These days they were heavily involved in local organic produce.

Sybil's digestion could no longer take the fiery spices she used to love. Now she read chipotle recipes and sighed with nostalgia. Asian food, in her view—and in Estelle's, too, Sybil believed—offered the most interesting and varied possibilities in every direction. Spicy to bland, simple to complex. In the context of their twice-a-week sex games and dinners, Austin's constraint on Asian food was definitely limiting. Politically and intellectually, she now remembered, she'd had her suspicions of Austin from the beginning. He'd made jokes about her membership in the Gray Panthers, for example, and listened to NPR only to deplore their absence of "opposing points of view." He drove a bulky Imperial. How could she take seriously a man who supported the Republican administration? Also, he was stingy. He refused to read *The New York Times* because, he said, it was "too thin to be so expensive."

She admitted she'd known right from the start that they weren't exactly star-crossed lovers. Bread on the table indeed. She admitted that she'd wanted an admirer and some sex and an excuse to buy the green silk blouse. But Austin himself didn't quite come up to the mark. Why should she pretend? What she wanted most at this moment was to lie back on Dr. Beitner's adjustable leather chaise and close her eyes as the resources of modern dental science were gathered together to fix what had gone so awfully awry.

Finally, finally, Sybil zipped up the Gilman off-ramp in plenty of time, she discovered, to stop at home and shower. Freshly dressed, the ordeal over, she walked through the familiar door to find Dr. Beitner's staff all abuzz with talk of the fire. Sybil was warmly greeted, however, and given a hug by Denise, Dr. Beitner's red-haired assistant. Sybil was very fond of Denise, who at once made her comfortable in the big chair. Dr. Beitner soon removed the original plastic implant peg and replaced it with a better, stronger, metal peg. His minuscule screwdriver had a long thread on the end, presumably so that it could be retrieved if patients swallowed it.

"Good thing this happened now," he said. "Better plastic than porcelain."

While they worked, Dr. Beitner and Denise talked about the fire. Sybil learned that no lives had been lost, though at least three houses had burnt to the ground. Denise lived in Contra Costa County and had been concerned about getting home. However, the BART was now running. She'd previously thought she might have to spend the night in Oakland with a friend. How had Sybil gotten back here anyway? Sybil, her mouth propped open with a rubber block, forbore to answer.

"This ought to do it," Dr. Beitner said. Denise opened a brown cardboard box and showed Sybil the replacement shell that the lab geniuses had hastily molded from the original impressions. It had a tiny threaded core into which the final pin would be screwed. There was a long concentrated period while Dr. Beitner and Denise fitted it to the break-proof peg and used the miniature screwdriver to secure the pin tightly. Then the new tooth had to be filed down. At last Denise handed the mirror to Sybil.

"Perfect," Sybil said. "Excellent." She had expected no less. She sat up.

"Eat what you like," said Dr. Beitner, "except, please, no walnuts." He gave her a thumbs-up sign and left the room.

"So how *did* you get here?" Denise asked again. "And what were you doing out in Walnut Creek?

Sybil hesitated. "It's a long story," she said. She fumbled with the chain of the dental bib. She had total trust in these people, didn't she? In her dental team? Hadn't her mouth, in some sense her most intimate part, been given over totally to their expertise?

Denise was looking at her with an interested expression. "I've got time," she said. "You're my last patient."

Sybil was feeling quite herself again. She stood up. This wasn't, after all, the appropriate venue for a discussion of romance and all the dumb things we do in the name of romance. She could wait until Estelle came home. Then she'd tell her her adventure. It was a genuine adventure, now that it was over. She'd even smoked a cigarette. She couldn't have planned anything more dramatic than the broken implant and, of course, the fire. She could almost hear Estelle's satisfying little gasps.

"Oh, well," she said, "not such a long story after all. I took 680 to 4. Went out to Hercules, and then just slipped home on the Bayshore." She gave Denise a sincere theatrical smile, showing all her teeth.

In Common

Up early, weeding the bed where pansies, saxifragia, and early white lobelia grew, their blossoms aided by last month's application of Osmocote, Bea crouched, a thick pad of newspapers separating her knees from the damp ground. She was thinking about her grandson, who'd just decided to drop out of college. Brad was his name, not a serious name in her view. But it hadn't been her choice. The boy himself was sweet, however, some hereditary tangles fused in the zygote, and his purposeful glad smile was sweet. He likes his grandma, too, she thought, and calls me Bebe, and borrows my books, and gets me high. The young men aren't like the old, they listen. How have they learned this? Not from my high-salaried competitive daughter, that's for sure; not from her dreamy husband.

The husband, Stan, is the kind of guy, she continued her reverie, dropping sneaky needles of grass into her bucket, and I would never say this to my grandson, never offend or insult him with an allusion to his dad, there's a kind of guy who's silent, who's passive, who will see a movie or eat a salad and seems to have no preferences. Can this be true, I've so often wondered, can there be nothing he wants more than something else? The word "prefer" is foreign to him. "Whatever you like," he'll say. And not a mutation either; this type of guy is countable, demographically visible, publicly known. Brad's dad. Brad knows, too, but hasn't been exposed to the concept of dad as a type, and I'm not the one to embarrass him—at this thought Bea's lips pressed together virtuously—not yet, not until he spells it out for me to confirm. And then his name, Stan, I always thought culturally unfortunate, flat, pale, a name that burns but doesn't tan. Stan. His parents presumably named their child Stanley. Dunstan? Wynstan? Stan seemed to Bea nice enough in his manners and smile, but trivial. He's pleasant, and asks me how I am and remembers if well or ill but doesn't listen to why, can't listen to the interesting parts. Brad, though, he listens. A young listening man is a treasure, and how he got that way some magic unacknowledged by those who wiped his nose, or maybe unnoticed, probably unnoticed. In the wild spit of millions of genes? Or caused by television? I'm not the one to ask. Certainly younger men seem to be more interested in women's inner lives, including their problems, than do men of my generation, that is, older men, that is, men who were alive before WW II.

Bea's thoughts now rushed to the thrilling topic of Kenneth, and she decided, not for the first time, that when starting up a relationship with such a man, an older man, one's own problems must not be disclosed. One must instead elicit the man's problems and listen with a helpful, compassionate, problem-solving, and, if possible, sexy ear. My problems, and this is well known by women my age, would probably scare him away. If he had the skill to hear them. I imagine that he, like other old lovers, would listen with increasing horror and unease to, for example, the story of my conflicts with my daughter, or how I can't afford a well-fitting bridge, let alone state-of-the-art dental implants, because my ex-husband and his smart-ass lawyers cheated me out of thousands of dollars that were rightfully mine. No, no, he can't be told, certainly not in the beginning, not before we've established a bond so compelling and passionate that he'll do anything, listen to anything, to get into my panties.

Do younger women know this? It might not be necessary for them to know this. Men are certainly wonderful, and interesting, but they live in a tent without windows, canvas blind spots; they're camping out, and the meadow beneath them is flooding, and they're sinking, more and more, into the damp muck of an obstinate refusal to know.

Bea pulled up one last weed and stared proudly at her work. The mass of pale flowers, pink, lavender, shadowy brown, and yellow, shimmered as she stood. Her knees creaked and then throbbed as she poured the bucket of pulled weeds into the compost, out of sight in the backyard. Her friends were due for Sunday breakfast, soon, at 9:30 a.m. sharp. They'd be hungry, but Bea also wanted them to stop and be impressed by her flowers. The pansies looked good. These pansies, Antique Shades, are just darling, she thought. She lingered to imagine the admiring comments of Lolly and Sybil. Her khaki trousers were still clean, thanks to her foresight in laying down the newspapers. Of course she'd already picked up the bagels, first thing. It was a matter of only a moment to set them out, still warm, in a basket, near the low-fat cream cheese, the spring fruit salad (strawberries, mango, kiwi), and the coffee cups. Bea had bought extra bagels today, for her new boyfriend, a person of her own generation, a person who fit very well, she knew, the characteristics she had pondered in her reverie. Her grandson Brad was also expected. The time of his arrival was uncertain. He'd promised to visit before heading back to school, and he'd maybe have eaten breakfast already—but this boy was still growing.

Out the window she saw Lolly and Sybil, prompt as always, stepping fastidiously down the cement path. They paused a moment to point at the pansies. Bea was gratified, and began to pour out the coffee, which her friends seized and drank thirstily the minute they entered the house.

"There's no melon in the fruit salad," Lolly noticed.

"Certain foods generate more garbage than the original mass of the food." The three women spread cream cheese on their bagels, and began to eat.

"Like corn?"

"Yes, and melon, turkey, artichokes."

"When is Kenneth coming?" This comment from Sybil was uttered in the tones of someone who was getting to the real point. Bea knew her friends were eager to meet Kenneth, especially after Bea's carefully exiguous announcement that she'd actually made love. All three women were fervent followers of each other's personal news.

"Very soon, very soon." Suddenly shy, Bea refused to say more.

The three friends drank more coffee. They traded pages of the Sunday paper, and threw them, digested, onto the floor. When they were well into this cozy ritual, Kenneth arrived. He was meeting Lolly and Sybil for the first time. As Bea greeted him at the door, she was relieved she'd told her friends. Otherwise she wouldn't really have been able to touch Kenneth: a touch would be an abrupt, even intrusive, announcement. Yet when Kenneth moved to kiss her, she shook her head, indicating the others.

Both Bea's friends were assertive, commanding women, and smart and talkative, each in her own way, and considered contentious in their intimate circle. But they were agreeable and mannerly when introduced to Kenneth, and they spoke of their eagerness to set eyes on Brad the grandson, an old favorite of theirs. For Bea's guests, Brad was a neutral leading topic.

Kenneth, clean-shaven, his hair slicked down, commented that younger people were more highly evolved than their elders. The dissatisfactions and failures of the older generations had performed an intellectual mutation on the younger, who now built on the information they'd received while simultaneously pointing out its flaws. Bea agreed with this opinion, which seemed to echo the thoughts she'd had while weeding her pansies. Lolly and Sybil emphatically did not agree. Bea knew her friends were honorable to a certain extent, but by no means above inventing data or making up statistics to prove a point. Bea herself had done this. Lolly, who had always been very judgmental and rigid, Bea now perceived, said with a sniff that young people appeared to live only for pleasure. Her very own daughter had run off to Denver, Colorado, with an airline pilot, she explained. Lolly's daughter Paulette had, in actual fact, Bea knew, been offered the Denver job at a salary that made all the older people gasp. The airline pilot, she was quite sure, had come later. However, it was true that Paulette, nearing forty, had left Lolly all alone. Sympathy mixed with schadenfreude was what Bea felt at her friend's apparent failure to recover, a casualty of the difficult but essential separation, put off until too late. And Sybil, while conceding that successive waves of culture carried generations through change, made a case for the essential, the very depth, of human nature as more or less immutable and eternal. Bea herself did not hold this view, and said so, leaning forward toward Kenneth, holding herself in a posture that indicated she was prepared to listen closely. To her surprise, Lolly and Sybil assumed nearly identical attitudes. Their eyes were bright, their faces a little pink, with the intensity of their interest.

"A new perception of a thing may be equivalent to a new thing," Kenneth said tentatively.

"It's certainly true the culture of the young rewards sophistication," Sybil replied.

Bea sat back a little. "You mean ours didn't?" she murmured.

"Oh, no. We were encouraged, molded, really, to be

innocent of a good deal of real life, and to avoid thinking of much of the rest of it."

Kenneth turned toward Sybil. "That's certainly so," he said.

"Self-esteem and flexibility," Sybil went on, "those were my goals in child raising." Was she criticizing Lolly? Was she criticizing Bea?

"Having a good time was mine," said Bea. "But the kids, they know so much more than we knew, maybe more than we know now—"

"Oh, no, Bea, that's just not possible." Lolly, who had addressed her remark to Bea, smiled at Kenneth.

Kenneth smiled back. Bea hated him then. It was his attitude of entitlement that got to her, sexual entitlement, complacency, as if the three women were fawning over him, flirting with him, hauling on his attention. Which they were. Disgusting. Responding to Bea but addressing his remarks to Lolly, Kenneth said: "The kids do know certain things we don't, MTV and VR for example—"

"Initials," Sybil hissed.

"—but these are just fashion. The actual processing, interpreting, analyzing, is infinitely more complicated and sophisticated in us. How can it not be?" Bea forbore to answer. Kenneth stood. "I'm going out on the deck to smoke. Anyone join me?"

Sybil pushed her chair back and stood up, Bea noticed, without grabbing her cane. Vanitas. She took a rubber-banded baggie out of her purse. "I'll join you," she said.

"I thought you quit." Lolly sat tall, disapproving.

"Oh, you know, I always keep one for emergencies." Sybil removed a cigarette from the baggie and looked meaningfully at Kenneth. "Got a light?" she asked.

"Well," Lolly got up hurriedly, "I'll join you, too, but only for a breath of fresh air." As though the air in this room, in this house, were stale, Bea thought in amazement, rejected, her arguments apparently stale, her position not fresh enough. She watched the three file out through the glass door onto the deck, which this morning was looking particularly spring-like and fresh with its pots of flowering nemesia and mimulus, with diascia and blue-flowered rosemary tumbling over the sides of larger pots containing tulips and ranunculas. She watched Kenneth leaning on the railing, while Sybil and Lolly sat in the two plastic chairs. She saw him looking from one to the other, as each in turn vied for his attention. Bea could hear their voices, which became increasingly girlish and seductive. Disgusting. She sat back, appalled but also amused. She fished the strawberries out of the fruit bowl with her fingers, then the chunks of mango, and finally the slices of kiwi. Then she drank the remaining juice from the bowl.

She'd only been to bed with Kenneth once, so far. Their love-making was a little difficult, a bit of a bore, probably about average, Bea thought, for old folks. Sex with Kenneth, in short, wasn't great. Aside from the sex, she felt profoundly ambivalent about every aspect of his person and personality. But she was astonished to find she wanted the difficult, boring, not-great sex with him so very, very much. How glad she was that he'd decided to extend his visit, stay in town a little longer, hang around for an indefinite period. And yet how doubtful she was too.

Women my age are so great in bed. And we're complicated and refined sexual beings who know a lot more than we, that is, I, can show to a man I'm newly interested in. Details of his appearance are like headlines in a newspaper. Minutiae of his facial hair, type of shirt, age of shoes, protuberance of gut over belt, these things tell me volumes. Then, in the restaurant, his willingness to try new foods and order more wine than we'll drink, his preference for the familiar, his shocked glance at the prices, his meticulous and stingy figuring of the tip, the way he treats the waiter—and I've got inadvertent information, I know things he'd never reveal.

For example, it was interesting to me the way Kenneth talked about his ex-wife. He never once said he loved her. Not once. But he spoke freely, almost happily, about her culinary compulsiveness, how she had to straighten off every measured tablespoon with a knife, and how it drove him crazy. Yeah, well. He told me stories about their vicious divorce, how she had run off with another man, leaving him, poor Kenneth, to raise their daughter and their son.

"I was the original single parent," he said, his voice husky with self-pity, "I was a good daddy." While Bea listened, listened, listened, Kenneth talked, talked, talked.

It was because she loved the not-great sex so much, she admitted, that she put up with Kenneth's less desirable manifestations. But she considered him her new boyfriend, and had told him so, and he'd laughed and said, "God, I love you, Bea," which to Bea's mind carried powerful intention.

Kenneth was jowly and paunchy and tall. Behind thick retro glasses his eyes swam, magnified and moist. Bea would have liked him to be more inventive in bed than he was, but his intense gazes were better than sex. She wanted to display herself, all of herself, even her semi-toothless mouth, and press her skin tight to his forever. And also she didn't. Why should she? Why shouldn't she continue to make love naked with him, and send him home afterward, and never have to confront her own image, her self-image, of sexuality? I mean, why not? If only he, right, if only he, it's him, it's not my fear, it's not my cowardice, it's his! Good work, Bea. Once again I've managed to deflect responsibility, and transform it into guilt and blame so that I won't even miss it. But I'm ashamed. Ashamed all the same. I'll extract my partial denture, wave it in the air, that strange appliance with its six little teeth, it's like an amphibious creature described by David Attenborough, I'll disclose my naked gums to the world. I'm not the one to dissemble. And why not? It's only dentistry. It's only the work of the dental surgeons, showing by this hole in my mouth that they don't know very much, don't know what they're doing, don't know why they're doing it. If I expose my undentured mouth I'll expose the dental profession. My flaw is their flaw.

All the same, she'd held his head with both hands and given him cushy, delicious, close-mouthed kisses, partly because these were her favorite kind, and partly because she didn't want his tongue exploring her mouth and discovering the hidden metal that crossed her palate and held her elaborate six-toothed denture firmly, or semi-firmly, in place.

Later he'd asked her, as they lay side by side, sweaty and affectionate, "Do you want me to stay over?" Bea would have loved sleeping all night long with a lover after such a long dry interval. She imagined herself in the morning, springing up when she felt him stir. She'd run barefoot to the kitchen to start up Mr. Coffee, she'd jump into the shower with a brand-new cake of Neutrogena, hoping Kenneth would join her there. And when he did, she'd pull him back to bed. If only she had the teeth.

"Mm." Noncommittal but not really. "Maybe not tonight?"

With his big thumb Kenneth rubbed her spine, in assent. When, after some time, he rose and began to dress, Bea slipped on her robe and helped him button his shirt. Kenneth squeezed her and groaned, "Ah, god." Bea was ecstatic. This was a peak moment, she knew. She wanted to remember it, play it back all by herself. She was tired, too, and wanted him to leave so that she could remove her partial, drop it into the cleansing solution, and rinse out her mouth. She wanted to be alone so that she could think about him, think about them together, think about his groans. She imagined sinking into the warmth of her bed, rolled up in her soft comforter, replaying Kenneth's loving exclamation, over and over.

After he left, she'd cleaned out her mouth and sat smoking the end of a joint in a hemostat Lolly had given her years before. Love or something like it was back, just when she'd learned to do without it, back for another transitory immersion in wonderful and terrible new memories. As though she didn't have enough. But, she mused, maybe there's never enough. But I don't believe that.

Her new boyfriend and her two old women friends came back into her dining alcove, banging the door behind them and smelling faintly of cigarette smoke. Bea watched, scornful, above the fray, as her friends flirted with her boyfriend, competed for his attention. Yes, disgusting. How she wished, now, she had told them how crazy she was about Kenneth. But why should she have? Why shouldn't she have a secret, a new secret? The secret was delicious, it made her warm all over, it was better than the sex; thinking about it was better than doing it. As with so many things. If the sex had been better, would she have told her friends? The imperfect connection between Kenneth and herself was what she wanted, she was pretty sure, just as it was, private still and still confined to one intimate evening. But there'll be more. And eventually I'll have to tell. I'll want to tell. Oh, god, yes, I will. But by then I could be bored with Kenneth. But then I could pass him on to one of them. Bea smiled benevolently at Lolly and Sybil, who were still vigorously charming Kenneth. Only a hormonal rush can conquer the fatigue of age.

Brad arrived, wonderfully tall and slim as a creature from a sitcom, shaggy haired as befit his college student status, but wearing clean jeans and only one visible piercing, in his ear. Bea sprang up from her chair, and with delight embraced her grandson, who graciously bent over to receive her hug and to clasp her quickly in return. Lolly and Sybil greeted him familiarly, and rapidly began quizzing him, showing off, Bea thought, to Kenneth their privileged, long-term knowledge of the boy, whom, after all, they'd known since before he was born. Brad's long, sweet mouth, opened now in a pleased, polite smile, was full where his dad's was thin. Genetics, Bea thought, the most suspenseful show in town.

Lolly, of the four older people, was the only one a little bent. With her uneven arthritic gait, dyed red hair, and erratic use of cosmetics, she looked a little bizarre, Bea realized, when to the accustomed setting was added a young person. Sybil, her once blonde hair now gray, her tall figure and straight-backed posture at once imperious and resourceful, kept casting sideways glances at Kenneth. Disgraceful. Bea was the shortest, plumpest person in the room. Comparing her clothes with Sybil's elegant long rayon skirt and dark silk blouse, she felt squat and dumpy in her baggy khaki pants. In honor of Brad's visit she was wearing the UC Davis sweatshirt he'd given her, maybe not the most appropriate garment for a grandma. But why not? I'm not the one, she thought automatically, to criticize a gift. It was a clear soft blue. Blue is one of my best colors. She ran a hand over her springy white crewcut, trying to pat it down. Brad and Kenneth were finally introduced, they shook hands, two tall men shaking hands. There was more conversation about college. Brad announced he was dropping out for a year after he finished up this semester. All the older adults congratulated him on this decision. Bea felt a bit miffed. She'd thought his move would not be highly regarded, and that she would be Brad's only advocate. In the background, grandmother Bebe, wanting only what was best for the boy, not what convention decreed. I want to thank my wonderful grandmother who always encouraged me, even when my actions were not popular ones. Oh, well.

Lolly and Sybil left, after inviting everyone to join them at a matinee of *Farewell My Concubine.* Only Kenneth accepted their invitation, but hung back for a minute to remind Bea of their dinner date later on. He hadn't embarrassed her with handholding or kisses, and Bea was grateful. Also she wasn't grateful. Why hadn't he been affectionate, demonstrative? So her friends would know better than to fawn? Underneath these indignant thoughts Bea knew very well that Sybil and Lolly were eager to know Kenneth out of concern for her. But the situation allowed her to wallow a little in these unaccustomed protestations. Unable to determine which move of Kenneth's she would have preferred, after all it was her decision too, full disclosure inevitable and soon in any case, Bea turned her attention to Brad. Taking a year off, good idea, no matter how many people thought so. Travel, work a few minimum-wage jobs, meet a different class of people. Couldn't hurt. The boy was smart, thoughtful, more sensitive than his parents, but sheltered.

To Bea the existential dilemma, one of many existential dilemmas, consisted of coming to understand that other people are irrevocably different and other than oneself. With the realization one always felt betrayed. Shock and disbelief, outrage, refusal to accept, amusement, and repugnance. But evolution is the traitor here. But to Brad, because he was a kid, a smart kid, true, an early reader, but still a kid, every other being was a supporting actor, probably improvising to his lead, the only real character, the star, the center of the universe. Of course he felt alien, unutterably alien, no one could know the depths of his weirdness. Could they?

Obsessed with the manifestations of hormonal gush, fairly recent after all, and presumably disturbed as well, with the alarming increase in musculature, appetite, shoe size, need for sleep. Was it because of this that he could listen, because his heedless ignorance of Out There-ness also signified an interest, not quite a concern, but a curiosity, about the characters who moved in and out of his vision? What would they do next? What were they like? Wasn't that what she'd been like?

Bea was dying to know why he'd decided to drop out. What she said was, "Have you been thinking about this for a long time?"

The context of Brad's response turned out to be his new girlfriend. "Not exactly, but yeah, I have. And it turned out later she was interested too."

Bea's response was immediate. "Tell me about her." I know some things, she thought. A woman of my age, I know.

"She's a senior, she's a couple of years older than me—"

"A year or two doesn't mean anything—"

"She's really mature." Brad went on to tell Bea critical information about his inamorata Zoe: her major (women's studies), her postgraduate plans (more women's studies), her job (daycare), her eye color (really, really blue), her athletic inclination (rock climbing), the subjects of their late-night soul talks (mutability and angst). The data, a lot of data, streamed past Bea without engulfing her. "She grew up in Oregon," he finished, gasping for air.

"My new friend comes from Oregon too," Bea divulged, suddenly excited. "You know, Kenneth. He's here visiting his daughter." She choked back the daughter's job and name and marital status, and the color of Kenneth's car. She gave Brad a bagel and watched him eat it. He declined her offer of coffee and pulled a bottle of Ty Nant from his backpack, which was hanging by one strap over the back of his chair.

"Oh, and here's a little something for dessert, Bebe." He

handed her a baggie containing a walnut-sized marijuana bud.

"Ah. Thank you. Shall we do it up now?"

"Definitely." They exchanged a confidential look. "So, your new ... friend. From Oregon. He's going back when?"

"It's not clear." Into a white dinner plate Bea cut tiny shards off the redolent red-threaded bud. "He was going to visit a couple of weeks, but then we got together, he thought it over, he changed his plans, he's not sure." Bea continued to cut with the orange-handled scissors. With not-too-clean fingers Brad broke up the larger of the clumps. He pushed a seed over the edge of the plate onto the table. Bea's face was hot. Talking about Kenneth made her nervous, but she wanted to, wanted to talk about his worn Pendleton shirts, how they made her eyes wet with nostalgia, his concentrated arousing gazes, she was dying to tell everyone, tell the world, tell her grandson. She reached out and opened the top drawer of the sideboard cabinet, and pulled out a pack of Zig-Zag.

"I've got a bong, Bebe."

"Would you rather?"

"It's up to you."

"Okay. Get your bong. I'll try it."

Brad stuck his grubby hand into the long side pocket of his backpack and pulled out a cardboard tube, which he unrolled to reveal a garish orange plastic water pipe decorated with stickers of skulls and breasts. Bebe had never seen anything like it, and if god was merciful, she never would again. However. Exchanging secrets with the grandson. Special treats. The bong it would be. They lit up.

Brad. Hardly a name. Maybe a special kind of carpentry tool, or a brand of cheap athletic shoes. Rocky Horror: "Oh, Brad." Probably Brad had sounded like an appropriate offspring of Stan. Sad, how the best genes skipped a generation. But Brad. Ah, Brad, hoop shooter, guitar player, science-fair winner.

He exhaled. "I'm glad we're friends, Bebe—"

Oh, me too. Her chest was hot with dope and love. Darling baby Brad. "Likewise." Definitely.

"—Because it's good to have another person's perspective, you know what I'm saying? Someone who knows your mom and dad from a different perspective."

"Mm."

"Dad was cool about Zoe, though."

"Oh, good."

"Yeah."

"And your mom?"

"Well, she can be embarrassing, you know what I'm saying?"

"Sure." Bea definitely knew what Brad meant. But she wanted to hear the story. She nodded her head encouragingly. Brad, however, in a sudden reverie, perhaps of merging with his beloved Zoe, had clearly sent his conscious self elsewhere. Bea wondered if he was hearing in his stoned ears his favorite song, a popular lament sung by Galen Doom and The Dregs: "Don't think you're smarter than me/Don't think you're cuter, See/I'm just like you,/Wondering who/I am, you're just like me." To Brad, who had explicated and paraphrased the lyrics to Bea more than once, the song expressed an important philosophical truth, in its clanging minors and riffs, that was almost visible to him, just around the corner; and each time he heard the mournful shrieks of The Dregs, he'd told her, this time, he thought this time he'd surely get it. Bea took a hit off the bong and waited him out.

His face was finally cheerful. "She'll come around, you know what I'm saying? I mean, won't she?"

"Of course." My daughter, well, I've had my times with her. We've had our close times. We've squabbled. I'm not the one to deny this. I've noticed her husband Stan never argues. Someone to contend with is frosting on the cake.

But not my daughter.

Brad had to leave. Bea walked him out. They stopped to admire the newly weeded beds.

"Your pansies are beautiful, Bebe. I liked those blue ones you had last year. I liked their name. What was their name?"

"Maxim Marina. Yeah. I love those."

"Do these guys have a name?"

"Antique Shades is their name."

"They need a better name. Know what I'm saying? How about, like, Fade to Pale?"

"Perfect." This was what she'd wanted—was it too much to ask?—some real focus on her flowers.

"And what are those neat little white guys?"

"Lobelia."

"Lobelia." They stood gazing at the lobelia. "Well, Bebe. Next time."

Bea hugged him again, her darling, her darling baby Brad. Now he had a girlfriend, her name was Zoe. He still shared secrets with his grandma. And listened. Bea stood on her porch after he left. Did she have time to take a nap before meeting Kenneth? Yes. A nap would be good. And she'd decide later about the sleepover and exposure. It occurred to her, for the first time, that Kenneth too might have a reason for wanting to sleep the night alone. What would his reason be? How can I get him to tell me? I might have to tell him first, tell him about my teeth. On the couch, Bea closed her eyes. I can do that, she thought.

Women my age, at this moment, on this quaking crust of beach, this crumbling seaside patch of planet, were thrown here just like everyone else was thrown in their place. We can't help it. We have all the chromosomes intact, the DNA spiraling as nicely and randomly as evolution could design, the eyes as blue as spawn from a barbarian ancestor decreed; but are creatures of the energy source of the zeitgeist, the recycled mud of the hovel, sleeping animals in the yard, the hovercar in which we zoom, foldable tents of finest wool and beads from Kirghiz, television announcing a frothy digestive aid, drawings on the wall with a bit of coal, a restaurant dinner with wine. Creatures, created things, products and seed. Women my age mutter about the accidents of birth and abortion that have brought us, that brought me, to this place, this time, this click of the clock, this cheap worn rug, this sputtering pen, this worrisome ache in my knee. And what's around me is all I know and also all I don't know. Gasping, thrown on the rocky sand, drowned by the seventh wave, I'd like to know the wave, but too late: it's already engulfed me, it's become me, and I can't know it now. Before, before I approached it, before it rushed over me, I saw it, almost understood it, caught its nature, thought I'd know it, but no, too far inside, too much of it, with it. When it's gone, I'm drenched and stunned, drooling, bruised, in need of warm blankets, gazing at the sea the wave presumably came out of, was extruded from, but there's no sign, and now perhaps I'll never know. But I've been in it, and that's something.

Kay Kay and Jay Jay

I WAS DOWN TO no friends and two acquaintances. My longtime boyfriend had just dumped me, and I'd moved out of our house into a cramped, dark apartment. Because the split, the inevitability of which I'd somehow ignored, was abrupt, my descent into rented space was hasty. I was heedless and unlucky. The new place was awful.

Neal—the boyfriend—had been fairly brutal. "I don't want to see you, Kay Kay. I don't want you to call me. I don't want any communication with you," he'd said toward the end of our last couples counseling session. I reminded him that he owed me a huge amount of money, my part of the house. "You'll get every penny, Kay Kay," he said coldly. I was devastated, and had to tell my story over and over to anyone who would hold still for it. I was also inconsolable, and I blamed my friends for their egregious inability to console me. I soon became, if not non grata, certainly non invited.

I nearly found myself asking staff and colleagues at the clinic if they'd like to grab a bite after work. These were the very people from whom I had previously declined invitations, on the grounds that I didn't need new friends. But now I did.

Before I started working at the clinic, I'd been in an obstetric practice with two other physicians, with whom I socialized and drank beer after work. The practice had been more lucrative and also more difficult. But I'd always been active in the women's health movement: I'd been on the board of the Women's Health Clinic, fundraising and so forth, before it opened, and when I was offered a position there I really couldn't refuse. I had no idea, of course, that I'd soon want my old income and my old friends.

I kept thinking there was a good person inside me that my friends couldn't see, that Neal couldn't see. When I looked in the mirror, I couldn't see that good person either. Maybe I'd hurt Philip's feelings by leaving his party early so that I could rush home to watch *The Sopranos,* but so what? At least I'd lied and said I didn't feel well. At least I didn't want anyone to know. At least I wanted to *appear* good. The truth was, I was having a lot of trouble being who people, my friends, wanted me to be, and also who I wanted myself to be. My true self, sarcastic, attention-grabbing, bossy and opinionated, out for only my own good times, kept breaking through. I was inexorably, unfortunately, myself. Remorse washed over me again and again, and I kept wishing that everything had been different, that I'd been different, that I'd been kinder, more sympathetic, more sensitive, more likable.

On another level I thought, fuck them, who needs them. I was perfectly satisfied with myself as I was. That was a lie. I was miserable.

If it weren't for them, meaning my ex-friends, I could have been happy by now. If it weren't for them I could have recovered after the breakup with Neal and resumed my previous single life. That life had involved agreeable sexual partners from time to time, but no one as significantly other as Neal. What had happened to my old friends? Ellie could have cheered me up, she used to cheer me up, but she didn't have time for me now. No doubt she had other friends she liked more than me. They were probably vapid and shallow, and flattered her, and never told her the truth as I did. Pitilessly abandoned but clear-eyed, I now saw Rachel as another inadequate friend, unresponsive and unfeeling, always interrupting me to say something irrelevant and inane. As for cruel Philip, he was way too busy being the most important environmental lawyer who ever walked the earth to console one of his oldest, probably his very oldest, and most loyal friend, who was in terrible pain. They'd all discarded me and betrayed me.

I thought these stony thoughts as I lurked in the new, heartbreakingly charmless apartment. The kitchen area was completely without windows. The living/dining area had French doors that opened out to a depressing strip of concrete patio bordered by a light-stopping concrete wall beyond which was a shrubby garden and the street. The wall-to-wall carpeting, which I was so far too dispirited to pull up, was so woolly it made me feel quite demented. Not too demented to be angry, however: at Neal, Rachel, all of them. Treacherous narcissistic pigs. All of them. All.

I'd been in the apartment since spring and it was becoming unbearable. There were a few cool days before Labor Day, and afterward too, but then Indian summer hit, and I thought I'd die. I was so irritable and grouchy that I cut down my hours at work, and soon had every afternoon to fling myself into despair, in addition to every evening. To compound matters, in the aftermath of having been dumped by what was probably the last great love of my life—I was in my fifties, and what did I have to look forward to?—I was seriously considering buying a house of my own.

Why, I asked myself, dismayed by my own attraction to risk, why would I want to endure such a difficult painful process when I was already in a difficult painful process? The answer came to me that I was trying to dampen the anxiety of one experience with the anxiety of another, not unlike the law student who gets pregnant right before the bar exam. In any case, I'd looked at houses all summer long during my walks on the empty hot afternoons when I was trying to discharge my painful grief. These walks usually began with a stroll up the hills, to my wonderful pre-Neal apartment building. I often stood looking at it, wishing one of the old residents would happen by, wishing I lived there again, and that the years with Neal had never occurred. After that obliterating fantasy, I'd walk back through west Berkeley, threading my way through every street, tree-lined or barren, curvy or straight. I passed tall shingled Victorians and short stucco bungalows. I couldn't help noticing that a lot of houses were for sale. There were three or four I really liked.

The October weather continued hot. I suffered at night. My colleagues and I snapped at each other during the day. There was a turnover in clerical and technical staff, and a surge of HIV-positive cases, always complicated and sad. Pregnant twelve-year-old girls came in for exams. My heart melted and opened to them and their situations, and I counseled them to terminate the pregnancy; then, after they'd refused, I counseled them on prenatal care and on the other services offered by the clinic. I was so unaccountably depressed by their nonchalance that I called a realtor friend and made an appointment to talk.

One afternoon I found a card in my mail addressed to Jay Jay Ringer. Nonprofits got my name from the roster of the clinic, and they assumed, because of the M.D. after my name, that I was rich. Then they commenced a monthly, sometimes weekly, dunning, which lasted until I shot them off a note, begging them, in the foulest language I knew, to save a tree. This actually worked for a couple of years. Then they started up again. Maybe they thought I'd forgotten, or been born again. But these big computerized mailing programs often made mistakes. The most common was to address me as Mr., or, if as Doctor, to simply assume I was a man. This was infuriating. Another was to misunderstand my name completely, and to address me as K.K., or Kay K., or K. Kay Singer. My last name was frequently misspelled too. It had been rendered as Sinker, Stinger, Sinner, Singe, and Singh. Jay Jay Ringer! It was easy to see how each capital letter in my real name had been moved back one letter in the alphabet, thus producing a whole new person.

"Hi, Jay Jay," I said to my reflection in the mirror, "Hi there, Dr. Ringer." The reflected grin looked quite sweet, really, and not quite like me. There was a soft neon light over the mirror. Sometimes it looked pink and sometimes yellow. I thought the light gave me a blurred, benign look.

I'd worked full-time that day, and participated in a birth, and I was restless and pleased in a tense way that needed expression. I thought I'd walk out to a nearby café and have myself a cold beer in the company of my fellow citizens, none of whom, if I was lucky, would know me in my professional capacity. I'd been a doctor all day long, and now it was time for me to be, well, a non doctor. Persona non doctor.

I changed and stepped out of the apartment. It had been hot for several days, and my two large fans no longer made a difference. My old pre-Neal apartment had had windows on all sides, and a good breeze could always be coaxed indoors. In the new, dark, post-Neal place I'd lined up my plants in front of the rickety French doors, and they formed an agreeable green buffer against street sounds, but there wasn't nearly enough light or air. The apartment was on the street level, under four oppressive floors of a modernesque concrete box.

Wearing shorts, walking briskly, I quickly covered the half mile to the café. It had just gotten dark. Late daylight was an aspect of summer that I, a dedicated walker, cherished. I'd often worked late, and my evening walk home had been an energizing transition to my life with Neal. But there was no more life with Neal. This thought enraged me, and I walked even faster, and arrived at the café a moment before I was, strictly speaking, emotionally ready. Through the window of the café I saw Rachel.

She was sitting against the wall, laughing at the person on the other side of the tiny round table. The person was an older guy, practically bald, with gold-rimmed specs. Oh my god, the person was Lenny. When had he gotten back? And why hadn't he called me? I was struck by how pretty Rachel looked, her gray fuzzy hair curling around her pink smiling face. Rachel was having a good time. Lenny was laughing too. I watched them from the street, and tried to make myself invisible. This attempt was superfluous. They were so fascinated with each other that they didn't even look around. I was not within their ken. I slunk back across the sidewalk, between two parked cars. There they were, having fun, two old friends. They could so easily have been three old friends. They could so easily have called me, left a message on my machine, said they were just stepping out for a beer. My heart was beating fast, my stomach hurt, tears bulged behind my eyes. There was no real conspiracy here, I knew, but there was an apparent conspiracy, resulting in a real exclusion from the company of my ex-friends.

I lingered in the darkness, nearly getting run over, and walked disconsolately home. No sooner had I turned the key in the lock than a whooshy fluttering breath turned into something clawed and furry, about the size and shape of a small scarf. It flopped past me, scratching my shoulder, bouncing on my head, and disappearing behind me into the gloomy entry of the building. I froze. Cautiously, I left my door open, and hesitantly walked back the few steps to the heavy glass front door. I opened it about a foot. A shape, revealed to have pointy wings, fluttered in the corner and veered out the door. *It was a bat.* It disappeared immediately around the corner of the building. How did a bat get in? What was it doing there? I reentered the suffocating apartment, my initial fear now turned to puzzlement as I pondered the origin of the bat.

I turned on both fans and opened all the bedroom windows and the French doors too. It was so intolerable indoors with everything closed that I didn't care if a horde of bats winged in as though to a cave. More likely would be alcohol-crazed street people, roused from their sleep by the heat, breaking in and stealing my credit cards and my money, and my kit with its stethoscope, adrenaline and syringes, flashlight and reflex hammer. These random thieves, I imagined, would leave behind the much more valuable diamond wristwatch Neal had given me in happier times, which I now hated and wondered daily how much I could sell it for.

No bats returned, but later that night, half asleep, I heard a slight crepitation that might have been a moth. A little uncertainly, I said, "Was that you, Jay Jay?" My heart pounded loudly as I realized I'd forgotten to close all the windows and doors and turn off the fans. The discovery that I'd opened myself to danger was as scary as an actual intruder might have been. I closed up the house and returned to bed. I lay there, struggling to snatch at the tiniest creak of aging wood, the most incremental settling of the walls, the subtlest rustle of a leaf outside the window. Nothing. I leaned back on my pillows. My heart was still audible. "God, Jay Jay," I muttered, "get some sleep." I heard what I'd said, and had to smile.

I made up a story about the bat, that the bat had somehow sneaked into the apartment while it was being fixed up (the bathtub faucet still leaked, but the kitchen area had been painted) before I moved in. It had elected to hide there, maybe in the weird useless grungy area between the top of the kitchen cabinets and the ceiling, or maybe in the hall closet. It had lurked for several weeks and then, driven to action by the stifling night, made its successful scrabble for freedom when I unlocked the front door.

The next day I prowled the outside of the building. It was sprayed concrete, featureless, muddy and faintly cracked in a way that did not inspire confidence in case of earthquake. There was no sign of anything, although I wasn't sure exactly what to look for. I promised myself I'd seek out a book on bats, and learn about their urban habitats. I forgot to do this because I was thinking about Lenny.

As soon as I saw Lenny, my old old friend Lenny, I wanted another go round with him. We'd been lovers before, twenty years before. It wasn't that he'd been a great lover; we didn't exactly have godlike chemistry between us. (This thought led naturally to sharp memories of Neal, whom I missed with an acute sexual ache.) But Lenny was easy to be with, amiable, apparently eager to get along and let things go and not confront. He had, in fact, a lot of virtues, the best of which, as I saw it on that sweltering lonely night, was that I already knew him. I couldn't confide in him about being miserable and rejected and having no friends in the world or anything like that. His unspoken rule was to eschew anything personal. Not that he'd get pissed off or chastise you. He'd just slip out of it; you'd be on your own, out there, and everything you said swung you farther out over the alligator pool where the jaws gaped wider. Clearly it was safer to hang on to the relatively unthrilling, maybe even unsatisfying, but definitely safe territory of small talk. And despite all this arm's length constraint, Lenny was an excellent friend. He'd give you his last $50, he'd drive you to the airport, he'd take care of your dog. If you were sick he'd make soup, and return your videos, and bring you juice and aspirins. So I decided to enlist Lenny to get over Neal.

Now on some level I knew this was a dumb idea. A better idea was mind-altering sex. But I decided, the moment I saw Lenny in the café, that he was the way to lessen my obsession with Neal. How was I to do this if not with a relationship? Lenny couldn't get personal, I knew this, but he could have a relationship, and I knew this too.

A couple of nights later I was in the bathroom when I heard something falling off the kitchen counter. I pulled up my pants quickly and without washing my hands ran across the hall. Nothing. No one. What had I imagined? "Was that you, Jay Jay?" I called out. I let the warm water run over my fingers, and I soaped my hands again and again. Leaning over the sink, holding the soap, I fell into a kind of vertical coma, unable to move, watching the water gather into my cupped palms and spill over into the sink. Was there another presence here? What was it? What? A few minutes later the feeling of unease left me. I found myself able to move. I picked up newspapers and threw away beer cans, washed up the few dishes, and wiped the crumbs off the counter. "Oh, Jay Jay," I babbled, "please don't frighten me." It was nothing after all. I was just jumpy and lonely. If someone were here, if I had some company, it would all be better, calmer, I would hear nothing. Natural noises do occur in the world, but I wouldn't hear them because I'd be occupied with an interaction, a conversation, something real, something in the moment. I wouldn't be full of resentment and remorse. Neal was never very far from my thoughts, and I was also harboring deep, deep grudges against Rachel and Lenny.

Virginia Prinz, my realtor, was an old friend of Rachel's. During November she took me through the houses I liked, pointing out every advantage. But I was already willing. I liked west Berkeley. The houses were small but the lots were big, and I liked the idea of being separated from my neighbors. I'd had enough of living directly under them. Or with them, I reminded myself darkly, thinking of Neal. His first buyout check had arrived, and I put it aside for a down payment. I picked out the most suitable three houses, then the best one of those. Virginia was efficient. My offer was accepted. I looked forward to escrow and the move. The pretty two-bedroom cottage I'd just bought had a greenhouse window in the kitchen. I'd paint the kitchen matte white, I planned, with dark blue trim and bright brass fixtures. There were many roomy closets. Those alone, I told myself, were worth the price. Smugly, I compared the new house to my present dwelling, which had only two minuscule closets. Its dim kitchen area had hardly any cupboard space. Every day I felt more and more cramped and temporary where I was living.

After the night of the bat and the night of the strange vibes, the unusual noises recurred, usually while I was getting ready for bed, already in the reflective mood with which I commonly ended and assessed the day. Often these moods were harshly judgmental: why had I said that particular thing, why hadn't I said this other, nicer, friendlier particular thing? During the next week I came home twice to find a closet door open, and once to find the bathroom cabinet open. Small objects were where I didn't remember putting them. It was disquieting, but I assumed I was under stress and had forgotten. It was when I got into bed with my book that I heard really sinister noises. Breathing, I heard breathing. I heard one breath, or one breath and a half. "Is that you breathing, Jay Jay?" I whispered, "Please, Jay Jay, go to sleep now." It wasn't funny anymore.

During the day I was beginning to pack and make lists. I was thinking a lot about my ex-friends. Ellie and I had had our falling-out for reasons I'd never understood. She had just ended another disastrous love affair. Why this one affected her more strongly than the others I could not fathom. We'd always been close, but I couldn't make myself available to her in what she claimed was her extreme time of need because Neal and I were by then involved in the first big fight of a series that ended with the end of our relationship. I was absorbed by those quarrels and Neal's unwillingness to negotiate. I'd also just started working at the clinic. We were all excited to be starting this new enterprise, and every day there was a meeting of the entire staff. It was exhausting. That, together with the hassles with Neal, used me all up. There was nothing left for anyone else.

Thinking about my loneliness made me understand I'd alienated all my friends by being abrasive and intrusive, and that made me think I'd probably alienated Neal in a similar way. Not exactly the same way, because Neal was a workaholic and a statistician. What he studied was the waves of random combinations and interactions of the chemical alphabet of DNA, and the chaotic movement of neo-Mendelian genetic components, which he translated into bits of theories. When we were first together, Neal had thought about this stuff a lot, which was good for his disposition. Later he thought about it too much, which made me jealous and restless. Finally he thought about it to the exclusion of everything else, which plunged me into petulance, then exasperation, and at the end screaming demands for attention. But that was then.

At last I called Lenny. We agreed to see the new Scorsese flick. Getting dressed, I realized this was the first time I'd been out with anyone since I left Neal's house. That had been several months ago. I stared at my reflection in the mirror. Without my glasses I couldn't see with great clarity, yet I knew that face well. I looked different. Had my eyes degraded another optical notch? They were maybe slightly bluer than I'd remembered, and the shape of my face was less puffy around the chin. I'd definitely changed. Splitting up with Neal had probably aged me. I put on my glasses to correct this impression. With my glasses on, my eyes looked definitely blue. I'd thought of them as being sad, maybe a little dull. But no, they were definitely bright as well. I pulled my mouth sideways in a habitual movement. In the mirror this faint grin, which all my life had turned my mouth down in an expression of faintly comic disapproval, was now an actual smile. My mouth was turned up. How could this be? "This is your doing, Jay Jay," I scolded. The smile became very slightly wider and, if anything, more smile-like, without my conscious volition. "Oh, Jay Jay," I said, more gently, "Jay Jay, this has got to stop." I didn't mean it, of course. Although the smile looked unfamiliar, I liked it.

That night was easier than I'd expected. I felt my mouth turning up like Jay Jay's mouth. I knew just how to be with Lenny. We both knew our lines. Our behavior had been many times rehearsed. Of course I saw right away that it wasn't enough, and that my plan to escalate my old affection for Lenny into an actual affair was a silly and embarrassing fantasy. In fact already I was just as lonely as before. After the movie we walked west on University Avenue, and went to my local café, the café where I'd seen him and Rachel on the night of the bat. The night of the day I had gotten the card addressed to Jay Jay Ringer. Sitting in the café, I wondered if someone was looking at me through the glass, watching me and Lenny chatting together, and sipping our late-night cups of tea, and breaking off fragments of our late-night oatmeal cookies. Maybe Jay Jay was looking at us. But she wouldn't be feeling left out. She wouldn't be feeling rejected. She'd be glad to see us. She'd be happy for our good time. Jay Jay could do this because she wasn't like me. She was a smiler. She had sparkling blue, snapping blue eyes. Jay Jay, I knew at that moment, didn't even wear glasses.

Lenny and I finished off our evening by walking back to his car, which was parked near the movie, so he could drive me to my place, which was near the café. "I had a good time," I told him, getting out of the car. "Do you want to do this again next week?" "Sure," he said, affable as always. I didn't ask him in. I had had enough social interaction, and wanted to sleep. Also, though I felt stupid, the way you always feel when caught in the fanged grip of a vaguely unwanted and unexpected compulsion, I had to know if my insight about Jay Jay wearing glasses was true. I rushed into the bathroom and turned on the light. In the mirror my face was pink with excitement. I leaned closer. I took off my glasses. There she was. She was definitely not a glasses wearer. I'd been right. I smiled. "I had a good time, Jay Jay," I told her. She smiled back.

Getting ready for bed I thought about Lenny. He'd remained companionable but remote. I had to face the fact that our connection was so light it revealed as unattainable the weight required for even minimal passion. That is to say it wasn't there. How I wished I could just conjure it up! I was dismayed at my ambivalence. On one hand, I had had a good time. Thin soup, perhaps, but easy to swallow. To keep the flow, we neither of us had acknowledged the flow. No, Lenny wouldn't do. On the other hand, I'd upgraded my status to one friend. If I got sick, I knew, I could call Lenny to bring over some thin soup. My new official status was reassuring. Something was better than nothing.

I'd unplugged the fans before I left for the movie, and I turned them on now, hoping to release the rooms a little from their airlessness. I recklessly opened all the windows and doors. An unaccustomed shuffling noise repeated itself slowly. Was it the newspapers stacked on the floor? "It's only you, Jay Jay," I said, "right? It's you." I brushed my teeth, took my calcium. I was in a good mood. Lenny hadn't turned on me, and I'd behaved myself. I hadn't told him how inadequate his method of relating was, or how it could be improved. I was a little relieved, actually, to fall back into my accustomed isolation.

In bed, after thoroughly locking up, I picked the top medical journal off the stack on the night table. I stared at the contents page. Nothing on women, nothing on reproduction.

I tossed it aside. Just as I reached for the next one, I heard a board creak in the other bedroom, the uncarpeted one. "Jay Jay?" I said softly, "is that you?" Too distracted now to read, I turned out the light and lay in the dark, listening, for a long time. My ears were strained to the point of nearly ripping themselves from my head, but I heard nothing further.

I woke in the morning, groaning at my aches and pains. My eyes had an obscuring pre-shower film, and every muscle was stiff. I'd stayed up way too late, listening for scary sounds, and hadn't slept well. Moans came from my foul-tasting mouth: "Oh," they said, "oh, no, oh, oh." Muttering this woeful mantra I stepped into the shower. I walked to work, I worked, I deplored myself. Nothing had changed, really, except that hope had vanished.

When I got home I was still tired, or maybe tired all over again. I poured out a glass of wine, hoping to feel a good deal better in the morning. "Have a drink, Jay Jay," I said out loud, and then, "Thanks, I think I will. How about you, Kay Kay? Won't you have a drink? Why, thank you so much, Dr. Ringer, I do believe I will just have a little drink." The glass was a large one, and then there was another, and soon I was pleasantly tiddly and it didn't seem to matter so much that I was all alone and would never be in love again.

I heard more noises. I heard sighs and settlings and building creaks. They had a purposeful sound or rhythm. They sounded meaningful. They sounded sentient. They made me self-conscious as I threw takeout cartons into the trash, scuffed off my shoes, watched my favorite cop show on TV. When I'd realized Lenny couldn't do it for me, my yearning for companionship began to dissolve. I couldn't take, didn't want, any more disappointments. I could barely handle the breakup with Neal, now so many months in the past. That was enough, it was more than enough. Other people always let me down.

I told myself I didn't care. Even if my worthless friends never called me. The little red light on the answering machine shone steadily, never blinking, when I came home from work. I never spoke with the other inhabitants of my awful building, who were, in any case, rarely seen. Also I was eating and sleeping a lot. I felt depressed. As a Californian, I well knew depression was frozen anger.

I saw Lenny again the following week. We saw a movie, drank tea, laughed, played our parts perfectly. I wasn't nearly as lonely as I'd been before I'd bought my new house. Indian summer was gone gone gone. The weather had definitively turned. I still missed Neal, in a sorrowful meditative way different from the gut-ripping way I'd missed him when we first parted. Things had gotten calmer at work, and I promised to work a full load as soon as I was in the new house. I packed boxes and gladly carried them from one location to the other. I could hardly wait to move in. December began cool.

While I was packing I talked to Jay Jay practically nonstop. I packed up my photo albums and found an old college snapshot of Ellie and Rachel and me, all with long, long hair, our arms around each other. "Remember this?" I asked Jay Jay, as if she'd been there. I debated for a long time about the kitchen equipment I'd lugged from my old apartment to Neal's, and from Neal's to the dismal apartment I was now escaping. "Shall I take this?" I asked Jay Jay, staring at a beautifully shaped but dented and rusting old yellow colander. "Nah, throw it out," she answered in my head, "get yourself a brand-new one." I put the colander in a box of things destined for the Goodwill. "How about this box of mugs?" I fretted, "What should I do about these?" I'd carried those old mugs in that same box from house to house and never unpacked them. "To the Goodwill," Jay Jay said. She helped me throw away the suede trousers I'd never worn but always wanted to. They were clearly too small, I saw that now. Together we threw away big-knit sweaters, knee socks, scarves, lace slips. I took a pleated plaid skirt, a fitted pink coat, and a truly venerable pair of bell-bottomed pants to the vintage clothing shop, and got quite a lot of money for them. This, I decided, was money for the new house, and when I moved I'd buy something Jay Jay liked. I was surprised by that thought, since until that moment I hadn't realized that I wanted Jay Jay to move with me. Was it possible? For one thing, she wasn't real. Was she? For another thing, she belonged to the cramped apartment, an integral part of the bathroom mirror. Didn't she? She'd originated at that address; in a way, she *was* that address. Wasn't she?

I continued to pack, more efficiently now, but I asked Jay Jay fewer questions. I knew most of the answers. When I spoke out loud, the apartment fell silent, and my voice dominated the space. An intentional momentum pushed me along. I took my old things out of storage and scattered them around the new house. I thought dreamily of how comfortable the next summer would be. It could be hot. Because of all the pretty windows I would get a cross-draft in every direction. And I'd sit out on the shaded patio among my flower-beds and little patch of lawn with a tall iced gin drink in my hand, or a couple of tall iced gin drinks, and feel sheltered from the heat.

The actual move went quickly. I was in before the new year. My first night in the new house, there were a million eerie noises as I unpacked. "Hi, Jay Jay," I said from time to time, after a box fell over or a rap! rap! came from the spacious cabinet to which I was bringing load after load of bowls and teacups. I started a new list: "cabinet under sink," it read, "plant food, loose doorknob, dish drainer." I was eager to fix things and buy things, whereas in the dark apartment I had been reluctant.

My bed was already made up. The coffeemaker was plugged in, the curtains were hung, my clocks were set. The closet, or something near it, creaked as I went into the bathroom to brush my teeth. "More noises, Jay Jay?" I murmured, my mouth full of toothpaste foam. "Just noises." I rinsed out my mouth and looked in the mirror, which had a harsher, whiter, light over it. I'd have to put that on the list: softer light in bathroom. I wasn't exactly expecting to see Jay Jay. But I wanted a vision of her most enabling emanation: me, but happier than I knew myself to be, more accommodating and supportive, a good friend, the best possible but somehow unachievable scenario of me. In the mirror I saw my old, old face. Deep lines parenthesized my mouth. I grinned a somber grin. My reflected face scowled back at me. I heard the front door click open and shut. Probably the wind, an unstable latch. Put it on the list to be fixed. "Hi, Jay Jay," I said sadly. My face in the mirror reminded me I was alone. No friends, no lovers. I stared at myself.

And then I heard a voice behind me, my voice. "Hi, Kay Kay," she said.

Getting Rid of Randall

I PUSHED HIM DOWN the stairs, Polly was thinking as she guided her grocery cart past the fish counter. He broke both his legs and both his arms. No, just his legs. But he could get to the bathroom without my help. He had to sleep in the house, on the living room couch, and he got in everyone's way. Soon he was driving me and the boys crazy.

Polly was shopping at the Coop and getting more and more depressed. She looked at her list and then at the deli case. Could she get away with buying deli desserts for tomorrow's party? She decided to try. Into her cart went pink bakery boxes containing an amaretto cheesecake, a chocolate almond torte, and lemon cookies.

Polly then bought leeks and zucchini for Randall's dinner, and Gruyere for the boys. After she stowed her groceries in the car, she did not drive directly home. Instead she took a route over the bridge to Coralville, twenty minutes away. She went to Wittski's Gun Shop, which she had previously looked up in the *Yellow Pages,* and bought a handgun. The man who sold it to her was wearing a yellow necktie and a white short-sleeved shirt. He had Daffy Duck tattooed on his forearm. "You can pick it up in fourteen days," he said. She paid in cash. Then she drove home.

Polly's position in Randall's house was still uncertain. They had fallen in love ten years ago, just before Polly's bead business failed. She was making good money at that time. There was a big demand for handcrafted beads. Randall, who taught sociology at Columbia, had come to Berkeley to attend a conference. They met at a party. While their friends shouted and drank and danced, Randall and Polly walked around the block, then around the neighborhood, and finally to Polly's car. Polly sent the babysitter home. In the morning Randall was captivated by Polly as she fed her boys and drove them off to school. She came back with fresh bagels, and made Randall the best cup of coffee he'd ever had. He had already given his paper, and found he was able to skip the rest of the conference. A few days later he left for New York.

Polly couldn't understand why she stopped getting orders. She fired fewer and fewer batches of hand-rolled porcelain beads in her kiln. She ground fewer and fewer bone and soapstone beads. Still the boxes of beads, packed in cotton, piled up in the corner of her bedroom. She thought about Randall constantly. She had trouble paying the rent. It became clear to her that she had to visit Randall in New York. Her sister lent her the plane fare and agreed to take the boys, then four and six years old, for a week.

They were happy together in New York. Randall gave a big party, and Polly prepared the food. She made dozens of intricately decorated deviled eggs, and a lavish California-type green salad. Randall's friends and colleagues loved her. She was an asset. Randall thought they should live together, in New York of course.

"I have no money," she told him, "no one's buying beads anymore."

"It doesn't matter." Randall was uncharacteristically passionate. "Come anyway. I can afford to support you, and Theo and Mikie. I need you, Polly. Love is more important than money." Polly too felt that love was more important than money. During the Christmas vacation, in Berkeley, they discussed conditions and made agreements. This time when Randall went back to teach, Polly stayed on only to pack up her things and consider what she could salvage from her sinking business. Not much, as it turned out. But Randall had said he would support them. Randall had lots of money.

I told him I would drive him to the doctor, Polly thought as she left Coralville and drove back over the bridge. I parked in a deserted mall and got out of the car. "Where are you going?" he asked. His voice had that same executive tone he uses when he says, "Polly, haven't I told you I hate mushrooms in my food?" I walked away from the car without answering. I turned to look at him. He had already opened a book and was reading it, sitting in the passenger seat. I left him in the car for hours. However, he continued to nag. The next day I crumbled four Valium and dissolved them in his favorite low-sodium French-style salad dressing. He complained all the more, although in a distinctly calmer, even somewhat satisfied, voice. I had to do something final about Randall. I hanged him from a tree with his green-striped necktie.

Home from Coralville, Polly unloaded her groceries, and was soon making a quiche out of leeks, zucchini, and two kinds of parsley. The custard was composed of nonfat milk and fake eggs, and the crust contained whole-wheat flour and toasted sesame seeds. Polly loved leeks, and as she sautéed the cut-up pieces in a little olive oil, she couldn't help tasting a bit here and there.

Polly was cooking dinner in the kitchen of an old frame house in Iowa City. Ten years had passed since Randall announced that love was more important than money. The boys had become huge, heavy-footed, croaking-voiced teenagers. Randall slept and worked in a two-room cottage in the back. Love had gotten sparser and harder to come by through the years, but Polly vigorously filled the void. The big house was crammed with yard sale chairs and rugs and lamps, and heavy coats and boots from the Goodwill.

Randall's quiche was in the oven. Polly began two other

quiches, using real eggs, and ordinary low-fat milk, and Gruyere cheese. These were for her boys. Before they went in the oven, she sprinkled over them all the leftover shreds of leek and parsley she hadn't been able to use in Randall's quiche. Then she added little strips of red pepper laid on top to form a T on one quiche and an M on the other. The quiches for the boys looked much more attractive, she thought.

Polly sliced tomato and cucumber. She was apprehensive, a familiar feeling. She did not look forward to Randall's coming home. The house was so cheerful without him, especially when she sat in the kitchen with her boys and their friends. The young people, whose posture was uniformly terrible, slouched over the table or stood like wading birds on one immense Reeboked foot, pulling little pieces of leftover lasagna out of a platter in the refrigerator. She listened to stories they told her with their mouths full. In fact she dreaded Randall's arrival. When six or seven kids lay around the living room, the TV their only illumination, listening to their loathsome heavy metal music and eating chips crumbling from garish bags, Polly sometimes sat with them and laughed at their silly cryptic jokes. No such gatherings could occur when Randall, busy and serious, was present. Polly felt constantly inadequate. The money that Randall gave her to run the house, admittedly a large amount, wasn't meant to be spent on the boys' friends. Was it? He glared at the kids, studied the contents of the refrigerator, tore her monthly checks out of his checkbook with a snap, and examined them carefully before handing them over. All his entertaining, including the departmental reception on which she'd splurged buying fancy desserts, was of course included. In spite of her budget she was generous with food for the boys and their pals. It was hard to feel physically close to her sons these days, they were so tall, they took up so much space, they left so many dirty socks on the floor. But when they gathered with their friends on the living room floor or in the kitchen with the refrigerator open, their shouts and guffaws and dirty words echoing through the house, she felt happy that they were at home, had brought their social life home, accepted her attendance, and ate up the cold lasagna.

The boys played their terrible music over their powerful stereos, and Polly heard it clearly in the kitchen. Their favorite band, which Polly had learned to identify, was Galen Doom and The Dregs. To her ears this group sounded like a heavy pre-typhoon surf pounding behind the splintering of smashing furniture and young men crying out in pain. "The Dregs," she would murmur as the boys came through the kitchen to snatch a round of carrot from beneath her knife. "Mom likes Galen Doom," they told their friends.

When Randall walked in, everything changed. It was magic the way Randall weighted the vibes in the room, brought them down suddenly to the floor, so that even the young high-school faces with their fresh fuzzy jaws sagged with the heaviness of Randall's presence. "Hello," he said briefly, pausing for a minute with his briefcase in his hand before going out to his cottage to do his mysterious and important work at his desk there. He didn't look around him or comment on the general state of the house, but Polly knew he perceived its deep chaos through his pores, and if he stayed within it too long he would absorb it and fall sick from its toxic clutter.

That the house was messy was undeniable, but Polly felt comfortable with heaps and stacks of papers on all horizontal surfaces. She could usually find what she wanted. She didn't see the need for the kind of swivel-hipped broken-field walking that the boys used to get from front door to kitchen and from there to the stairs. They avoided the little forests of tables, floor lamps, tiny rugs, circles of chairs, and baskets of tree-like house plants; they headed unerringly for what they wanted. Into the open refrigerator they reached long arms and without looking pulled out gallon jugs of milk.

This semester Polly was heavily involved in the details of Theo's graduation. She met with a group of the other seniors' parents to discuss safe driving on prom night, consumption of alcohol on graduation night, storage of perishable salads at the senior picnic, and other topics of concern. Mikie meanwhile was entering the Science Fair and thought he might run for class president. Days went by during which Polly and Randall brushed past each other in the kitchen with only a few words, Polly's polite and diffident, Randall's cold and abrupt. He was always working. The lights in the cottage burned late. Yet, whenever Polly sat in the kitchen at night drinking tea with a few seniors' parents, or helping the teenagers make pizza, Randall invariably came through on swift, hostile errands of his own. All conversation stopped as he came in to pull his carton of nonfat yogurt from the refrigerator. "Polly," he demanded, "did you buy Ivory soap? Polly, will you please pick up *The New York Times?* Polly, please write down the Dean's Dinner in your book." Polly was beyond embarrassment. She began to find his lordly manner a little comic, as though it were a kind of retaliation that backfired, like Wile E. Coyote in the Roadrunner cartoons.

While he slept, Polly thought as she poured a bit of Randall's low-calorie dressing on the salad, while he slept I released mosquitoes into his cottage. I thought perhaps he would move to a hotel. It did not work as I planned. None of these things worked. Indeed they affected him not at all. I began to concentrate on shutting him up for good.

Polly heard the cottage door slam and then the sound of Randall's shower. The feeling of anxiety was stronger now. His tiny bathroom was only three or four yards from the kitchen door. He would have arrived all sweaty after his run. He liked to eat after he was cleaned up.

Her mood slowly became recognizable as the confused dismay with which she routinely contemplated her relationship with Randall. She checked the oven and pulled her hair into a knot with a chopstick.

Polly's long straight coarse black hair had bright threads of white, and was of a texture that resisted attempts to smooth it. Unless it was braided in a few skinny tails, it seemed too heavy for her short, slim frame. Her very dark eyes still had the softness and sweetness with which she had attracted Randall. For his benefit she had always dressed in long flowered skirts and bright silk shirts, under which she wore little, if any, underwear. Her taste in clothes had not changed over the years, and now Randall, who was next in line for department chairman, sometimes frowned when he saw her.

He came in the door with his hair still wet. Randall was a small, well-shaped man, and although he was going bald on top he didn't look his age, which was forty-five. He wore black-wire-rimmed aviator-style glasses. Polly could see the defined muscles in his arms. He had equally impressive sinewy muscles in his legs. Jogger's legs. Randall ran on the track four times a week, Sunday and Monday, Wednesday and Thursday. In addition to this unalterable schedule, he jogged home from work, when weather permitted, with his work in a backpack.

"Polly," Randall said, crunching his salad and washing it down with swallows of white wine, "You haven't forgotten our reception tomorrow night, have you?"

"No, Randall. I'm getting everything ready."

I ran over him with the car. He was loading up the trunk with his list in his hand, standing in the driveway. On the pretext of looking for the map, I got into the driver's seat. Quick as a wink I gunned the engine and threw her into reverse. Randall's legs made a satisfying crunch as the tires bumped over them. But why do I keep breaking his legs?

Then I knocked him down and jumped on him and smashed him in the face. I was getting meaner and more violent. He rose, blood like in the movies trickling out of his torn and cut mouth, staggering a little on his fractured legs, but unhurt in that deep, protected way that babies are unhurt in their mothers' wombs and careless drivers in expensive cars are unhurt in their billowing airbags.

Randall pointed to the pink bakery boxes. "What's in there?"

"Desserts for the reception."

"Oh?" Randall was wary of bakery-made cakes. They had too much butter for him, too many eggs. They had cream and custard and sugar in abundance. He loathed and feared anything containing cholesterol. Ordinarily, Polly baked fruit crisps for parties, and bought store cakes only when Randall was at a conference out of town. However, Randall did not follow up his concerns about the deli desserts. With his special pencil he checked items off his list. Wine. Coffeemaker. They'd never yet run out of anything, but this was Randall's way of participating in the preparation. Napkins. Wineglasses. Dish soap. When people thanked him and Polly for the lovely party, Randall smiled his close-mouthed stretched smile and said, "I'm glad you came," somehow taking at least part of the credit. Flowers. Mineral water. Randall looked at her over the rims of his glasses to make sure she was checking her list, too.

On the morning following the party, Polly woke up exhausted. Immediately after their reception, several of the junior people, some of them distinctly older than Randall, had invited him and Polly out for a drink. Polly couldn't refuse. They had gotten home rather late, and together cleaned up from the party, murmuring sentence fragments to each other. "Big chair." "Tablecloth." "McGuire's jacket." "Outrageous." "Flowers?" "Margaret's boyfriend." "Couldn't be over twenty." "Saran wrap." Then, Randall had mysteriously elected to sleep with her in the big bedroom upstairs instead of in his cottage. When she realized his intention, she swept clothes off chairs and quickly straightened objects on bureaus. She put a new cake of soap in the bathroom and threw the slivers away. Her books, shoes, dirty underwear, clean underwear, all the heaps on the floor, got kicked into her closet. With a swoop she made the bed. There was no time for clean sheets.

In the morning she left the neat, compact lump of Randall still asleep, and went downstairs in her black silk kimono to make coffee. It was Sunday, her easy day, but she was groggy, her shoulders and neck were stiff, her eyes were slits, and from inside she felt frown lines in her forehead. She had been unable to respond to Randall, whose sexual ardor seemed to her more calculating, more attentive than it had before. What was he looking for? Did he find it? What did it mean? She brushed her teeth in the downstairs bathroom and put handful after handful of cold water on her face. When her coffee was filtered, she drank it standing up and began to feel a little better. As she put a slice of leftover quiche into the microwave, her tall son Theo came down the stairs.

"Yo, Poll," he said. He kissed his mom on her jawbone. "Any more coffee? We still on for this afternoon?"

"This afternoon?"

"Stanford reception, remember? You wrote it in your book."

"Reception, of course. For incoming Stanford freshmen and their moms. *Parents*. Of course."

"Hey, if you'd rather not go—it's not, strictly speaking, necessary. Just a lot of propaganda about how great the school is and how lucky we are to go there. Probably eat some boring cheese with really weird foreign crackers. You know."

"I wouldn't miss it." Theo would be gone next year, and

then, in a couple of years, Mikie. And then what? Could she revive her old bead business? Maybe she could set herself up as a caterer and hostess so that single faculty members could entertain as expertly and graciously as Randall. There might be money in that if she could ever organize it. It seemed like a brilliant idea to housekeep on a freelance basis as she now did on an indentured basis for Randall. She slowly tried to pursue this new and grown-up line of thought, but more engrossing images took its place.

Before I pushed him down the stairs I put ground glass in the biscotti dough. I chose biscotti because they're naturally crunchy. On reflection, I also cooked up some walnut brittle, and threw half a cup of ground glass in there, too. He ate three biscotti over a period of two days. They didn't seem to bother him. That's when I pushed him down the stairs.

Mikie entered the kitchen, scrambled four eggs, and ate them while telling Polly in detail the plot and special effects of *Alien,* which, she forbore to remind him, she herself had seen. Car horns honked and both boys left. As she rinsed the last dish Randall came in. He was carrying his desk calendar and his special pencil.

"Good morning!" Polly said, her mood greatly improved.

"Let's do some scheduling," Randall said. He wasn't meeting her eye. She sat with her calendar in front of her, poised to make lists. "I'm going to Chicago next week." What this meant for Polly was a vacation. When Randall was out of town there were no receptions to prepare or attend. She could cook meat and let the errands slide. She didn't have to pick up *The New York Times.* She wrote down Randall's instructions for hours, it seemed, until he had to leave for a meeting.

Later that afternoon, back from the Stanford reception, Polly sat with another Stanford mother drinking tea and discussing SAT scores. Randall walked through with his brisk angry walk, and she forgot to introduce him. She felt a moment of extreme disorientation when she realized what she had done. The other mom did not seem to notice, and left without commenting in any way on Randall's existence. Polly, slightly frightened, began to wash up the teacups. She heard Randall returning to the house, and then, louder than his footsteps, the music of Galen Doom over Theo's stereo.

Randall entered the kitchen. "Polly," he said, "we've got to talk." Polly could think of nothing to talk about. "Polly, I really believe we can work this out."

"Work what out? What are you talking about? What do you mean?"

He came into the kitchen while I was washing the teacups, Polly thought as she listened to the agonized cries of Galen Doom coming through Theo's door. The pounding of the surf was actually soothing in a way. She could see why the kids liked it. He spoke to me. Polly, he said, We have to talk. Did you write down the Deans Dinner for Saturday in your calendar? Did you write it down, Polly? I wiped my hands on a paper towel. In the pocket of my apron was the gun. I took it out and cocked it in the way I'd learned at the police department class. I pointed it at him and held it steady with both hands. Randall was still looking in his calendar, holding his special pencil, when I shot him. He dropped the calendar, which fell onto the counter and slid into the sink, but continued to hold his pencil in his hand. He looked at me impassively as he fell to the floor. His glasses slipped from one ear. He jabbed or gestured with the pencil and then dropped it and I knew he was dead. Then I had to get rid of the body. Later I cut my hair off short. After an appropriate interval I got all of Randall's money, and the boys and I just went on with our lives.

Polly smiled at Randall as he went on talking, telling her what he wanted her to know.

Want Not

SUSAN CAME TO COMPOST late in life. After Curtis left all she did was go to work and come home again. She was remorseful and anxious. Learning something new was the last thing on her mind. She sat on her couch and stared at TV with the volume turned off. She couldn't stand the sound of anything but Charlie Mingus. Cautiously, she signed up for the compost workshop because it was spring and also she missed Curtis, and compost seemed a tenuous tie.

The workshop was held on four first Wednesdays, 7:30 to 9:00. At the first meeting Susan learned the difference between hot and cold compost. Curtis had done hot yard compost which, it turned out, was the aristocrat of the compost world. Hot compost killed all known plant diseases, discouraged plant pests, and was a general tonic for the yard and the entire neighborhood. It was clearly the ecologically superior form of composting. Layers of leaves had to be spread on layers of twigs, topped with layers of green grass clippings, horse manure, and even food scraps, all divided by more layers of more leaves. Combining food scraps with yard compost was tricky, said the workshop leader, because compost in the Bay Area had to be rodent-proof. Susan imagined dark menacing shapes, big smart rats, *Rattus norwegicus,* common on Potrero Hill, advancing at night to tear at her tea leaves, her onion skins, her asparagus ends. *Bon appétit,* she thought darkly.

At work she perceived herself as much the same but more tired. Her coworkers at the lab knew Curtis had left her. Verna, the graduate student who was always hassling with her husband, took Susan out for coffee breaks and talked steadily about the perfidy of men, the bitterness of love. Verna was doing research in gas exchange membranes. Susan was the tech. She fixed the machines, ran the machines, pulled and logged the results, swept the floor and washed the glassware when the student didn't show up, answered the phone when the secretary didn't show up, edited the protocols, and proofed the papers. It was easy work, and Susan, dreamily checking references and printing out articles, had plenty of time to brood. When the new graphics system was installed everyone got excited, but Susan, thinking about Curtis, was calm as she deftly punched in the numbers and generated the illustrations and charts.

Every Tuesday she left the lab at 4:00 p.m. and took the bus to the Potrero High Adult School for yoga class. She put her hands together as she entered, and bowed slightly to Amrita, the yoga teacher, who sat in a perfect effortless lotus position at the front of the room, smiling at each student who came in.

At the end of the hour, Amrita took them through savasana, Susan's favorite exercise. The students lay flat on their mats and listened to their teacher relax their bodies, muscle by muscle, cell by cell. Amrita's sweet low voice persuasively directed them to "relax your palms, your wrists. Relax each finger, starting with your thumb. One, two, three, four, five. Now the other hand. One, two, three, four, five." Susan lay in a little trance, her body obeying Amrita while she, Susan, was somewhere else, on vacation maybe, reliving the time before and after Curtis.

In the years before Curtis she'd been celibate. She put it to herself this way: I was celibate for all those years. It was a sad thought. She didn't know if she'd done it by choice. She thought maybe not. It didn't seem like something she'd have chosen, especially after her marriage, in which the sexual good times were the only good times. There was something neat about celibacy, a kind of clear sad perspective, but she couldn't think of one person she admired who'd been celibate: Mozart, Haydn, Bach, Matisse, Emma Goldman, Charles Darwin. Nope. Incompatible with greatness. Then the City of San Francisco had left a leaflet in her mailbox. It said she could drop off yard waste at the Ecology Center. She filled bags with leaves and took them down. While she was there, a class schedule caught her eye and on the spot she signed up for a container-gardening workshop. Curtis, whom she'd never seen before, was teaching the class. She listened intently to every word he said. Afterward, she lingered while the others left. Impelled by a rush of unaccustomed risk-taking, she looked him directly in the eye and described her yard. Her backyard especially was a wild place then, heavily populated by squirrels who leaped about and watched the colonizing neighborhood cats from above. Two weeks later she and Curtis were lovers, and soon after that he moved in. She was forty, a distressed recluse working in the organic chemistry lab on campus. His wife was two years dead, and his daughter was a pediatrician in Boston, married to a hematologist. He was lonely too, or so he said.

When they'd been together a few months, she noticed the house had become cheerier, more colorful, more comfortable, even more beautiful, but also somewhat cluttered. Her shelves, formerly nearly naked, filled quickly with books. She'd preferred to use the horizontal surfaces for a scatter of rocks, a low spreading plant, a votive candle, and similar icons. She'd thought of her space as having a kind of irreplaceable empty serenity. Now her pieces of bric-a-brac were precisely arranged between rows of neatly stacked books, no less important in their reduced space and charged with an opulent connection. The house looked warm and inviting, sexy even, where before it had been austere, self-conscious, and a little cold.

Another benefit was a certain cachet in living with an ecologically oriented landscaper. She found she could talk knowledgeably, with her friends if not with Curtis, about corms and enzymes, drip systems and yarrows. Both yards underwent a startling transformation. In the back a deck was built, from which she and Curtis, lolling in campaign chairs and drinking wine, observed the wildlife. Everything was a good deal greener, and the shapes of flora more interesting than oak came into view. A hitherto invisible apple tree was pruned to a languid umbrella shape, and burst into gorgeous bloom in the spring. It had never done that before. As the seasons turned, other marvels were revealed. Two pink rhodos made themselves known. Exotic Japanese maples flanked a now elegant camellia. Bluebirds and sparrows were no longer hidden as they flashed to and fro in the big oak, which had been opened up to expose the sky. The front yard, which got a lot of sun, slowly became a terraced wonderland of vegetables and flowers.

Curtis suggested they get a cat to deal with food scraps. He hated to see anything wasted. She'd seen him feeding the gang of neighbor cats and had put her foot down. Two large stiff wire bins then appeared in the backyard. They were rapidly filled with yard trash. Curtis obsessively tended these piles even in the coldest most terrible weather.

That was how it was for five years, before Curtis fell in love with another woman and drove away. He had clearly prepared. All his tools and equipment were already in his truck. When he was truly gone, Susan packed away what he'd left in cartons, which she then stored in the basement. The house began to look lighter, calmer. It was a lot quieter.

She played only Mingus, Diz, Monk. Curtis had tired her of Mozart. OD'd. She hated him for that.

Amrita ended the class with another bow, and Susan walked the few blocks home, thinking about compost. That very night she began to do kitchen-scrap composting as encouraged by the compost-workshop leader. This required a five-gallon bucket, free sawdust from the lumber yard, and a certain amount of attention. It was the most intimate form of compost, as it involved actual food: coffee grounds, bread crusts, grape stems, banana peels, carrot scrapings, all the detritus of the average meal. Susan's kitchen scraps relied heavily on grapefruit rinds and tea leaves, and she was eager to see if the resulting compost was different in any way from the kitchen compost they had constructed in the first meeting of the workshop. She didn't add even one scrap of meat, not that there was much meat hanging around the house anyway, and no fish or fish bones. Definitely not! She knew from living with Curtis it was wrong to overburden any system.

She put together layers of her food scraps alternating with sawdust in the plastic bucket she'd cadged from the health food store. Then she set herself to wait for one to five months when it would be compost. She had to take off the lid from time to time and stir it up. This was easy, it was doable, she could do it, she was doing it. It wasn't the compost of her dreams, which was a huge, tidy, Curtis-like well-tended bin in the backyard, full of all her leaves, her billions and trillions of leaves, leaves as numberless as the stars in the heavens, mixed beautifully, perfectly, with green grass clippings, horse manure, and food scraps. That no doubt would come when she achieved her compost apotheosis. But not today, not this week. No.

It seemed obvious to her that some enthusiasms or undertakings had a momentum supported by change, and others had a ragged erratic progress that sputtered and died. Her relationship with Curtis was one and compost was the other. She didn't understand what she could have done differently with Curtis. It was hard to fail, though, with kitchen compost. Maybe "fail" was the wrong word. Something seasonal, some mysterious timing device or principle ran through things; and she, inexorably withering, celibate again, was a creature of entropy, consciously furthering the course of something else, some stinking mysterious alchemy, stirring it and waiting.

She mentioned to Ti-Sheng, the project director at the lab, that a family of skunks had ousted a few of the feral cats who lived under her deck. He told her all the ways to get skunks out. Play a radio, he said: they hate human noise. Install a light under there, and leave it on: they hate light. These sounded like sensible and noninvasive ways to evict the skunks, but she liked the skunks. There was something about the skunks that appealed to her. She wasn't repelled by their smell, and they weren't aggressive in any way; au contraire, they had a strangely mournful look, skulking and hairy and dusty. They were smaller than the occasional prowling raccoons who sniffed around the tightly capped garbage can, and bigger than the indolent cats who feared them and whose sunbathing was the major activity of her yard. The skunks didn't bother her and she didn't bother them. Her very rare visitors commented on a musky, acrid smell. "Is that skunk?" they asked, and she answered, "Yes, there must be one prowling the backyard." The skunks and Susan politely avoided each other, two mutually respectful fauna occupying the same geographical stratum.

In the second meeting of the compost workshop everyone brought a question. Susan asked about different kinds of animal manure. She asked why horse manure was okay but not dog or cat. She had access to plenty of cat manure, now enriched by plenty of skunk manure. She was informed it was a matter of acid balance.

In the third meeting of the compost workshop the group learned about worms and worm composting. Susan rejected this option, as animal life was not what she lacked. They were also taught to construct or assemble various kinds of bins and containers. Students were by now confident and freely asked questions. Was it effete to buy a Smith and Hawken three-bin screened rodent-proof compost bin? Wasn't it more rugged and compatible with the spirit of compost to layer your materials within a column of wire? And turn it with a real pitchfork?

At the fourth and final meeting they inspected the kitchen-scrap compost they had begun at the first meeting, three months ago. It was fertile, textured, loamy stuff, and each workshop participant got to handle it and admire it. Susan smelled it intently. Wasn't her own kitchen compost just a bit more sweet-smelling, a bit less, well, oniony?

She was sorry the workshop was over. Had anything changed? Now she had two buckets full of decomposing organic matter in her house. She felt just a little macabre, and she felt desolate, too, still thinking about Curtis, who had left her for someone else. She stayed up late listening to the jazz station. Her friends, to whom she had previously complained about Curtis and cohabitation, seemed like cardboard black-and-white images, smaller than life-size. She was lonely in a new post-compost way, and also in an old discouraging way.

The yard too reverted. Vegetable beds grew mushy and crusty and disgusting. The terraces deteriorated and sagged back into the hilly impossible terrain from which they had been carved. Did everything look the way it had before Curtis? From time to time she sat out on the deck, and cats slept on it in the short afternoon sun, and underneath it when it rained.

In the fall she signed up for another semester of yoga, as she had been doing for years. Yoga never changed.

"Let's begin with some breathing," Amrita always said. Susan had a hard time with the breathing. She was not sure she understood what exactly happened in her lungs. The class members sat in individual imperfect variations of Amrita's perfect lotus. "Breathe in prana," Amrita said. "Breathe in life force. Breathe into the bottom of your belly, fill it with prana, right up to the top of your chest. Let it out, exhale in the same order, first from the belly, then the abdomen, finally the chest. And again. Three deep cleansing breaths. Now we will do some slow stretching." Amrita stood up. The class stood up. Amrita raised her arms and the class raised theirs. Susan breathed as she was instructed. Was it her imagination, or was her breathing getting smoother, deeper, more yoga-like?

The dry Indian summer leaves fell and fell and the entire yard and deck were covered with layers of brittle leaves, which crumbled and then emitted a dusty, scratchy vapor into the hazy, thin October sun. She let the leaves lie where they fell. She didn't have the heart or the energy to rake them up. Her kind of compost was indoor compost. Curtis had done the outdoor compost.

Susan's little house was on Potrero Hill, built back from the street on a sloping lot. The backyard was relatively level. All the backyards on her street faced the towers of downtown, the Embarcadero, and the bay. That is, they would have faced these charming prospects were it not for an erratic uncontrolled growth of very tall trees, redwoods, oak, and eucalyptus, which blocked the view. Curtis had to some extent tamed these trees, and he and Susan had often sat on the deck looking through curly frames of branches and leaves at the darkening silvery bay and the East Bay hills. Under his scrutinized regime the yard had resembled a partially trimmed copse in a casually tended corner of the Elysian Fields. Dense dark-green ground cover marked the irregular open spaces between trees. Begonias flowered here, and darkly red rhodos. In the winter there were violets, and they cut their own branch of pine to hang Christmas lights on. For a while after Curtis left, the drip timer he had installed kept the greenery lush, but then the timer broke. Susan was a little frightened by the overpowering sudden dehydration. Autumn leaves fell continuously and massively from the trees. She didn't know how to fix the timer. She didn't want to water anything. She didn't want to look at Curtis' handiwork anyhow. She secretly hoped it would all die. Meanly, she hoped for a dry winter and thanked god intensely that not one other Californian knew she'd had that bad thought.

In her kitchen, now denuded of the Ecology Center posters Curtis had put up, Susan sat in her chair and stared out the window at the unpruned menacing roses. She thought of her sexuality as a kind of waste. Sentimentally, she envisioned herself as a fruit, an apricot perhaps, fallen ready from the branch, rotting on the ground. She reminded herself dutifully that it was the apricot's destiny, its genetic thrust, to decay and expose its seed so that it could explode its energy in root and trunk and eventually, inevitably, in new flesh protecting a new seed. She wondered what possible seeds could be in her solitary flesh. She looked okay, she thought, not heavy exactly, maybe soft and bulging a little around the middle, but with long and pretty legs and arms now tanned a little from sitting gloomily on the deck. How pleased she'd been, and how surprised to be pleased, that she'd waited for Curtis. Being with Curtis made her see her celibate years as a definitive waiting.

Still she'd often yearned for space. Curtis took up way too much space. He was stocky. He had solid treelike legs, and wide flexible flat feet with plump toes like bubbles. He had a lot of energetic coarse graying hair, and big wire-rimmed glasses. All these parts of him, clothed in his T-shirt, his padded vest, his khaki pants, had a kinetic solidity that seemed to draw all the energy in the room. Now his warm glowing static was gone. She cursed her dumber previous self. Why hadn't she appreciated what she had? But would it have made a difference? She had plenty of space now. She gave herself up to stumbling misery and groaning sighs so dismal she was startled at their woe.

Partners probably left home every day to move in with their new lovers. The person who remained was forever perplexed and disappointed, resentful, guilty. Alchemy must be undertaken, devious and unrelated. Nothing was inert. Everything was something else.

In the spring a few straggling sweet peas, which had apparently wintered over, fluffed out sudden fragrant pink butterfly petals on the ends of twisted stems. What tenacity, Susan thought. There were other unexpected survivors too. A little copse of tall purple bearded iris suddenly commanded a corner of the former vegetable garden, as in the days of Curtis. Grandiose chard stretched out. Skinny vibrant lobelia. White freesias. Susan squatted on the deck in the sun, spreading a moist fresh gallon of food-scrap compost onto a newspaper. She could smell the freesias. What would she grow with her wonderful compost? She had already filled half a black plastic trash bag full of the gritty organic super-dirt. She wanted to use it, but not in the yard, where green things continued to emerge, then burgeon. They grew and grew. Then it was summer and they grew some more, got gawky and trashy looking, began to die. In the black bag, compost waited.

At the lab she was promoted from tech to assistant. She did all the same things she used to do, but for more money, some of which she spent on a very large orchid. She thought she might take a class in orchids. They needed sphagnum moss and rich soil. Maybe she could use her compost. Verna's membrane experiments were finished and the results exciting. Together Susan and Verna prepared beautiful charts of data representing individual molecules oozing or squeezing through various microscopic pores. Ti-Sheng signed Verna's thesis, and everyone in the lab went out for pizza. Susan, who had been nowhere except work and yoga and compost, had a wonderful time. She thought she might try going out again sometime. But not soon.

Impatient to use her homemade compost, she planted radish seeds in a large terra cotta pot. She used one part compost to one part ordinary dirt, as she'd been taught in the workshop. Radishes, she knew, were a never-fail crop in any season; still she was surprised at how fast hers grew. They were delicious. She ate them with buttered bagels, sitting on the dusty planks of the deck, in the last stripe of afternoon sun. She figured out that after a year she'd somehow accepted her de facto celibacy. She still didn't understand Curtis' defection, or the time they'd had together, but she understood how her kitchen compost had come about, grain by grain. Beneath her the slumbering skunks were silent. There was a radiant haze over the bay. The radishes had a sharp crunch, a pleasant bite, and a smooth sweetness she imagined as having passed directly from her grapefruit peels and soggy chamomile tea leaves.

In the semester's last yoga class she surreptitiously looked around while doing the plough posture. Her legs were extended over her head, so far as she could tell, at a more elegant and natural angle than almost anyone else's. They weren't supposed to be competitive, she knew. She was ashamed. They were supposed to examine their own muscular reactions with as much subtlety and sensitivity and interest as they could manage. Susan conscientiously did this, and at the same time wanted to excel. She wanted to do yoga at least as well as anyone else, but maybe gloss over a little the self-awareness and discipline required. She had already signed up for the following semester. She couldn't imagine life without yoga.

Amrita directed them to prepare for savasana. Susan slipped between her mat and her striped beach towel. She placed her arms straight at her sides, on the outside of the towel, palms up.

"Close your eyes," Amrita instructed, "and take three deep cleansing breaths. Inhale prana, the life force." Susan inhaled to the sound of Amrita's voice. "Now slowly exhale." Susan slowly exhaled. As Amrita spoke to each part of her body, softly telling it to relax, Susan breathed carefully in and out. She drew prana into her body. "Breathe into your elbows. Your elbows are relaxed." Prana was sparkly pale blue, and filled her lungs. Dreamily she let it stream out through her elbows. The yoga students lay flat on their mats in rows, their eyes closed. Amrita sat in lotus posture, or so Susan wanted to believe, in front of them, speaking seductively about warmth and relaxation and prana. Susan could imagine shimmering prana floating from the air in the room into her body. It was invisible when she exhaled. All the glittery stuff had been absorbed. She supposed it was the life force, now at work oxygenating her blood. But she was definitely exhaling something, some indistinct vapor was gently flowing from her nostrils. "Relax your knees," Amrita said, "your left knee, your right knee." Susan's knees relaxed as she exhaled the skeleton of prana, and tried to identify what it was between in and out.

The Lost Objects Box

WHEN I BEGAN TO resent people who called me on the telephone, I knew it was time to get an answering machine. I would call them back when I had a sink full of dishes to wash or a complicated and time-consuming casserole to prepare. Lasagna, for example, could accommodate four medium or two very long phone conversations. A pie was good for returning several days' accumulated calls.

I felt uneasy about staying home alone all the time. When I went out for dinner with a friend I considered myself socially virtuous and gave myself a secret gold star. I didn't like to ask people in for dinner, as they invariably stayed too long, even the most sensitive of them. The least sensitive had to be actually requested to go. "I'm starting to fade," I would introduce the topic of their leaving; and then a half hour later, "Gee, I'm so sleepy I can hardly hear what you're saying." Sometimes to encourage their departure I picked up an object at random, a videotape, a shell, a sweater, and gave it to them. "Here, I want you to have this," I begged. Their shocked embarrassment hastened them out of the house. If they left something by mistake, a glasses case or a set of keys, I put it in a cardboard box kept by the door. The Lost Objects Box, I called it, and friends rooted around in the box whenever they came over, which was less and less frequently.

Sometimes I asked people to pick me up for dinner or a movie, to give both of us the illusion that people were not unwelcome at my house. I knew I was trying to expunge the substance of social interaction from my life while retaining its appearance. I didn't like the sound of the words "morally lazy," which is how my friend Naomi described those who stayed home watching TV, woolly slippers on, eating peaches out of the can with their fingers. On the other hand, I didn't want to do what my friend Kay Kay called "making an effort," that is, putting on clean clothes, paying attention to the affinity of these clothes with one's shoes, and collecting one's accouterments (sunglasses, checkbook, book to read in the event that waiting became necessary). Making an effort also meant that before walking out the door I had to check the various appliances (the coffee warmer had an irritating habit of burning to a disgusting crispy layer any half inch or so of coffee that was inadvertently left while in its ON state) and lock the door, and then drive the thrilling few miles, fraught with the dangers of the outside world, to the restaurant on the other side of town.

Again and again I put off my friends. I said I had houseguests. I said my cleaning person was coming for the day and could not be disturbed. I said various meetings were being held at my house, my oil spill-cleanup group, my poetry-writing group. This latter claim was true. I had discovered that another way I could punch up the pretense that I was still socially extant was to allow meetings to be held at my house. Meetings were usually short and always formal, that is, they had a predetermined starting time, around 7:30, and ended around 10. As soon as the group left, I immediately eradicated all signs of their having been there. I washed their cups and emptied their ashtrays. Then I watched that night's TV shows, which had been silently recording during the meeting.

Consulting my calendar one day, I found I had put off Naomi for three weeks. Simple guilt obliged me to drive to her side of town as opposed to her driving to mine. I resented this concession (though it was more than fair). When I reached the café, I used all my charm to establish a connection between us, a rapport, so she would be convinced again that we were very good friends and loved each other dearly. I listened sympathetically to her trials with the boyfriend, though secretly I deplored such a situation and shuddered lest I find myself in love again. There was little chance of this eventuality, however, since I had stopped going to parties. Also, my one remaining "admirer" had recently married and could no longer be considered even the slimmest possible excuse for, or simulacrum of, a boyfriend. The woman whom he married, in direct contrast to myself, was friendly and hospitable and upbeat and generous.

My dad got cancer at the beginning of the summer, and had to have treatments. I drove him down from Ukiah to the UC hospital in San Francisco so that I could keep an eye on him. The doctors said he was dying. My sister came to town, and then my brother. I did my best to encourage them to stay elsewhere but was not successful. Certainly I did not want the entire burden of my father's hospitalization to be on me, the thrice-daily visits, the shopping expeditions, the constant conferences with the oncologist, the internist, the neurologist, the surgeon and the other surgeon, the pharmaceutical consultant, the radiologist, the nursing supervisor. Fortunately, my siblings were willing to do as much as, if not more than, I; in our new amicable adult affiliation we efficiently shared the work associated with the care of a sick and demanding elderly parent. We stayed up late at night discussing distasteful alternatives, such as a nursing home, a rotating residence with all of us, round-the-clock nursing care, and so forth. We disclosed our most intimate financial secrets and in an unprecedented burst of cooperation pooled a large amount of money to be placed in a separate account for our father's needs and comfort. My sister LeeAnn, a lawyer, wrote out a little agreement for us to sign, and we all signed it.

Still, it was hard having them in my house. They walked in and out of the kitchen while I was cooking. They sat down at the table to talk with me while we ate. I always brought my book to the table and always opened it, but soon under the onslaught of direct questioning was forced to put it on the sideboard, where I gazed at it longingly.

One day I went down the steep back stairs with a basket full of laundry, and screamed when I saw my brother Gary bending over the washing machine. I had temporarily forgotten he was here, forgotten who he was, and for a moment it seemed to me that a hostile stranger had invaded my laundry facilities. Another time I came home from a long dreamy solitary walk to find Gary and his ex-wife, now an outsider in our lives, sitting at my kitchen table. They were drinking beer. The ex-wife had put her handbag on the table, and a small package in a white pharmacy bag. I fixed myself a cup of tea and thought about joining them, but, with a reduced availability of space on the table, I felt I had essentially no place to put my cup. I went out to the porch instead, and sat on the top step. I read my book until the ex-wife left.

My dad got worse. LeeAnn flew back to Vancouver and spent two days there arranging a leave of absence from her firm. Gary, who was a freelance film editor, asked his assistant to take over the movie he was working on. Now they had no other obligations, and were free to spend all their time sitting with my dad, running errands for my dad, making arrangements for my dad, or hanging out with me. They both had friends in San Francisco, as we had all grown up here, and those friends began coming to the hospital to visit, and then to my house. I understood that they were paying their respects, that they formed an important support system, that if it weren't for them my siblings would be so miserable and put upon they would probably leave and I would have to do everything, but still. Where was the wonderful solitude of yesteryear? I yearned for the numbing isolation, the desolate calm, the restless lurching trance.

For LeeAnn and Gary, this was a time off from work. But not for me. My new job at the library was 69 percent time, a proportion chosen so that workers could select their own shifts but could not receive benefits like compassionate sick leave. I resented their freedom and my wage slavery.

Grasping solitude in bits was how I saw myself, my special spaces seized by those most powerful of Porlocks, one's own family. I had to give up my yearning to have all the dishes washed all the time. What I couldn't give up, however, was my uncontrollable need to sit in *my place* at the round kitchen table, between the window and the china cabinet. Whenever I gazed through the small panes, framed in white painted wood, and I did this often, I saw the dense pittosporum growing up the hill and the three large inadequately pruned pink rose bushes. Thus I comforted myself.

This essential centering pleasure, the very ground of my solitary contemplation, was threatened—no, vanquished—by people who dropped over without even a warning phone call. I admired them and wanted to think of them as my friends, but not actually coexist with them in the same room. They sat at the kitchen table with me, tearing sections of *The New York Times* from my neat pile, and crumpling them in a pretense of proper folding, before tossing them on a chair. They stayed up all night, watching videos, toasting muffins, playing Monopoly. They often brought food. More than once the smell of ribs or pizza got me out of bed in the middle of the night, in my best gray silk kimono, to join them at the table—*my table*—and to talk and laugh my way into a sociable second wind. The next day at work I was lethargic and irritable.

Often I wondered, how can my siblings tolerate such a crowd in the kitchen? I stared at them sitting at the kitchen table, leaning against the wall, opening the refrigerator, and extracting cans of beer. One was my brother's ex-wife, another was her present boyfriend, and yet another was her present boyfriend's friend. The Taiwanese detective, a former classmate of my sister, was there, and the man who taught Mosquito Indians how to build boats.

They were exciting people, but they loomed, they seemed to cluster around me, around the table, around my special space near the window. They blocked my view of the china cabinet.

The china cabinet contained no china; or rather, only two plates, souvenirs of New York City, one with the Statue of Liberty depicted. On the top shelf were photos, standing around the three sides of the shelf as though facing the single crystal candle holder, and a few open packs of cigarettes that visitors had left. The cigarettes could have gone into the Lost Objects Box, but I liked having them in the china cabinet. Sometimes late at night I smoked one of them, meditatively, as though I were DeQuincy staring at a ribbon of smoke from his opium. On the second shelf were fossils, geodes, a sparrow's nest, and other hokey treasures of the natural world. The bottom shelf had my miniature *Tyrannosaurus rex* collection (plastic, rubber, glass, china, wood). Behind the doors were tablecloths. It was just an average china cabinet, but I needed to sit near it. I can't explain this.

My sister began to bring home flowers several times a week. They were potted azaleas, cyclamens, and mums from the hospital. My dad begged us to take care of them. Then, as they made such a lively difference in my spare, possibly grim, little house, she began buying them. She could afford it. Irises, lilies, stock, glads, godetia, carnations, eucalyptus leaves, curly willow, peonies, stalks of cymbidium. They were gorgeous.

In the movie *Girlfriends,* Melanie Mayron, moving to a new apartment, puts a tiny vase, with one skinny flower sticking out of it, on a pile of cardboard cartons. She has not yet unpacked. She steps back to look at the vase, at the blank white wall behind it. She approaches the vase and moves it about an inch to the right. She looks at it again, satisfied.

In this scene you get the essence of the notion of totemic chattels. They're the little-seen corner, the space between two windows, the arrangement of toys on the mantel. I considered certain bare spaces to be totemic chattels. The emptiness of a corner was a space I cherished and protected. It had a sacred quality.

When Gary or LeeAnn dumped his/her stuff in the empty corner, I felt it as a violation. When I, on the other hand, deliberately left the living room littered with newspapers and videos on the rug beneath crumpled beer and soda pop cans, they didn't even notice. Sometimes they cleaned it up, sometimes they didn't.

One day I entered the kitchen and looked suspiciously at the sink. Someone had washed up half the dishes and left the rest. I stood still and tolerated this chaotic situation, feeling myself to be virtuous and flexible. I opened the refrigerator. My sister had brought home salads of strangely shaped pasta, interspersed with shrunken midget vegetables that looked like marzipan, in disconcerting containers that you couldn't keep to use another time, but also couldn't recycle. Everything they did in my kitchen presented me with a dilemma. But I could accommodate. I could adjust. I could compromise. I washed up, brooding self-righteously about how I always left the kitchen clean for the next person. My habitual tidiness, which was hard-won and not at all something that had come naturally to me, was surely a virtue. Resentment made my fingers twitch.

There was nothing for it. I called a meeting. Actually, the meeting took place as we sat together at the kitchen table, each of us eating his/her own idiosyncratic food. My brother was eating a huge French dip roast beef sandwich from the deli, with a side of sauerkraut and a can of beer. I was drinking beer too, but in my case it accompanied a tuna and tomato sandwich I had made myself with celery and onions and cucumber. He had a dill pickle, crunch crunch; I had a sweet pickle, crunch crunch. My sister was eating a pure white chunk of lasagna out of a plastic container, and had poured herself a second glass of white wine. For once, we each had a book or magazine in front of us. I was reluctant to break the cozy silence.

"You guys," I began, "we have to figure out a way to keep the house cleaner." They looked up. My brother was reading the *Bay Guardian,* my sister a thick Peter Matthiesen novel. They stared at me politely. I imagined them thinking: "What can she be ranting about now?" I kicked my courage gear one notch higher. "This isn't the way I normally do things," I said. "I haven't been feeling completely comfortable. I'd really, really like the mess to be kept more at bay so that I could be more comfortable..." I paused but went on, "in my own house."

My house was a slanting rickety bungalow clinging to Potrero Hill. On its top, street level, were the living room with its tiny front porch, the kitchen, and a sort of closet with a toilet and sink in it. Below that were two bedrooms, one of which was mine, and a big bathroom. Then on the lowest story, which abutted the last alley in America, were the garage, which I used as a laundry room, and another sort of box room, where my brother was now sleeping. It sounds like a lot of rooms, but really it was all very small, and the top level especially, where I normally spent all my time, got quite crowded with the three of us going about our separate pursuits, eating, cooking, entertaining ourselves, entertaining our friends. And, as I have already described, I normally did not entertain at all.

"Sure," Gary broke the uneasy silence. "What can we change?" It had probably suddenly occurred to him that he was paying no rent. "What can we do to make things more comfortable?"

"Well, in the kitchen I usually just reach out my hand for the knife, the wooden spoons, the salt, and when they're not where I put them, I have to take time out to search. I'd like these common ordinary household utensils to be kept in one particular place."

"Good idea," said LeeAnn, "I think the salt should be kept on the kitchen table." I blinked. This wasn't what I had in mind.

"No," Gary said, "the salt should be kept on the stove. That's where it's used, after all."

"Maybe we should have two saltshakers," my sister said, "one for the kitchen table, one for the stove."

"That sounds good," my brother said. They looked positively benign. "What do you think?"

"Let's have three saltshakers," I said, giving up on some level but hardening on another, "One for the table, one for the stove, and one in the place I always put it—the sideboard." They agreed and returned to their books. "Wait a minute." I felt a little desperate. "There's also the knives, the newspapers, the shampoo, the cheese. There's the dirty plates in front of the TV. There's the loads of dirty towels. There's the trash. If there are three of us living here, then we all three ought to share the work." They were stunned, I could tell, perhaps never having contemplated these radical notions.

Gary rallied. "Let's take turns bringing home dinner from the deli for everyone. The one who brings it cleans up," he said. That was certainly easy.

"I'll wash and fold everything we all own for one week starting tomorrow," I volunteered.

"No, no," LeeAnn said. "I know: we'll each of us do all of our own, plus once a week one load of household stuff."

"What household stuff?"

"Well, towels. You know, the odd potholder. The bathmat." My goodness. This was certainly beyond my wildest dreams.

"Right," I said.

"Right," said Gary.

"What about the stuff with Daddy?" LeeAnn spoke briskly.

"Actually, I think that's been working very well," I said. "Each of us doing one shift per day, I don't see how it could be better."

"Right," said Gary and LeeAnn together.

"But will you fold the towels in thirds?" I couldn't help myself.

They howled. I felt myself grinning. Finally I began to laugh too. What surprised me was not how good it felt but how familiar.

LeeAnn is the oldest and the heaviest. Gary, though he is the tallest, is skinny and stringy, a swimmer, and weighs less than I do. I'm in the middle, always have been, always will be. LeeAnn has dark hair, Gary has light hair, I have medium hair. And whereas as children and teens we were all gregarious and popular in that same descending order, now we had diverged. It was Gary and LeeAnn, the two extremes, who were united in sociability and generosity; and it was I, the median, the norm and the normative, who skulked at the other end of the scale.

We continued through my clenched list of chores. I got into it, at least to the extent I could. It was fun. I didn't expect it to be fun. We quickly finished off all my grievances, the soda pop cans, the crumpled newspapers, occupancy of my special chair. They had no complaints of their own. *Well, as long as they're here, why not?* battled in my breast with *oh thank you, thank you, you darlings.* They were more easygoing than I was. Just as soon do it one way as another. I saw things quite differently. I was attached to preference. Had it always been like this?

That night I watched TV until they went to bed. Then I moved to the kitchen table. It was 1:00 a.m. I stared out through each pane separately, mesmerized by the wavery reflection on the neatly delineated rectangles of me and my hands and through them the pittosporum growing wild down my slope. The house was mine again, briefly, for a late-night hour. Two huge roses ruffled extravagantly from a dense dark blue vase. The surface of each curly pink petal had a neon shine under my table lamp. I felt I was getting away with something. I'd tidied the kitchen, not to my usual reclusive standard, of course, but to a state of coziness and order far more satisfying than it had been in days.

I turned the pages of tomorrow's *New York Times,* which had just been delivered. Stillness draped me like a shroud. I could barely move. I breathed in and put my feet up on the table. Ah. I stared at the window. A frizzy-haired person, pallid in the yellow light and wearing a black sweatshirt, stared back at me.

The house whispered up its subtle and familiar creaks. An old, cold, comfortable loneliness formed a lens before my eyes, and I looked out at peace, at the momentary cessation of demands, at the easy spiraling association of the mind. This tiny reprieve, I wondered, is it enough to restore me for tomorrow?

My dad, confounding everyone, got better, got stronger, got well. His crony Malcolm Lock was driving down to pick him up on Friday. On Thursday my dad got formally discharged from the UC hospital and formally transferred to his local hospital in Ukiah. That night we cooked a dinner for him.

I roasted a chicken and steamed a pot of brown rice with squash grated into it. My brother made a tomato salad with Japanese cucumber and watercress, in a lemon dressing. My sister made coffee meringues to eat with oranges and Peet's Premium decaf. While we cooked together, sharing the kitchen, we moved smoothly, humming snatches of old Beatles tunes, singing a few bars together. *Golden Slumbers. Good Day Sunshine.*

"God, it's like a fucking ballet," my brother said. I saw that it was, that it was possible. Only a thin line, though, separated all this mutual love and trust from solitude and its attendant introspection. I wanted the family. Didn't I? Why had I been so hostile? Why had I watched with horror (instead of, e.g., delight) their careless dismantling of my intricate life-support system? Was I less happy now?

My dad said it was the perfect meal for a recovering cancer patient. He drank a glass of wine, too.

I was filled with guilt, remorse, enthusiasm, love. "Lets all do Christmas here," I shouted, impelled by that rush.

Beat. "Sure." "Okay." "Wonderful." "Yeah, all right." "We'll do it."

My dad made a little speech. "Kids," he said, "LeeAnn,

Susan, Gary—I'm very glad to be here, to be alive. I felt your love, and your love pulled me through, and I love you all." I looked around the table, through the two tall candles I had lit, at the three pairs of brown eyes exactly like my own.

That night I gave up my room to my dad, and bunked with my sis. I got out the foam mattress and lay down on it inside my stained college mummy bag. I, the finicky sleeper, was out cold in minutes.

My dad left before I got up. Malcolm drove him back to Ukiah, to his "senior" condo on the edge of a golf course. My brother's ex-wife came by, alone this time. Likewise the detective. Gary and LeeAnn talked on the phone all day. That night we watched a video of *Blade Runner,* a movie whose lines we all knew by heart.

Gary went home the next morning, driving away in his rental car, and left us with a whole summer's worth of *Newsweek, Time, Sports Illustrated, Esquire, The New Yorker, Atlantic, Playboy,* and *Vanity Fair.* I swept out his room, washed the linen, remade the couch. I was absolutely fulfilled in these tasks, in the restoration of order. I begged my sister to take her time. I thought the sudden disappearance of my entire family might leave me abandoned and paralyzed.

The kitchen magically was neater. I was amazed at how easy life had become. My sister spoke on the phone as she packed. I cleaned out the refrigerator. Late at night I sat almost comfortably at the table. In the living room LeeAnn was watching a *Will and Grace* rerun as she packed and talked into her little headset. She never even once clicked the remote.

It was wonderful. I felt my body spread itself out and become longer. My space had retrieved something of its old latent fecund inspiring emptiness. I hugged the sense of it close. I knew what it meant, oh yes, I knew.

I'd over the course of two days cleaned the entire house. Magazines and catalogs were piled neatly in a box for recycling. All my laundry was clean and folded. The bathroom was immaculate. The house grew sparer, it had more depth, the yellow lilies LeeAnn had brought fairly vibrated with totemic recognition.

The night after my sister left, I sat up late writing a poem. The Lost Objects Box by the door was bulging with things I actually recognized and whose ownership I knew. They'll be pleased, I thought. At Christmas they'll be glad to see their old stuff. I thought of my dad, how delighted he was to recover. He'd been given a new life, he said, the best gift of all. But he was pleased by the dinner too, and by our gathering together. Everything was a gift from here on in, I thought, every day. God how trite, what a cliché. But true really.

I knew there were messages waiting for me on my answering machine. I felt as though I lived in the best of all possible worlds. I brewed a cup of tea and sat by the china cabinet with my book. Stillness. Freedom. Splendid isolation. Was I lonely? What an interesting topic. I blurred my vision into a speared haze of ribbony green leaves and two passionately red gladiolas. I gave myself over to it, the complicated loneliness, all of it. Really, this was all I ever wanted.

The Alley View

Before my tree was cut down, I'd almost never gone into my backyard except to take out the trash. In happier times the ex-boyfriend and I had loafed on the deck, drinking wine, pointing out special leafy glimpses to one another. We'd had a few sweet relaxed hours but not too many. My house was built down the side of a hill in the Potrero District. The deck protruded from the bottom of the house over a small, dappled yard, and looked out at a glint of a view through a few thickly leafed trees. Then there was the alley on a leveled terrace before the hill dipped down again to Sylvan Lane. From my kitchen window at the top of the house I could see the trees below and the bay through the foliage.

On a gray December day, with a soft sparse rain, I went down to the deck. The City of San Francisco had cut down the tree, which they said obstructed vehicular traffic through the alley. I assumed they meant the trash collectors. I stood under the roof overhang, out of the wet, and looked out at the house across the alley. A kitchen window, lit against the cloudy sky, was now exposed. People moved back and forth within the frame. I'd lived in this house for eight years, and had never given a moment's thought to the world across the alley. I saw a man in a gray sweatshirt rinsing or washing something in the sink. Then a dark-haired woman in a red shirt spoke with him. They looked friendly, intimate even. They were joined by another woman with longer pale hair and a light blue shirt or sweater. The intimacy was if anything slightly more intense. The man moved out of the picture and the two women stood talking, their heads tilted toward each other in an interested posture. Right away I began to wonder how I could meet them, any of them.

At this time I was trying to recover from yet another failed romance. All my ex-boyfriends had some trivial flaw that, at some stupendously inappropriate moment, compelled me to see them as blemished, inadequate, and disappointing. From that moment on I was lost, I could do nothing right. They asked if something was bothering me and I sullenly turned away. Sooner or later they got tired of this treatment and dumped me; and I, who had gotten what I asked for, yearned remorsefully for the latest defector. The most recent ex-boyfriend fit the pattern perfectly. He'd had a haircut, and I suddenly saw him as skinny and boring. What could I do? I tried to wait it out, remembering previous similar occasions. His hair would grow, I reminded myself, I'd love him again, but it was no use.

I'd spent weeks puzzling over the demise of my attachment. How could I have been in love one minute and not the next? Such thoughts dogged me, and I was diverted by the seemingly compatible trio across the alley. In order to be closer to them, I began to do a little yard work, raking leaves and so forth, but this was difficult because it rained for many days. Also my view of their window was best from the elevation of the deck. I was drawn to their kitchen window as to a theater. A few sunny days rendered my viewing impossible, as they did not turn on their kitchen light. One night, driven by a despondent restlessness, I sat on the deck, wearing my down coat and woolly boots, and watched the house across the alley with binoculars.

The inhabitants appeared to be engaged, connected. They talked, laughed, argued, cooked, washed dishes. I thought the dark-haired woman, who wore romantic red shirts, and whom I named Melisande, might be the wife or girlfriend of the man. He was my favorite. Through my binoculars I could see that his gray sweatshirt had a *Star Trek* patch on the breast. I loved him for that. I was fond of Melisande too. She wore sparkly earrings and drank beer from a long-necked bottle. This seemed to me a charming, funky thing to do. I wished I liked beer. I found my old *Star Trek* patch and considered sewing it on something. I tacked it instead on my kitchen window frame, near the prism over the sink, and it became another resonant icon, reminding me sharply of a vague but definitely adjacent fantasy.

That winter I was frightened and jumpy about earthquakes, riots, and other apocalyptic events. In my solitude, in my quiet distance from the disasters of homelessness and climate change, out of boredom, curiosity, laziness, and terror, I began to zero in on my old on-and-off history with gardening. I had read a million gardening books but I really knew nothing about gardening. It defeated me. It was too hard. What does one do about snails? Can a single woman do yard compost? What about pruning shears? Thinking these pragmatic, difficult thoughts, I sat in my kitchen throughout the winter, eating choco-grahams and flipping the pages of the *Sunset Western Garden Book*.

In the spring, Melisande and the man dug a garden near their backdoor. Surely this was synchronicity. They planted seeds, whose paper-packet flags were too far away for me to read. They also planted a small bush, which as summer approached was revealed to be a pink azalea. Melisande came out from time to time, sometimes accompanied by her fair-haired woman friend, to pull weeds and water her patch of garden. Another time I saw the man taking out the trash. From my kitchen window far above the alley I could see only a corner of their yard, and signs of life were rare. They probably lived mostly in the front of their house, as I did in mine.

I was very lonely. I didn't know what to do with myself. Finally, to convince myself that I could have a life if I wanted to, I put a personal ad in *The Bay Guardian.* I spent a long time writing the ad.

> CONTEMPLATIVE STYLISH LIBRARIAN,
> 40, SEEKS SEXY WELL-EDUCATED MOVIE-
> LOVER FOR DINNERS AND CONVERSATION.
> GARDENING EXPERTISE HELPFUL. WILL PAY
> MY OWN WAY.

When it was printed it drew only three responses. It was probably too specific, or not specific enough, or not seductive enough. In a way I was disappointed, and in a way it was two more than I wanted.

At the library, my job was running the office. I catalogued new books, traced lost ones, updated and revised the patron database. But sometimes, often, when Antoinette was sick or not up to facing the public, I sat at the front desk and checked books in and out. I'd always thought of the desk as a sort of tiresome place to work, but now it seemed fraught with possibilities. Maybe the man across the alley would walk in the door, or Melisande, or the woman with pale hair. I'd recognize them immediately, I knew, and strike up a friendly conversation. The idea that this exciting encounter could actually occur propelled me out of bed in the morning, and my manner with the patrons became pleasanter and more solicitous.

From surreptitiously driving and walking along Sylvan Lane, a scarf on my head and huge sunglasses hiding my face, I knew they had a deck in front of their house. Their deck was big. They had outdoor parties there. I could hear laughter and music, and I could smell chicken sizzling on their hibachi. Why had I never noticed these parties before? Were these people new in the neighborhood? The parties sometimes lasted quite late. I was annoyed, I was jealous, I writhed. I took home more gardening books from work, and tried to read them. After days of desolate indecision I decided to call the guys who'd answered my personal ad.

The first letter was straightforward and low-key, a little diffident. I called the number and was disappointed when I didn't like the man's voice. It was too high or something. Too breathy. There was a hesitant, tortuous rhythm to his speech.

"Do you want to meet?" he asked. We'd already discussed movies and he didn't like Hitchcock. I was put off.

"No, I don't think so," I said, surprising myself. For a moment I feared some kind of hostile reprisal for my honesty.

"Okay," he said, "well, better not then." He added that it was nice talking to me.

"Take care," I said inanely.

The second guy, who'd sent a hand-calligraphed letter and seemed extremely literate, wanted to talk about his sexual preferences. I was interested and offended at the same time.

"We haven't even met yet," I said.

"Let's get naked soon," he invited, "and get it over with. Then we can decide."

"I don't want to," I said. By now I was disgusted.

He got a little testy. "False advertising," he accused. There was a long silence. Then I hung up. Meeting new people involved weirdness; I'd known this.

Finally there was the third guy. His name was Michael, and he'd enclosed a photo of himself. He had a scar over one eye, pulling his eyelid out and over in a kind of sinister but attractive way. His very blue eyes looked directly at me under the scar.

Dear Contemplative, he began his letter. *I live alone. Although I'm set in my ways, they're nice ways. You'd probably like them.*

I'm long divorced and have two kids in college. I'm a lithographer, I teach art at Peninsula Jr. High, I'm 48 years old, I know a really good Thai restaurant near Potrero Hill. I'll pay my own way.

Guy #1 was too shy, guy #2 was too bold, guy #3 was just right. I looked at Michael's photo again. His face was square-shaped, with a big swoopy nose and a cheerful expression. I liked his looks. There was something reassuring and familiar about being able to see him without his being able to see me. On the phone he was funny and nervous, which I appreciated very much. We decided on dinner the following week.

Even as Michael and I were making our date on the phone, I was aware that there seemed to be a larger party than usual across the alley. I'd tried my binoculars early on, but the side of their house blocked even an oblique view of the deck where the festivities took place. After Michael and I hung up, I jumped into my car and cruised Sylvan Lane, once north and once south. I was right. The party was a big one. The crowd had spilled over onto the stairs leading up to the deck, and even onto the narrow strip of front lawn bordered by low-growing, hedge-like azaleas bigger than the one in the back. It was 10:00 p.m., and the guests were shadowy figures, partially illuminated in the light from the open front door. Their pale summery clothes shone a moonlit silvery pink.

I found myself wishing the guy across the alley would answer my ad. His name would be Sylvan, after his official address on Sylvan Lane. He had such a wonderful look. I wanted to know him, I wanted him to know me. I wanted to know his two interesting housemates. Were they his housemates? What was their relationship anyway?

If he'd answered my ad, I thought, he might have invited me to one of their parties. Of course he'd have no idea I was his neighbor. *We can check each other out,* he'd say; *a lot of people come to my parties whom I don't know,* he'd explain; *you could introduce yourself or not, as you choose,* he'd offer. In my fantasy I'd immediately agree to this proposal.

I was already half in love with the three of them, Sylvan and Melisande and the fair-haired woman too. I liked the way they clustered around the sink, chopping vegetables and drinking wine. Sometimes they seemed to argue fiercely, sometimes to shout and interrupt. Certainly they were often excited. I was beginning to recognize their visitors, who apparently made up a casual coterie. There were two older men, one gray and one bald. The gray one seemed to be romantically involved with Melisande, but she was sometimes sexy and romantic with Sylvan too. And there was another man, a short, rotund, bearded man, whom Melisande kissed on two occasions in a distinctly meaningful way. This man looked very familiar to me. I knew I'd seen him in the library. I vowed to work at the front desk every chance I got. There was also a very large woman who visited frequently. She brought champagne once. She opened it right in front of my binoculars. I loved champagne.

My view was far from uninterrupted. Gesturing, they moved abruptly away from the window. They crossed to other parts of the room, maybe to the refrigerator or a pantry, and returned with bottles and boxes and covered bowls. And they were by no means in the kitchen every night. Many times the window was dark, or only lit for a moment as Sylvan or one of the others came in, fetched something, and went out.

After I saw them gardening, I decided to plant flowers around my deck. I went to the nursery and bought dianthus, pansies, lobelia. These were all low-growing blooms, and I imagined little spreading areas of color, like patterns in a rug, laid out in pointy rays from the short pilings of the deck. What I wanted was to initiate a routine of casual greetings to and from the inhabitants of the house on Sylvan

Lane. I'd seen them plant their herbs, their petunias. Tall irises grew from their back steps up the edge of their small backyard. Had they put the bulbs in last fall? Several years ago? The irises were lush, soft, cloth-like falls of a bluish purple, with almost imperceptibly glowing yellow throats. They bloomed at the very top of the stem first, and then as the days passed, huge secondary and tertiary flowers erupted farther down the stalk. I wanted irises too, but worried they might be too tall for my tiny rockery plantings of lobelia and alyssum. I spent several late afternoons setting out my flats, arranging them as elegantly and wittily as I could. No one appeared from the house across the alley, not even to take out the trash. At least I had the flower beds, a consolation prize, which, however, took a good deal of effort as I had to weed and water them frequently. This chore too I welcomed, as it gave me opportunity to await any activity by my neighbors. Several times I heard conversation from their kitchen. I could make out a few fragments: "Geraniums or pelargoniums? ... Pizza ... Get the phone!" Once I thought I heard the words "Hitchcock movie." I saw no one. Of course the light was never turned on during these long bright late-summer evenings.

A revival of *Rear Window* was playing at the Red Vic, and I went alone. Scandalized by what I saw, I drove home regretting I'd ever spied on my neighbors. Really, I didn't want to know anything. I wished I'd never looked in their window. I wished my tree was still there. I no longer knew why that particular movie had seemed a good idea. I couldn't imagine what I'd ever seen in Hitchcock. Spring was terrible in a way, there was disappointment hanging in the expectant air, a tense pollen. I could understand why Eliot wrote that

April was cruel. But summer could be awful too. I knew any season could be bad, plenty bad. I knew there were dues to be paid with every relentless planetary turn.

Meanwhile I was nervous about my date with Michael, guy #3. On that Friday night I had a terrible clothes crisis and was unable to dress coherently. I was aware that I'd end up with my old faithful outfit, pink silk sweater and black rayon pants printed with pink and green flowers; but I also tried on jeans and leggings with a variety of shirts, and even a gauzy summer dress. I thought of the dress because Sylvan and his housemates were having another party. It was a warm, still night. I could hear ice clinking, just like in the movies. Something savory was on the barbecue. I didn't know how tall Michael was, so I wore flat sandals. I painstakingly applied lipstick and fussed with my hair. No matter which way I combed it I didn't look right. Finally I pulled it back in a clip, which left my face naked and mournful. No question about it, I wasn't looking my best. I walked down to the restaurant, which was only a couple of blocks from my house. I hadn't told Michael where I lived, or my last name either. I was prepared for our encounter to be disastrous.

We sat drinking cold beer and eating Styrofoam shrimp chips with a sweet chili sauce. We were formal, courteous, anxiously trying to put the other at ease. I could feel an awkward stretch from the inside, emanating from the base of my skull, spreading through the trigeminal nerves, and pulling what I'm sure was a laughably fake smile onto my stiff mouth. It was an effort, and when we both gradually recognized this, we relaxed a little.

"You know," I said, "I had a really good time writing that ad and reading the letters." I hoped he wouldn't ask me how many responses I got. "In a way," I added, "that was the best part."

"Anticipation is preferable to experience?" I could tell

Michael was a little put off and also a little amused.

"Well, yeah, in a way."

"Myself, I like the thing better than waiting for the thing."

"I can see that. Sure. But before I met you I imagined myself as saying all the right things." My heart beat fast. He was looking at me intently. His eyes were really blue. In person his scar was hardly noticeable. I arranged my face in what I thought was a sweet interested expression. "Sometimes I go for days without talking to anyone," I confided, "except at work." Why had I told him that? Now he'd think I was a registered wacko. Stubbornly I went on. "So I don't get person-to-person contact. Response. And I feel myself getting invisible."

"Do you feel invisible now?"

"Not so much anymore, now that I've said it." It was true. "I really loved your letter."

"I loved your ad." We smiled. After a pause he said, "You mentioned gardening?"

"Oh, well, I want to, I'm just starting." I was uneasy again. A drink of small talk after a cough of intimacy. "But do you do gardening?"

"Not exactly."

"Not exactly?" It felt good to put him a little on the spot.

"I'm doing a series of lithos of flowers that grow in my yard. Canna lilies. Birds of paradise. Big prints, about two feet by three feet, up close and enlarged." He hesitated. "The one I'm working on now is pink rhododendrons."

"There's a pink azalea across the alley from me."

"Similar."

"Tell me about the picture." I was more comfortable. I was interested.

"They're shadowy pink trumpet-shaped flowers. The buds are soft, cushy, a darker color pink. Then there's clusters of antennae, really bright pink antennae, shooting out of the flowers' throats. One antenna is always slightly larger and paler, like a pseudopod. Each flower has five sort of scallops, not quite separate. They're ruffled and stiff. They're connected, they're not actually discrete petals." I was stunned. He was an observer on a scale I hadn't imagined. He continued. "One of these non-petals, always just one, has a scattering of red freckles. I wonder, you know, what this is meant to convey. So meticulous. So flamboyant. Bees and other insects must be drawn to plainer, less elaborate blooms. So the beauty is kind of botanical largess. I wonder if it's part of the design."

I was rapt. "Whose design?" I murmured.

"Whose design? It's mine now."

We arranged to meet again the following week, same time, same restaurant. He said he'd call me in a few days. It was clear there was an attraction between us, maybe something important. This made me nervous, so nervous I knew I'd spoil our rapport if we didn't end the evening early. I told him I'd brought my car, but I walked home. I got more and more excited thinking about Michael and how well the dinner had gone, and how, without meaning to (but surely I had meant to? surely I'd had to have had some intention?), I'd jumped back into the terrible space where coupling is done and undone. On the way home I pulled the clip out of my hair. The minute I entered my house I raced to my bedroom and threw open my closet. I tossed summer dresses on my bed. I applied perfume and eye makeup, my goodness, I hadn't used eye makeup in months. I put on lipstick and was dazzled at how charged and sexy I suddenly looked. As I chose a dress, a drop-waisted, gauzy, dark blue dress with big shimmery purple shapes printed on it, I planned my entrance. I'd walk down their side-yard steps and unobtrusively insinuate myself into the crowd. "I'm with Michael," I'd say if anyone asked. Michael was a common name. I pulled on a pair of high-heeled sandals and combed my hair back with my fingers. I looked wild, electric. That's it, I decided, as I let myself out of my back door, I'll say I'm with Michael. It was amazingly credible and it had a solid voyeuristic truth. I ran across the deck and the yard, over the alley to Sylvan's house. I raced down the steps. My hair was all down to my shoulders and I could feel it bouncing a little as I ran. "I'm with Michael," I practiced saying, as I rounded the side of the house across the alley and crashed Sylvan's party.

In the Eyes, In the Mouth

ONE NIGHT MY CHINESE cooking class was stir-frying prawns with a free choice of fruit and sauce. Never before had the students been permitted to choose two important elements of a dish. I wanted to be partners with Calvin, whom I'd cooked with before. I was thinking nectarines, I was thinking mangoes, I was thinking casaba melon. It was summer, and our teacher, Thomas Hwang, who had an unorthodox approach to his subject, had arranged a huge platter of exotic produce. I looked around for Calvin.

"Partners," coughed Mr. Hwang. He was a chain-smoker, and had a terrible chronic cough. But he never smoked in class.

Calvin was absent that night. I gloomily teamed up with Sam Montoya, a skinny, mustached lawyer. I was suspicious of skinny men. I knew him slightly from before, as he sometimes came into the library where I worked. He'd always addressed me as Ms. Keller. But when he showed up the first night of the cooking class, I was so surprised to see him that I told him to call me Susan.

"Apple," he suggested.

It was a good idea but I didn't want to admit it. "Better plum than apple," I said.

"Papaya," Sam offered. I considered.

"Not too mushy," I warned. "Not too sweet," I fretted. We picked out a fragrant but hard papaya.

"Begin when ready," said Mr. Hwang. He left the room

to cough and smoke in the hall, where we could consult him if necessary.

Our prawns with papaya and a sugary lemon sauce were excellent, but not quite so exciting as the prawns with kumquats and a ginger sauce done by another team.

My best friend, Naomi, was on the phone. "Do you miss Rick? Is that why you're taking a Chinese cooking class?" Rick was my ex-boyfriend. He was thin. He'd already moved back in with the girlfriend he'd had before me. One thing I knew about her was that she was rich.

"Yeah—well, maybe. I've stopped reading his horoscope."

"That's a good sign."

"Ha ha. But I occasionally have this urge to ask someone about their inner life. Do you mind if I ask about yours?"

"Not at all. Delighted. Flattered."

"Oh, good."

"Now? Do you want to hear about my new painting?" Naomi taught at an elementary school in Daly City, but in her meager spare time she was an artist.

"No. Not now."

Naomi sighed. "Oh, well. What's the class like?"

"It's great. We get to eat everything we cook. It's like a party every Tuesday night. Sometimes we have to bring ingredients."

"I wish I could ask the second grade to bring ingredients."

"There are two single guys in the class. One of them, this lawyer, I've seen him around. At the library. He says he's semi-retired."

"What does that mean?"

"For a lawyer it probably means he only works fifty hours a week." Naomi snickered. I loved Naomi. I went on, "The other man is cute. He's kind of fat and has a beard. He's young, much younger than me. He and I are partners a lot."

"Does he make you feel warm and pink?"

I didn't even have to think about it. "Yes," I said.

"What about the lawyer?"

"Cold and pale."

I sat up late, listening to Bach's preludes and fugues. Half tranced by the complex music, I slumped in my chair and focused my gaze at a spotted dracaena in the corner, which seemed to be metamorphosing into tree-hood. Trees enabled and supported many little lives. I thought of insects, whose tiny and meticulous organs, excretions, wings, for god's sake, gauzy little wings, seemed to reproach my own grosser proportions.

If I were much, much smaller and less obtrusive, if I were as small and as self-sufficient as a beetle or a housefly, I would need no possessions. No refrigerator, no Nikes, no houseplants. But I loved the mysterious dracaena. It looked good in its homemade pot, which I had made several years ago in a series of pottery classes. The neighboring sanseveria, from whose stringy roots erupted a burst of leathery yellow striped leaves, also resided in a pot I had made. These short-lived enthusiasms had permanent consequences.

I was gratified that plants cohabited with me, in my artificial ecosystem. Against the opaque white plaster walls a gravity-defying palm tree rose in miniature grandeur from another hand-turned pot. A tree. Indoors. Apparently thriving. I sucked photons from the palm in through my eyes, and fell forward into the knife-clean daggery fronds of a green so profound, so saturated and light absorbent, that the stiff curving stem vibrated slightly within my visual field.

I was also in a writing class. I had gotten tired of writing poetry and thought I might try fiction. The writing class was on Monday nights and the Chinese cooking class was on Tuesday nights. All my other nights were free, free, free. I had nothing to do but stare at various species of flora. This was what I did for fun.

In the class, my stories were criticized for over-identification with my characters. "You need a more distant voice," said Robert, the teacher. Robert wore cowboy boots. He had written a mystery novel, now out of print, and urged us to concentrate on plot.

I read my stories over and over, perplexed by their imperfection. I wrote new ones, imagining and reaching for that clean authoritative seductive voice, the voice that wouldn't get in the way of the story. Nothing I wrote seemed to mean very much. Nothing happened in my stories. *Plot?* Robert wrote in the margins. Things happened in movies and in TV shows, which I watched avidly, and also of course in books. Car crashes. Deaths of loved ones. Marriage, divorce. Mostly divorce. But in my writing, none of these things occurred. Someone might take a walk. Someone else might cook a meal. But the universal drama of these events, and I did not doubt that it was there, escaped my skills. Information about the characters interested me and I wrote it down: their flowery sheets, their preoccupations and reveries, what they kept in the fridge to eat at midnight. Surely this couldn't be The Real Thing, this motley description of the imaginary person. Couldn't be. I thought I had a glimmer of what it was, I could recognize it in the work of others, but it eluded me. What about just telling a good story? I wondered. But I didn't think it was in my nature.

It wasn't exactly an argument, but I was having a moderately contentious exchange with Calvin, the attractive bearded man from my Chinese cooking class. We'd made hot and sour soup earlier that night. Now we were drinking decaf in the café across the street. Calvin was talking about his two cats and how much he loved them and considered them to be wonderful creatures and so forth. He implied that he was a superior being because he had empathy with his cats. He said that people never considered animals to be as important as themselves, but that heck, we were all living creatures on the planet.

"I agree," I was enthusiastic. "Definitely. Humans, cats, plants, spiders."

"Spiders?" He laughed.

"Sure," I said. "I consider them some of the most beautiful, elegant, and cooperative of the planet's mobile creatures. I'm using the word 'mobile' as opposed to those biota, like oak trees and carrots, who're rooted in the ground." What was I saying?

Calvin looked at the table. "Are you a vegetarian?" he asked.

"No." There was a definitely awkward pause. "What do your cats eat?" I asked lamely.

Calvin's cats ate the same food he did, which was lucky, since there was a plethora of gardeners in San Francisco, and Calvin's business had suffered during the recession. He supplemented their leftovers, he told me, with dry cat food. I fed the spiders in my house nothing and felt no need to. When I swept their fly-laden webs from the walls and corners they presumably scurried off with a full stomach. Now I regretted I hadn't come up with a more socially acceptable insect, like butterflies or cute little honeybees. I liked them all, really, iridescent beetles and crickets and hairy cautious tarantulas. Nor was I afraid of moths, as was Rick, my ex-boyfriend, as were most people for reasons I could not fathom, though I agreed they were distracting, careening around the lamp when I was trying to read.

But when Calvin laughed at my admiration for spiders, I couldn't help feeling defensive. I was afraid of the poisonous ones, black widows and their ilk, and I'd had my share of itchy spider bites just like anyone else, but I wouldn't kill one on purpose. I was especially affronted at Calvin's simultaneous defense of mammals and disdain for insects. What did he think an animal was? Maybe Calvin was one of those persons who said one thing and did another, like Rick. When I'd first met Rick, he said he'd chosen to live frugally, because he was an artist and time was his greatest treasure. Yet the very first thing he told me about his ex was that she was rich. He also once said to me, "Money is sexy." When he went back to his old girlfriend, I immediately thought: *Hypocrite!* So maybe I was looking for hints of hypocrisy in other men, in all men. It was a possibility.

Rick had always hated and feared moths. When we split up, Naomi and I planned a devastating revenge: moth quiche.

I myself had never eaten an insect. Now after my talk with Calvin I began to think about it. Insects seemed to lend themselves to Chinese food, to Asian food in general. I imagined a spicy Thai salad, crisp sprouts at one end of the plate, cabbage and mint and chopped peanuts mounded in the middle, and batter-fried grasshoppers at the other end.

This idea didn't disgust me. I was a meat eater. I'd even eaten and enjoyed the inner organs of animals—brains, kidneys, tongue, liver. But organ meats were a different class of flesh from insects. Grubs, I seemed to recall, were regularly consumed by human beings. Ugh. Not for me. But fried grasshoppers, or moths, a nice little crunch. Would they be bitter? Would the wings melt into powder on the tongue?

Still I was reluctant to think of them as food. It went beyond the question of how they'd taste. It was their scale. There was a difference between a piece of chicken and twenty deep-fried crickets. Maybe eating twenty animals, any animals, was excessive.

I began writing a story about a woman who struggles through each day at her dull job only to rush into her bed at night and dream. The idea was that the dreams would elucidate the woman's oppressive life, and vice versa. This woman, Margaret is her name, works in an office. She's weary of her autocratic and demanding boss. Every day she walks home from work, her only time alone. She walks slowly, peering into windows, stopping to buy bread or a few peaches. At home she and her teenage son Carlos prepare their dinner. Carlos is surly and uncommunicative. He prefers the company of his equally churlish friends who play loud, and to Margaret's ears terrible, music in the garage. Margaret has a glass of wine, reads the paper, and goes to bed. There she dreams and dreams. Each night she has mysterious and intense dreams that reveal important but elusive messages. I hoped the reader would decipher them.

The first dream I wrote for Margaret was a numerical dream, of the type so beloved by Groddeck and Jung. Margaret finds herself in the dreaded diagonal elevator, accompanied by the familiar feeling of anxiety that this elevator always elicits. It shoots past her floor, which is 22. Maybe I should go back down to 19, she thinks, or 18 or 12. She suddenly wants a cappuccino and a chocolate chip cookie. The restaurant is on 12. She's very, very hungry.

I then wrote that Margaret wakes from this dream and looks at her digital clock. It's 3:30 a.m. She sits up in bed. The dream has confused her. What have I got to eat? she thinks. Are there any cookies? No. Cheese? No. As she tries to remember the contents of her refrigerator, she drifts off again and dreams again.

In Margaret's next dream she finds herself turned into a slim silvery dolphin. She's moving rapidly, with rhythmic thrusts of her powerful tail, into the ocean's depths. She's accompanied by her tribe of fellow dolphins. They're murmuring and whistling endearments to one another. Everywhere are coral glades, shifting balletic fronds of kelp, and the constant neural flash of fish swimming, swimming, toward some dreamy mindless living meal. Margaret feels the tides of the water through which she swims resonate to the rush of her blood and the beating of her heart.

When Margaret wakes again she's definitely awake. She pulls her soft quilt up to her chin, her eyes open. Her terrible workday looms.

Among my favorite Chinese foods were steamed and sautéed dumplings containing a sausage mixture of pork, shrimp, onion, ginger, and cilantro. I had for some time been formulating a crass but dazzling vision of a kind of won-ton lasagna. The middle layer would be the sausage mixture, very loose and fluffy. Above a sheet of overlapping egg-roll wrappers would be a stratum of crisp snow peas and water chestnuts, covered with another sheet dipped in or basted with a classic soy-sherry mixture. The bottom layer, between egg-roll skins, would be juicy black mushrooms. I had never dared to confess my idea to anyone, nor had I dared to try it in the privacy of my own home. Something about the scale was wrong, disgusting even. I thought about my imaginary lasagna as I stared at cut flowers, and at other times too. Did it violate the spirit of Chinese cuisine? Form and content were such mysterious entities. You could discuss them as conceptually separate, but in real life there were no such interesting distinctions.

One day I called in sick and took a morning walk. I wore dark glasses and a big-brimmed straw hat as a barrier between myself and the rare thick sun of San Francisco's hottest summer days. The still heat had wakened me throughout the night and finally roused me early from a restless sleep. The hat and the glasses helped to block the glare, which made the sidewalks shimmer. I stopped to look at a fence covered with jasmine. The dime-sized white flowers, edged in purple, formed clusters. The fresh dark feathery green leaves glistened faintly as if moist. I was transfixed. How shady it was, how refreshing. I was hot and sweaty though I was only wearing a man's black undershirt over my brassiere, and a pair of threadbare, nearly transparent jeans. I walked on, searching for another sensation of coolness, of forest glade, of dim filtered light and the fragrance of green. A flash of emerald caught my eye—there—to the right. I turned. It was a perfect spread of dichondra, growing all by itself within a square of bricks apparently built to accommodate it. I felt an immediate affinity with the matted velvety symmetry. The tiny leaves seemed perfectly adapted to their brick box, confined by it yet flourishing within it.

Robert, my writing teacher, said there were only two plots: (1) a stranger comes to town; and (2) someone takes a trip. Was he joking? I wondered if Margaret's dreams constituted a trip. There has to be some progression, Robert said. I knew what he meant: the same old problem of something actually happening. Poor Margaret went to work every day and nothing changed.

I loved writing down Margaret's dreams. They flowed from my pen. Soon I had twenty dreams, written as if by a prolific spirit guide. When I read them over I was a little stunned. Did I write this? I wondered. I couldn't identify within myself the source of these facile portent-laden dreams, which had appeared suddenly, like real dreams. Their antecedents, if any, were shadowy and ambiguous.

Baroque chamber music was playing on late-night radio, the violin trills as elaborate and soothing as a formal contract. I sat up smoking a cigarette. I stared at the big-bellied, brown-spotted jar of lavish hydrangeas. Their florets, which varied in size, had a palette ranging from pale green down to white and then up to a fibrous pale pink hinting of lavender without touching it. From this mass a few stridently green serrated leaves poked out. I was happy. This was definitely my idea of a good time.

Great writers wrote about significant encounters, it seemed to me. Their characters either underwent a life change, or the unexpected consequences of some thoughtless act culminated in a resonant and scary adventure. Love was flawed, and passionate entanglements got wrecked or exposed. The characters meanwhile were thinking the most extraordinary thoughts about themselves and the other characters. I didn't like depressing stories. I liked stories in which the main characters got something they wanted. Or found out what they wanted.

Fiction was a serious undertaking. But the point of fiction was entertainment, or amusing ideas and connections, or fun, yes, that's what made it so compelling. Writing was like a current lover, as hopeful and fantastic as Calvin from the cooking class, as historically unalterable as Rick.

Mr. Hwang showed the class how to poach a chicken.

"We used to simmer until pink and juicy," Mr. Hwang said severely. He coughed. "Now we simmer until white and juicy. You can't depend on chickens. Even from Clement Street. Cook them well-done."

The class watched the three plump chickens bobbing in the pot, barely covered with a frothy broth that emitted a wonderful smell. Mr. Hwang looked at us grimly. "This does not apply to vegetables. As you know." I knew. Sam Montoya shot me a look that said he knew too. Mr. Hwang could be positively harsh when confronted with an overcooked vegetable.

"The chicken tastes very good well-done." Mr. Hwang raised his eyebrows very slightly, perhaps to indicate surprise. "Very good."

One of the literary problems Robert discussed was that of tense. Many modern short stories were written in the present tense. The class deplored these in principle. Where was the suspension of disbelief, we asked, the distance? Where was the story, as in the sense of history? How can you imagine that this all happened if you're reading about it as it is happening? When you're sitting in your comfy chair? What's so important about immediacy?

Coral-colored gladioli looked ready to burst from their stiff green budding stems. The sexually charged color of the fluted petals emitted a light so inner that it looked instinctual, like a gorgeous neon prawn in the ocean's trenched depths. When I pulled the white columnar jar closer to the lamp, the moist, papery overlapping petals glowed orange, pink, brown. What a vibration. What a glow. The blossoms erupted to the turning of their own green clocks, stretching and reaching toward replication, even in death. What powerful structures. What a rush it was to apprehend these mysteries.

I hoped it wasn't morbid to offer my deepest attention to dead flowers, to watch them blooming as they tilted on their cut stems, as they drowned in a jar.

Each of the students in my Chinese cooking class was to bring to that evening's meeting an unusual ingredient, the spirit of which was appropriate to, and would inspire, the art of Chinese cookery. I strolled through the farmers market. The weather was still hot. I had in mind something green, something very dark green, very crisp. Chard? Cucumber? Parsley? I pondered parsley.

But when I examined the stalls of produce, I wanted to buy everything. Tomatoes, squash, apricots, chamomile in a pot, eggplant, mesclun. I stared for a long time at purple basil, and next to it papery-skinned tomatillos. Tomatillos? No. What was I thinking?

A tap on my shoulder.

"Susan, hello." It was Sam Montoya, dressed for his legal practice, in the middle of the day. He was wearing a necktie. "I was thinking of leeks," he said.

"Oh," I said. I was jealous. Why hadn't I thought of leeks? We turned together and walked to another stall.

"You could do turnips," he suggested in a helpful tone. "Crispy sliced turnips with velvet chicken."

"No," I said. I stopped to look at green zucchini, golden crooknecks, pale summer squashes. "Three squashes," I said slowly, "with garlic."

"Good idea," Sam Montoya was clearly relieved. "I'll get the leeks," he said. He paused. "I'll see you later." He was gone.

I bought the squashes but was uneasy. My contribution, I saw now, was boring, a featured player but not a superstar. On an impulse I also bought raspberries and baby beets. I had no idea what I could do to them.

I saw the petals of the variegated pink godetia as skin, stiffened yet flexible tissue. They were living extrusions of the thinnest most delicate gauze. They were most like the wings of butterflies and moths. The edges were a little carelessly made, I saw, when I examined them through my 5× magnifying glass. Conceived as straight-rimmed, these little curves of tender fabric ended in a half-ragged, half-erratically scalloped abruptness, which had a scale only the word "perfect" would describe. Each one was what it was.

I thought of the human race as multiple flowers on a stem, perhaps a stalk of foxglove. Some little cups were plump, spotted all over their purple insides with red. A couple more were smaller, looser. Still others were misshapen, broken, wilted, crushed, falling away to the ground. It was all an accident of fate, or of rumbling electric genetics, complicated far beyond human comprehension.

And no getting around it: some flowers were flat-out more fortunate than others. Peonies: more gorgeous. Nasturtiums: more cheerful. These godetias in front of me, thrust into a brown pottery vase, were dense, profligate in variation, in size, in age. One wilted blossom sagged. Another shriveled into a caterpillar shape. The others stretched up, up and out. "I want to fly."

I brought the beets, after all. I was partners with Calvin. He had brought chorizo. We were each startled by the other's choice. We talked in low tones while the rice steamed. He told me about a retaining wall he was putting in for his girlfriend, just a couple of blocks down the hill from me. I was disappointed to learn Calvin had a girlfriend. Not that I. Under any circumstances. Still. We chopped scallions, green peppers, broccoli. We minced ginger and garlic. We toasted sesame seeds.

"I was thinking of morning glory," he said. "The dark blue kind, to fall down over the stones." Together we cut the parboiled beets into neat julienne strips and sprinkled a little rice vinegar over them.

"What kind of stone?" I measured out the hoisin. Calvin carefully heaped the beets in the middle of a plate and surrounded them with strong ginger sauce. I scattered the sesame seeds.

"Gray. Used gray brick."

"I'd have passiflora," I said. "More upbeat."

"Too gaudy. This is a cool kind of backdrop area for the rhodos and azaleas. They're mostly pink."

I liked Calvin. I forgave him his snobbism toward the

animal world and also for having a girlfriend. We gently mixed thick disks of chorizo with the broccoli. We looked critically at our two plates.

"Not too bad," I said. To myself I thought, this looks fabulous. Why can't writing be like cooking?

I couldn't write any more dreams for Margaret. I tried to remember my own dreams or at least fragments. Even if they were distasteful and repelled me with their intimate gravity, I reached to clutch them behind my eyes and assign words. The words might evoke shadows of the images. Maybe I've written them all out, I thought, maybe there aren't any more. I knew this couldn't be right, and yet the details of Margaret's difficult job, her boss, her computer, her lunch break, became more and more vivid to me, and Margaret's dreams more elusive.

I called Naomi on the telephone. "Had any dreams lately?" I asked.

"Still working on the Margaret story? Well, a kid in my class reported an interesting dream. She said she was in a movie theater filled with chickens. The chickens were sitting quietly. I asked her what movie was playing, and she said it was *Home Alone.*"

"Chickens?"

"Yeah," said Naomi. "What a nightmare, huh?"

Nasturtiums glowed in a clear globular glass vase. Earlier, on another neighborhood stroll, I'd seen nasturtiums everywhere, thrusting their radiant savory flowers forward on skinny tensile stems. The leaves were the shape of sand dollars, a confident round of opaque dark green skin. Great long streams of nasturtium vine made assertive cheerful clumps and mounds spilling over fences, surrounding bus stop signs in a conical shape. I peered into individual flowers, pinkish yellow, with little claw-shaped streaks of orange emerging from the throat and bleeding out toward the ends of the five petals. Little hairs, bee attractants no doubt, fringed the bottom of three, not two, not four, always three petals, which emerged from the flower bowl on mini-stems. The other two petals always grew directly from the hip. I loved this elaborate discipline. Whoever thought up this stuff was maybe a kind of showoff.

Everything in the natural world was perfect. Each detail could so easily be other, each was improbable, each was inevitable. Yet on one stalk of foxglove, I reminded myself, some of the perfect blossoms were complete and radiant, others were shriveled and misshapen.

I gulped my tea. I was in a warm civilized cave. Surrounding me were the products of Western civilization and its evil twin, technology. Art, kitsch, convenience. I completely appreciated the skin between myself and the planet. I understood about shelter from the elements, about food preparation, about sleeping and bathing and the whole schedule of biological tasks. It was good to sit in a comfy chair that rested on a carpeted floor, and drink wine from a stemmed glass. On a chill night I was glad for electric heat and for my soft bed with its flannel sheets. What pleasure could surpass sitting comfortably with my book, listening to Mozart? No cave-dwelling hermit could luxuriate thus. Social cooperation, coerced and threatened, bought and paid for, had produced my state of being. Would I have it otherwise? I was a veritable beacon and hidden treasure of civilization. Outside my hut, the maelstrom raged. Viruses. Identity theft. Car wrecks. Earthquakes. Poverty and degradation. Nature red in tooth and claw. It was all going to come down soon, I knew. How was it thrown that I got to live in my house, that I had a job, that I had flowers and music and good shoes? And from the perspective of any other species, really, except maybe rats and lice, who benefited from humankind? Weren't people just a kind of ruinous infestation, a plague to strip the planet bare and choke it and flay it and mortally wound it and kill it? And what about the billions of galaxies out there? I shook my head, baffled. The nasturtiums glowed.

Naomi called to tell me she was working on a new painting. "It's like a dream in a way," she said. "It's got people's hands coming out of fruit hanging on a tree. It has a Hieronymus Bosch quality. I don't know what it means. But it's dreamlike, it's definitely dreamlike."

"What kind of fruit?"

"Pomegranates, I think. They could be oranges, though, or persimmons. Something spherical and reddish. But there are flowers on the tree too."

"What kind of flowers?"

"Big, flat, Frida Kahlo-type flowers. Hibiscus, I think. Gee, Susan, I'm not sure. I don't know the names of the stuff I paint."

How lucky she is, I thought.

I wrote down a dream for Margaret that I myself had had. But first I wrote that Margaret's son, Carlos, signs a recording contract. Soon his group has two songs on the top 40. He's bringing home so much money that Margaret can quit her job. With more time on her hands she takes a horticulture class.

This was my best attempt at a happy ending. Deus ex musica.

In this dream Margaret is in a luxurious train speeding toward a gorgeous and exotic destination. Perhaps Marlene Dietrich is on the train too. Margaret is not entirely comfortable, however. Unlike all the other passengers, she is not soothed by the vibration of the train. There's something stifling about it, something oppressive and imposed. Yet it is the condition of the journey.

I looked closely at the pussy willows in the vase in front of me. They were so improbable, with their larval yellow pollen-laden mammal toes springing out of the twigs and then drooping. I had tried to commune with plants, the palms, the dracaena. I always felt self-conscious and silly. Here now was a twiggy branch, erupting with woolly swelling little bulbs. I felt something like empathy, not the real thing of course, no way, but an appreciation, a focus, a view of the pussy willows as dots of planet cover, a frame of me as the same. The rustling, sighing, grunting, belching, rumbling, gulping surface of earth, a skim of growing and dying so complicated and random and connected, in which whole species escape the broken continent, evolve into the rain, and disappear forever. How did humankind get to be such a ravening, rapacious pest? Maybe the pussy willows wouldn't be doomed. Maybe they would thrive, in vast forests, from mountain to mountain, pussy willows. Not likely.

The pussy willows were now a formal Japanese painting exercise. Objets d'art, now, dead already, really. As are we all. As am I. Dead already. Even the redwoods. As I thought of those giant and courteous beings, dreaming their long, long dreams, I again felt a tangential nudge of my heart toward the gallant pussy willows, thriving in the vanguard of their decline. The inhuman non-selectivity of it, that's why humankind fears nature and messes with it and struggles with it and fucks it up. If we're all dead, what's next? I pictured San Francisco covered with ivy, from whose murmurous thickly leafed surfaces the disparate trees of this urban forest would stretch up and in time renew or remake the air. Yes. Cars would rust and crumble beneath giant ivy, the eater of the Golden Gate, now gorging itself on the city, brick by brick, block by block. In the faint long narrow depressions like rivers in the ivy's rubbery surface, groves of pussy willows would grow, in pairs and threes, seeding themselves up the hills of San Francisco, over the on-ramps to the bridge, and down toward the quiet bay.

Mr. Hwang gave the class instructions about the last meeting. It was to be a combination potluck and final exam. First we would eat. Then each student would explain, and answer questions about, the dish he or she had made. Mr. Hwang advised us to bring copies of the recipe.

My heart beat fast. This was my chance. But did I have the guts? Was my won-ton lasagna casserole, for which I didn't even have a good name, just too bizarre? Or was it a stroke of genius? And how was I to know?

Maybe I'd just pass on the whole idea. Yeah, maybe I'd just steam a red snapper and serve it with scallions and sautéed apricots. Much better idea. Simpler.

Mr. Hwang, coughing, said good night. I shuffled out the door of the Culinary Arts Building at Potrero High. The lawyer, Sam Montoya, tapped my shoulder.

"Susan. Whaddaya gonna do?" he said. "Wanna be partners?"

Caught in my obsession, I blurted out my crackpot idea.

"One layer's got to go," Sam said. He spoke with authority. "You can serve the greens separately. See what I mean?"

"Yes, I do." I did. Suddenly the lasagna snapped into the realm of delicious possibility.

"And the egg-roll skins? Too doughy, too solid. How about noodles laid out loosely between the stuffings? They can be wide noodles, the sheets can be, you know, raggedy." He shaped with his fingers the way the layer of noodles would go between the sausage and the mushrooms.

"Oh, yes. Yes. Yes."

We smiled at each other. I'm having fun now, I thought. He had a wonderful smile.

"About the name," I said.

"What name?"

"This dish should have a name."

"Okay."

"What name should it have?"

Sam smiled again. My goodness. "Make one up," he said.

In Margaret's last dream she hovers on the rim of a leaf, its green, moist surface trembling slightly. The leaf is as big as a hotel lobby. She drops over the edge, perfectly balanced on the strong silk thread emerging from her abdomen. The sky is blue, the sun is warm. Margaret knows this will be her best web. Deftly she anchors the thread and rapidly runs up it again to make another line. How beautiful her skeletal trampoline is. How it glistens in the sun. How the faint breeze pulls its intersection into a taut and elegant knot. Margaret is now getting hungry. What will blunder into my web today, she wonders dreamily as she works. The humming frenzied wings of a snared fly shine iridescent green.

About the Author

ADRIENNE ROSS has studied writing with Thaisa Frank, Dorothy Wall, James Frey, and the writers' group The Green Rug Club. Her work has been published in literary journals, anthologies, and on-line magazines. She was awarded a Literary Fellowship by the Carlifornia Arts council, and a book of her poetry, *Twelve Winter Haiku*, was published by Hit and Run Press. She divides her time between Berkeley and the northern California coast.

Acknowledgments

Many thanks to the patient and clever people at Lost Coast Press, especially Cynthia Frank, Joe Shaw, Mike Brechner, and Joel Mikesell.

Undying gratitude to the wonderful folks without whose help this book would not exist: Karen Balos, Zida Borcich, Alison Cadbury, Cecile Cutler, Sue Finkelstein, John Fremont, Janet Keyes, Deborah Lichtman, Claire Lobell, Bobby Markels, Bob Ross, Ayn Ruyman, Zoe Sheppard, and Sally Sommer.

Credits

The following pieces were previously published in slightly different form under the name A. D. Ross:
"The Feather in Data's Wing" in *Apocalypse 5;* "In the Eyes, In the Mouth" as "In the Mouth, In the Eyes," reprinted from *Prairie Schooner* (vol. 71, num. 3, Fall 1997 by permission of the University of Nebraska Press, copyright 1997 by the University of Nebraska Press); "Leaving Town" in *The San Francisco Review;* "The Transition Consultant" in *Wisconsin Review;* "Lizard Love" in *Ascent;* "The Lost Objects Box" in *American Literary Review;* "The Alley View" in *Sycamore Review;* "Want Not" in *The G.W. Review;* "The Dream of Ten Normas" and "Jack Bailey's Beach Story" in *Hayden's Ferry Review;* "Getting Rid of Randall" in *Breaking Up is Hard to Do* (The Crossing Press); "Being Her" in *Reed.*